Gothica

Romance of the Immortals

A Dark Fantasy Novel

by

Steven R. Cowan

This book is a work of fiction. Names, characters, places, and incidents are the product of the author's imagination or are used fictitiously. Any resemblance to actual events, locales, or persons, living or dead, is coincidental.

Copyright © 2001 by Steven R. Cowan
All rights reserved.
Southern Charm Press, 150 Caldwell Drive, Hampton, GA 30228
Visit our Web site at www.southerncharmpress.com

The publisher offers discounts on this book when purchased in quantities. For more information, contact:
toll free: 1-888-281-9393, phone: 770-946-4664,
fax: 770-946-5220, e-mail: info@southerncharmpress.com

Printed in the United States of America
First Printing: March 2001

Library of Congress Catalog Number
        00-109821

Cowan, Steven R.
        GOTHICA: Romance of the Immortals

        ISBN 0-9702190-5-9

Cover design by Ginuwine Graphics

Chapter 1

I

Sleek black fingernails lustfully traced his jaw-line as the vampiress's heart stepped up in its beat. He was neither mortal, nor vampire, and desire for him clutched her dark heart, controlled her shadow-spirit and rekindled emotions within her that, for centuries, had remained dormant.

He, too, was equally drawn by this exquisite creature of night—her broken English—the deep, clear abyssal pools that were her eyes— the alluring possibility of those twin daggers puncturing the flesh of his willing throat...

Each of the two deathless hearts, seared by the white-hot seduction of the other—were bound together—for all time.

A bright, classical guitar melody plucked away in his mind, as he stood behind the bedroom door with a thirty-four-inch Louisville Slugger—waiting for her. His heart quickened when he heard her key the front door, and cold beads of perspiration burst through the skin around his temples and on his forehead. She was coming. As her footsteps grew louder, he gripped the baseball bat, until his knuckles grew white and his palms effused sweat. He hoped he would not lose his grip when he connected.

"Oh, yeah," he thought. "Come right on in. All I need is *one* shot."

The hinges creaked, and a redhead with long curly tresses stepped into view and into range. He lunged and swung savagely. Her very life sprayed into the air, igniting it with a scarlet fog, as the bat crashed into the base of her skull. Her rubbery neck flopped like that of a slain game bird, unable to support the crushed, dead weight of a heavy head. He stood over her flaccid, twitching body and laughed maniacally. "One good turn deserves another, Mags…Maggie…naggy Maggie," he would say.

Calvin McLeish turned up a shot glass and poured the dark amber liquid down his throat. Another shot and his anger ebbed. "Well, there's nothing wrong with a little fantasy," he thought. "They can't very well lock me up for imagining what it would be like to take her out with a bat."

He looked at an empty computer box sitting on the floor. It was the reason his wife had blown up and stormed out with the kids, or it was the straw that broke the camel's back, anyway.

"Damn her," he whispered.

His wife's angry words echoed in his mind, like the gong of a clock announcing the final hour for a death row inmate. "That's it, Calvin…*finito*. When you quit your job at the power plant, it was all I could do to stay, but now you go and spend three grand on a computer and Internet service. Let's see, why was it you quit a forty-five thousand dollar a year job? Oh, yes, how could I forget? You gave up a good living and insurance to become the next great American author." She had scratched her head and rolled her eyes with exaggerated sarcasm. "And wait, let me think. How much do I make as a daycare worker? Oh yes, that's, right, fifty cents an hour over minimum wage. And how much have you made as a writer? Hmm...let me get the exact dollar figure in my head. Okay, I got it, now. The exact amount is...zip...nada...bupkiss, zilcheroonie...*zero*, Calvin!"

He sucked down another shot of Jack Daniels. The baseball bat fantasy was trying to come back. Calvin teed off and booted the empty computer box, like a soccer-style field goal kicker, its corner striking an upper windowpane. A spider-web fissure speeded concentrically in all four directions from the epicenter of the blow.

"Oh perfect," he sighed.

With his head hanging and the wind depleted from his sails, McLeish walked over to assess the damage. A figure near the street in front of his house remained unnoticed for a few moments. As he completed the window inspection, his focus turned more farsighted. Standing on the cracked cement sidewalk and craning her skinny neck to peer inside the house was next-door neighbor, Bitsy McCall. Bitsy pretended to walk a little rat she called a dog. No doubt, she had seen Maggie storm out with the kids and could not resist trying to see what might be going on internally.

"Well, I certainly have something that you can get an eyeful of, *Bitchy*. It's something that I've wanted to show you for a long time." Calvin pulled his sweatpants down to his knees and pressed his colorless buttocks against the bedroom windowpane.

Bitsy's lower jaw dropped like the trap door of a gallows Calvin might hang from, if he ever followed through with the baseball bat fantasy. Dragging the Chihuahua by its leash across the lawn, she fled, mouthing a rash of inaudible obscenities. His grin receded to a frown, as he pondered his marital situation and reflected on the previous months of trouble. Buying the computer and Internet service were not things he expected Maggie to be happy about, but still, he never saw this coming. Months of bickering and quarreling found the couple at odds over even less significant issues, but buying the computer proved to be Maggie's breaking point.

The curly redhead had her own closets and her own skeletons, though. While Calvin's eccentric behavior was enough to try any woman's patience, she had been building a case against him for the better part of a year, preparing for divorce. They married the day after high school graduation, and for Maggie, the thrill was gone. She would use his irresponsibility against him, and get what she wanted—freedom. Deep in the pit of Calvin's heart, he knew she was unfaithful, knew she was gone too often from the house, and knew that her alibis rarely held water. Instead of facing the death of their relationship, he opted to bury himself in writing. She had drawn first blood, though, and, now, he would unleash all his suspicion and pain. "Naggy" had made her bed as far as he was concerned. She could lie in it, wallow in it, and share it with whomever she might be screwing at the time. If she wanted to throw in the towel, that was fine with him. At least, his rage told him it was fine with him.

Headstrong determination, however, drove him to indulge, and he sat down to boot up his new toy for its inaugural journey into cyberspace. Popping the first of three Starscape set-up diskettes into the "A" drive, he followed the on-screen instructions. In a matter of minutes, he was surfing the net. He had rationalized that the computer might be a useful tool in the McLeish household and was convinced it would be instrumental in his quest for fame as a best-selling author. Had he been honest with himself, he would have admitted that tying to the web was not to research anything literary at all.

Articles he had read about the thousands of chat rooms on the net intrigued him—as did cybersex—as did online pornography. Curiosity, loneliness, and a yearning for adventure became his motivations for entering cyberspace. He did use the computer to re-type the first four pages of his current effort, *The Legend of Glynn MacTavish*, yet, a swift addiction to *cyberworld* and the bizarre new existence created for him there, ultimately, placed writing on the back burner.

Calvin found the Panorama search engine and clicked the box for search criteria. Flying fingertips spelled out the words *Chat Rooms* in the search field. The information query came back five seconds later with a list of over forty thousand articles, and/or, accesses. Running his cursor down the monitor's electronic page, he perused titles dealing with chat rooms. "Here's one."

The heading read, "Fountain Interactive Community- Come Join Us."

"That sounds friendly enough," he thought. "Let's give her a spin." Cal clicked his mouse on the highlighted title. It took him immediately to a Fountain Advertisement Page that read:

Welcome to Fountain's Home Page!

**Want to become a member for free?
Just click below and come on in!**

click here!

Indeed, it was easy. Once inside, the newcomer received his own home page where he could provide an alias, a nickname or handle, by which all other Fountain members would know him, his e-mail address, and the opportunity to give as much or as little information about himself as he saw fit. Calvin was suspicious of providing even his e-mail location, but finally did. As far as the open page to type a description of his personal tastes, and what he was and was not interested in, he passed. The information was optional, and he figured he could always come back and elaborate if he decided he liked being part of the online social club.

"An alias?" he thought. "What would be a good alias?"

Sharply snapping his fingers, he proclaimed, "Timetravellar!" After all, he *was* of Scottish descent and fascinated with time travel movies. *Highlander* was his favorite time travel film, and perhaps, his favorite movie of all-time. The misspelling of his alias would add a sense of mystique and immortality to the fantasy character. In the new realm, he could be a Conner McLeod, a romantic swashbuckler that traveled through time and space. Hours passed as he explored the Internet complex, scanning members' homepages, reading music reviews, and studying the various chat rooms' role-play formats.

Heightened curiosity met disappointed exasperation, when a Network error message popped to the center of his screen.

"What the...? What do you mean I've been disconnected?" He did not consider that an incoming call would disconnect him, until the telephone in the great room chirped. "Shit."

His heart transformed to cold granite and sank into his belly, as he listened to her greeting.

"Cal, I've filed for a divorce. Strom Gillespie is representing me. You're going to need an attorney, someone he can contact."

"Mags," he whispered in disbelief. The reality of the situation came crashing down around him, and all of his anger and pain vanished. "Think about this. I can't believe you really want a divorce. I know you're upset, disappointed. But honey, you're calling it quits too soon. Please come over and let's talk." Tears crested his eyelids, as he realized Maggie's serious intent.

"I love you Cal, at least I did, but I'm not coming over. I'd want to believe the promises you'd make. You, yourself, would believe them when you made them. But, you won't change. You've had more than ample time. Something has happened to you, something irreversible. I can't...no...I won't live like this any longer. You're interested in Cal, and that's about it. Just get an attorney, honey, I don't want to argue. I just want out."

Gently dropping the receiver on its cradle, McLeish slumped back onto the sofa. Trembling hands unscrewed the Jack Daniels bottle cap. The dark elixir had barely filled a shot glass, before it was racing down his throat. Three times he repeated the ritual, until his nerves began to calm, then three more times, and three more again. An estranged McLeish jumped on a twenty-four hour bender that found him still sick and vomiting the next evening. Dejected, he returned to the net, hoping to find someone to talk to, someone with a sympathetic ear. If possible, if such a person existed, he hoped to find someone as lonely as he was at that very moment.

Chapter 2

A darkened sarcophagus entombed by thick draperies and opaque window tinting was silent, save for the faint rustle of satin bed linens. A disposable lighter flicked and its small fire danced like a tiny ballerina above her closed fist. She ignited a single wick in a sea of bedchamber candles, the flame projecting surreal, ghostly shadows off the stone walls. Her naked silhouette glided effortlessly across the slate floor to the shift robe, where she removed a long-sleeved burgundy dress.

The silkiness of its material paled in contrast to her smooth, ashen skin, and while the vampiress lacked life's glow, her form and her image provoked a vision of desire and seduction. Two weeks since her last blood meal, her belly and dark heart rumbled to be fed. Cyber-conquests had allowed her to prolong the actual taking of a victim, but it had been too long. She desperately needed to feel her weapons pierce flesh and rejoice in life's dark scarlet wine cascading down her throat.

Sunset's final arc of flaming orange crested Ottawa's western horizon, as she booted up a twenty gigabyte Pentium. There was time enough to go to the meeting place before she began her hunt. Daylight could be tolerated, but was unpleasant. A few moments in Fountain's *Gothica* would keep her distracted from hunger, until daylight gasped its final breath. After all, her following was there, and just as she needed blood, so did she hunger for the adoration of the members that waited for her in *Gothica*. They were her flock, her disciples, and she had recruited most that were members. In a rather civilized way, those new-age vampires had come to provide her dark lusts with a quenching that allowed her to prolong the frequency between physical feedings.

Beyond the members of various clans congregating in *Gothica* were the visitors and spectators drawn to the dark side, those pulled toward the legendary Dark Princess—Vampyra. She went to them, flirted with them, and seduced them to vampirism. There, she nourished her dark lusts and her female psyche. Vampyra signed in rapidly, and her name suddenly appeared to the others.

In the Room: Mephisto, Stag, Queen Satania, Timetravellar, Vampyra and **the Sorcerer.**

Vampyra: Bonsoir, mon Prince...*kotc*...

Mon Prince was, Stag, master of the room. KOTC was cyber-language for, *kiss on the cheek,* one of many abbreviations used by the gothic chatters.

Stag: Good evening, Vampyra...*French kiss*...

Vampyra: A gift for the Prince... [IMAGE]

The French speaking vampiress instantly aroused McLeish. He had nearly decided against entering *Gothica,* but peeked in, simply as a matter of investigating all areas of the Fountain community.

"Who, or what the hell is mon Prince?" He speculated that the Prince she referred to might be Satan, himself. Tepid curiosity had led him to this room called

Gothica, but now, he found himself wondering what it represented. "Are these people for real?" Much of the conversation in the room seemed to center around what it was like to be Goth, or Gothic, something Calvin did not understand.

Proper grammar, at least technically correct grammar, appeared to have been abandoned by those posting messages. Sentences seemed most often separated by a series of two or more periods rather than just one. The following sentence or phrase rarely began with a capital, but it seemed to be the accepted technique.

Only mildly intrigued at first, he was ready to leave moments before the shrouded one's entrance. Something about her, though, her flamboyance, her coquettish accent, drew him and commanded him to stay. The interloper listened for a time, as she cajoled and toyed with several of *Gothica's* males.

Cal double clicked on the [IMAGE] the dark chamber's female had posted for the Prince. It was the back view of a voluptuous woman, naked, wearing a sheer, transparent gown. The painting was almost certainly a Vargas, and the fact that she had posted it spoke to Cal's sexual nature. Clearly, it implied promiscuity and lack of inhibition. That quickly, she had captivated Calvin McLeish, just as she had countless others who entered her lair. The novice *Gothican* clicked on the WHISPER button to convey a private message to the vixen of night.

Timetravellar whispers to Vampyra: I know the image was intended for another, but for myself and everyone else in the room...thanks...you made my night...

She instantly answered his whisper.

Vampyra whispers to Timetravellar: Monsieur...you night?...And how is it...that I made you night? ...*smile*...you like the night...oui?...

Calvin feared his heart would jump out of his chest and onto the floor. She had answered, and was friendly, at least, not unfriendly. The French flavor of her words magnetized him and bid him stay. It was not the real world, but indeed, it *was* a real fantasy world. Purely by replying, she had piqued his interest. He did not want to lose her attention and panicked for an adequate response.

Timetravellar whispers to Vampyra: Because...night is the essence of life...

His words appeared on the screen, as though being written by another, seemingly there before his thought was complete. He continued.

...And your gift, to the Prince...and to all of us...is an unexpected...night blossom...a sweet black orchid of...the darkness...an erotic fruit placed before us...on nocturnum's table...

His hands trembled, as molten lava streaked through every vein and capillary of his tense body. "What is happening?" he wondered. His fingers had hammered out an answer, while he helplessly stared at the screen in awe. Cold, frozen, he sat at the keyboard sensing the presence of another, one greater than he, one who spoke to the heart of night's most exalted seductress. McLeish watched in humility, as the Timetravellar seized command of the encounter. As Calvin McLeish, he resigned to only observe the immediate and intense bonding of the two cyber-characters. Unfolding like an opened flower, his mind released the captive immortal knight from imprisonment. The Timetravellar, an alter ego that he had only just created, now surged with life and grew in enormity with each rapid beat of his heart. A separate and distinct life force flowed into the traveler, nourished by each of Vampyra's silken words.

"My God, what is happening here?" he whispered in astonishment. Scotland's descendent backed away from the keyboard and monitor. Darkness surrounded him in the master bedroom, as his body radiated from the illumination of the terminal. An electronic blip caught his attention, another reply from the vampiress.

Vampyra whispers to Timetravellar: Mmmmm... *soft laugh*...I have said the same thing myself many times. It is the darkness to which I always return...it is my home...it is my hunting ground...as for the gift Monsieur...I am glad it gives you pleasure...*warm smile*...

Carnality seeped from her every word, and Calvin sensed that her focus was his. Unaware of his facial contortions—the one drooped eyebrow, the supreme confidence invading his eyes and the slightly cocked head, he scooted his seat closer to the computer stand, his fingers tapping out a response.

Timetravellar whispers to Vampyra: I saw from your posts shortly after I arrived...that you toyed with one named Mephisto...you described so eloquently...your taking of him...how your fangs punctured his neck...his weak attempts to resist...and his transformation to...the undead...and then...his embarrassing patronization of you after the throes of feeding and passion were complete...
Know this Dark Princess...the others are fools in the cyber realm...but it is I who sees your true heart...the others coddle you...submit themselves to you...whimper before you as dogs after a bitch in heat...but I understand your black heart...it is not their subjugation that satisfies you...it is the hunt...the challenge that thrills you...their

resistance...It is the conflict upon which your spirit feeds...and once conquered...they are hulls that you cast aside...

If Mephisto wanted to captivate you...he should not have submitted so easily...he is a buffoon...

Vampyra whispers to Timetravellar: *gasp*...You see into me...as one peers through a thin veil of mist...who are you Timetravellar...to know me so completely...when we have never spoken...*frown*...or have you been here before, as another?...is Timetravellar a new name behind which someone I know hides? Do you play me for a fool?!!...*hands in claw*...

Timetravellar whispers to Vampyra: I DO NOT PLAY GAMES! I am an immortal knight of Scotland, as I have always been...I DO NOT change my name...and I will not tolerate impudence from a wench...no matter how...desirable...I may find her...*tone softens...turns to leave*...

Calvin read with widening eyes, as the conflict heightened, his fingers the messenger of Timetravellar's words.

Vampyra whispers to Timetravellar: Non...Monsieur...*head down*...please do not leave. I beg you...I am deeply sorry...there have been others...others who...deceive...I see great strength in you...I fear you...because I am...attracted so strongly to you...

Timetravellar whispers to Vampyra: *drops to one knee and takes the hand of his desire*...I must leave my queen...but I will not abandon you...not now...not ever...I will be here for you...throughout eternity...*kisses her sweet stem...and disappears into the darkness*...

Vampyra logged out of the Fountain system and shut the computer down. Daylight was gone, and it was time to hunt. Most nights, she would have bolted out the door. Her belly churned to be fed, but this night, for what seemed an eternity, she sat quietly in the stone chamber candlelight staring at her computer. Knitted eyebrows relaxed, and a faint smile crept across her powder-white face. For a moment, there was the radiance of life in her eyes.

Shuddering gasps whispered from McLeish's separated lips, as he, again, jumped back from the computer. Dumbfounded at the events that had transpired, he struggled to calm himself. Timetravellar spoke—as McLeish would like to have written. Never before had he been able to extract the words or the emotion as he had when speaking to Vampyra. In truth, he did not have to leave her, as he said, but he feared continuing. Deep within himself, he knew that somehow he could have gone on all night. Calvin had intervened, ended the exchange, not the Timetravellar. The immortal warrior feared nothing, but because he was a manifestation of McLeish mind, he submitted to the mortal's will.

Cal gripped the slender neck of his Tennessee whiskey bottle. Spilling over the shot glass brim, droplets of dark brew beaded on the thick, glassy polyurethane of the coffee table. Expressionless pupils tracked the small vessel, as it approached his mouth. He marveled, savored his new experience in *Gothica*, and this...Vampyra.

Something had happened there, though, a transformation of sorts, he thought. Words and clear expression of feeling had flowed from his mind through his fingertips as running water, and that discomforted him. When he wrote, created a story, it was a laborious task. Nothing came easily. He groped for every descriptive syllable, every idiom of emotion. In Fountain, though, his mind truly *was* a fountain, a wellspring of limitless articulation.

The burning compound ignited his esophagus and calmed his nerves, yet nothing, absolutely nothing, could still his pounding heart. Should he go back in and find her—engage her again?

"That would be foolish," he thought.

Calvin sensed that he, as Timetravellar, had captivated the vampire, or at least aroused her curiosity. Every maneuver would be critical in establishing himself with her. He had been firm, and not cowered at her indignation. To go back now would show weakness. It would undermine the strength of character he had displayed. No, abstinence, at least for the moment, was his best volley. But, as provocative as their first meeting was, he had been stern. When next he met the voluptuous mistress, it was paramount that he approached her softly and sweetly. His words must drip as honey from the hive.

A gift! That was it! He had acknowledged her gift, the Vargas. Now it was his turn to provide a beautiful picture, but his canvas would be her heart and his paint would be the nectarous words in which she would willingly drown.

Calvin never stayed up past eleven thirty, and while his weary body dulled from the whiskey, his mind ran rampant. Intent on scribing a piece that would melt Vampyra's cloaked heart, he perched himself once again at the keyboard. That time though, Calvin alone tried to create a masterpiece, not the time traveler. Calvin alone struggled for just the right words, and he alone took credit for the final creation. Timetravellar stood as a spectator in the dark corners of his mind, while Calvin reached deep into his heart. Hours passed, as he painstakingly chose each verb, each noun, and each adjective.

The blue-black sky had paled to a deep gray when the last word was typed. Sunrise was but a half-hour away. The exhausted writer longed to slump onto his mattress and fade into narcotic sleep, but his quest would not be complete until he conveyed the tediously written love letter.

Logging back into Fountain, a drained McLeish found a tab that said, "Mailbox." A double click took him to a message center where he could receive and send messages. Addressing the mail to *Vampyra*, he posted his short prose.

*Timetravellar enters the Dark Princess's chamber and gaits across the marble floor to where she sits...he drops to one knee and pulls the left side of his cloak back behind him...

Reaching to extract the rose next to his scabbard...he quickly retracts his hand...a droplet of blood bursts forth, racing around the curvature of his forefinger...and hurls itself into space...finally achieving its own demise on the polished stone substrate below...

Now...more cautiously...more slowly...Timetravellar reaches again and removes the blossom...

Gazing ardently at the rose, Timetravellar begins to speak*...

"When grasped brazenly and without forethought, the body (the stem) retaliates, piercing the flesh with rapier-like fangs...But...when touched tenderly and carefully with light, properly placed fingertips, the body responds receptively and without malice...Above, lies the exquisite head, heart, and soul of the living entity...its majestic hue speaks to the life- force within each of us...it is the color of love...Intricate layers of petals create the complex design that uniquely identifies this floral creature...The petals...ah...the petals...

Words of my mouth are not adequate to describe their elegance...Any word falls miserably short of conveying their extraordinary texture...Save, to compare them to a woman's lips, her soft kiss; only then can one comprehend the exquisiteness of the rose's petals...

The fragrance of its blossom silently intoxicates the admirer...Is there anyone who can partake of its perfume and not be uplifted?...Is there anyone who can deny its immortal beauty?...I think not..."

Timetravellar hands the rose to the Dark Princess
"...a gift for you, Vampyra..."

Clicking the send icon, Calvin managed a weak smile and piled his aching body onto the bed beside the computer stand.

Chapter 3

Strong gusting blasts forced scattered raindrops sideways under a downtown Ottawa streetlight. The illumination of the street faded into the bowels of an alleyway near the heart of the Canadian metropolis. Monday nights were the slowest of the week, but still, that area provided the greatest concentration of people. Her timing was poor, but hunger came when it came, and she could wait no longer.

Vampyra's dark, morbid clothing was not so different from what it had been some four hundred ninety-seven years earlier. Light, brightness, and vivid colors offended the undead, and their garb spoke of that disdain. Clothing was worn more to avoid attention than to protect the flesh. The body was cold. No garment could warm it. Only the cascading of life's hot crimson liquid down her throat would thaw her chill and fill her desire.

Unfortunately, her modern-day existence had become more perilous than in years gone by. Hepatitis, AIDS, and a list of other transmittable diseases could be transfused, if she chose her meal badly. Communicable diseases would not vanquish the undead, but could induce illness, which in turn, would prolong feeding. If too much time passed without life's blood, great pain came, and even vampires avoided pain.

Standing camouflaged at the edge of darkness, in deep shadows, her cloaked form motionlessly eyed passersby, as they exited the clubs to return to their vehicles. The Dark Princess possessed a sense about the health of her prey and chose accordingly. Many passed that may have been adequate, but in her mind, were questionable. Two years earlier, she had taken what she thought to be a sound specimen, only to be bedridden for three weeks from consuming the tainted liquid.

Her right knee involuntarily quivered, as pangs of hunger and lust stabbed at her core. Panic drenched her, and she feared the movement might give away her blind. Good fortune found her moments later, however, as her gray eyes locked on a target. It was a young schoolgirl, perhaps seventeen, sweet and innocent in appearance. Vampyra surmised that she had probably sneaked out the house, and if this was not the child's first taste of freedom, it was certainly one of her first. Risk was minimal. The prey would lack strength, and promised to be healthy. The flaxen-haired youth turned into the very alley where Vampyra staged herself, heading for the parking lot at its end.

Quickening her pace, the teenager looked behind her. She sensed danger. A feeling that she was being watched instinctively put her on alert. Yet, she would not hear the predator's approach, nor would she see the strike. She would only whimper, when the porcelain stilettos plunged into her virgin throat and faint mercifully. Vampyra's bite was a feeding strike and not intended to leave the victim undead. It would quite simply leave the young woman stone-cold and blue.

Twentieth century vamps had learned to differentiate in the way their savagery affected the prey. Depending on the individual, they may choose to feed only enough to create a state of *undeadness* within the victim. That state may actually been desired by the bitten. Vampire recruits, for example, would seek such a bite as an initiation into the ghoulish world of the vampire. Attacking vampires would, on occasion, leave the victim undead, purely out of spite and jealousy. Being undead was not desirable to those who were. It was a condition that they had come to, but most would have traded their eternal existence for mortality and a few short years of—life.

While capable of such treachery, somewhere deep within Vampyra's lifelessness, a degree of compassion still lived. Indeed, there were those that she had stricken, leaving them to roam the nights of the planet for all time. But typically, they were those who foolishly lusted after vampirism, or enemies sufficiently unwise to stir her wrath. As barbaric as it would seem to those who found the young woman, to leave her undead would have been crueler still. The attack filled Vampyra's stomach, and mercifully left her target in peaceful rest.

CHAPTER 4

Scrolling down the list of members' names, Panthera studied each, hoping to find one that struck her fancy. Fountain boasted of having over a million members worldwide, so it seemed to her that they might at least attract some with imagination. Most members fell into very distinct chat genres. That is to say, their names readily identified them in one of the many role-play categories. An overwhelming number subscribed to raw, or at least unabashed sexuality. Then, there were the Arthurian knights of the round table lot, the occultists, the romantics, the pitiful sympathy seekers, and representing a smaller but fast growing subset, the vampires.

Panthera had made a home in Gothica, but she was not strictly vamp. She liked the people there and played the game, but was not loyal to any one room. Gothica was her nighttime playground, but daylight hours often found her milling around in *Sexual Fantasies.*

She was a brilliant mind, holding three bachelor's degrees and working on a fourth, computer technology. Diabetes, four kids, and a husband that continuously traveled overseas kept her from going out often, and the computer had become her closest friend.

"Hmmm, Timetravellar. Let's see. Well, he's not online, but at least the name is somewhat original."

Clicking on the royal blue alias, her Macintosh seemed to struggle and groan, as it loaded his homepage onto her screen. A full length painting slowly formed, block by block, below the immortal knight's handle.

"Mmmmm...I think I'm in love," she whispered in a sweet southern drawl.

It was the figure of a man from the neck to the waist, bulging triceps, a tattered shirt, and a tattoo of two entangled fighting dragons, one of which came out of the limb to which it was affixed into the third dimension. Its neck twisted backwards and bit the arm that it adorned. A trickle of blood streamed from the bite down to the elbow and dripped into infinity. Panthera, Cathryn Meeks, in the real world, guessed that it was a Vallejo, and indeed, she was correct. Many embellished their homepages with photos, or paintings stolen from other websites, and artist Boris Vallejo was a popular victim of such crimes. She had never seen this one, though. The owner of the page, in her opinion, had great taste in art, knew how to make a first impression, and, at least in cyber-world, came across as a babe magnet.

After soaking in as much lust as she could, she read Timetravellar's original verse below. His words painted a fascinating picture of their own.

I am a Scot of ancient lineage and have traversed the millennia for centuries. My quest is my own, and I grow weary in its cause. I waivereth not, however, for I am strong in purpose, and in will, and in body. My sword dulleth from its cross with the ancient ones, all of whom are now vanquished. The cyber is my new channel and it is strange to me. There are a few (not most by any count) whom are hostile and attack me with bizarre, secretive weapons. I shall learn their ways and...well, another battlefield, another time. After all, I am Timetravellar. I have all the time in the world.

There is one whom I should fear, but do not, and know not why. Her creed is of bloodlust, yet...she plucketh not my heart...she toucheth it with tender warm fingertips...

Immediately following the fantasy story, written in blue, McLeish had quoted verse from one of his favorite songs.

...the mist is lifting slowly, I can see the way ahead, and I've left behind the empty streets that once inspired my life...and the strength of the emotion, is like thunder in the air, 'cause the promise that we made each other haunts me to the end...I know you're out there somewhere ...somewhere...somewhere...I know I'll find you somehow, and someday I'll return again for you...

from Sur La Mer
Moody Blues 1988

His original intent was to leave that as the whole of his homepage, but he had remembered another song he hoped might intrigue the dark princess, if ever she visited his Fountain home.

Many times I've loved,
Many times been **bitten**,

Many times I've gazed,
Along the open road...

Led Zeppelin 1973
HOUSES OF THE HOLY

"Holy cow," Panthera whispered. "I gotta meet you, honey."

Tabbing farther down, she looked to see what Timetravellar had listed as his favorite chat rooms, who his friends were in Fountain, and what his interests were. Gothica was the only venue listed, and Vampyra was the only friend listed, nothing else.

"Hmmm...many times been *bitten*, eh? Seems you've been smitten by 'Vamp-whore-a,' just like every other male in Fountain and probably the entire cyber-universe. So here's a challenge. Let's just see if we can turn your head away from that bloodsucking slut."

Panthera popped over to the message center and began typing.

"Love your home page time warrior. The picture is...purrrrfect! Why doncha' come over and see me sometime big boy?"...*giggle*......Panthera

She could not have known that Calvin just finished constructing his homepage. Had it not been complete, she likely would never again have investigated his listing, and never played such a role in Cal's cyber-existence. Others would be similarly affected by his homepage and those femme would lavish him with their romantic attention. Panthera though, would become one of his favorites, second only to Vampyra.

Chapter 5

Maggie responded to a high-pitched, nasal voice that answered the telephone. "Bitsy?"

"Girlfriend! How are you hon?" Bitsy asked.

"Oh, as well as can be expected, Bit. The reason I called is because I have an apartment over near the old train depot, but I need to get a few things from the house. Since Calvin's always at home, I'm sure I won't be lucky enough to show up when he's out. Would you mind going over there with me? I hate to ask, but he was pissed when I left. I don't think he'd hurt me or anything, but I do think he'd be on better behavior if I had someone with me. Would you?"

With the zeal of a world class busybody, Bitsy rapid-fired, "Well, you know I don't mind. You just come on over. Don't blame you a bit. Wouldn't want to go over there alone either. He's not right, ya know. I wish I had your guts. I should have left Aaron a long time ago myself. Men are pigs—lazy, fornicating, deadbeat pigs. Why if I..."

"Bitsy, I hate to cut you off, but I have to go. The kids get out of school in just a few minutes and I need to pick them up. I'll be by around 9:30, if that's okay." Maggie's eyes lit up. "I've got a dinner date."

Squealing with fervor, Bitsy clung to each of Maggie's final words. "A *dinner* date? Oh, do tell, girlfriend.

Is it anyone I know? There is the most handsome new butcher at McPhereson's. I'll bet that hunk stands six-four or better. If I wasn't chained to this piece of deadwood I call a husband, why I'd..."

"Bit," Maggie snapped. "I have to go! I'll tell you about it another time...okay? Don't be mad."

"Why don't be silly Mags, if I had been through what you'd been through, I'd be ill too. I was just telling Ruth Anne the other day that I didn't know how you've stood it this long..."

"Bye Bit."

The dial tone droned, while Bitsy continued.

"Now don't you worry about a thing Maggie, I'll keep an eye on...hmm, we must have gotten disconnected."

She shrugged, hung up the telephone, and returned to the Wednesday episode of the *Young and the Restless*.

* * * * *

A kissy-faced Margaret McLeish wheeled into Bitsy's driveway at five minutes past ten o'clock. Her date had been hot, and she would not have pried herself away had it not been for her arrangement with Bitsy. That, plus the fact that she and the two children left with but the clothes on their backs, and she was tired of doing laundry every day.

"C'mon in Maggie!" Bitsy greeted. "I was beginning to think you weren't gonna show. Hot daddy, huh?" she said with a goofy-faced wink. "Why honey, I do believe your face has a flush."

Maggie bit her tongue. She liked Bitsy, but could only stand a little of her at a time. The two had gossiped incessantly during the five years that they had been neighbors. For Maggie, gossip helped get past boredom and her dissatisfaction with life. For Bitsy, gossip was life itself. It was a reason to get out of bed every morning and the last thing on her mind before falling asleep.

The thought of being the focal point of the neighborhood gossip crossed Maggie's mind, but she did not care. She knew Bitsy had been running her mouth to Ruth Anne, Veronica, and the rest. Bitsy would swear up and down to keep all secrets strictly confidential. It simply was not in her to keep a secret though, and Maggie smiled, as she considered what all might have been said about her and Cal splitting.

"You ready Bit?" Maggie asked.

"Why, of course. Did I tell you that I heard Ruth Anne is six months behind on her house note? One of the girls at the bank was telling me that..."

Bitsy's words floated unheard into the South Georgia night. Maggie was lost within her own mind, as she and her neighbor walked across the McLeish's shrouded lawn. A streetlight common to several houses provided the only light for that part of the block. She hated having to go to the house, and what was worse, knew she would have to make several more trips to secure all of her belongings. That night was just a necessities-run, allowing her to get the things that she and the kids needed most.

Calvin's car was there. She knew it would be. Her husband rarely left the house, anymore. As the two women tentatively negotiated their way through the darkness of the garage, Maggie's heart pounded. She dreaded the forthcoming confrontation, but knew that it was unavoidable. Perhaps Bitsy's presence would keep it civil.

The doorknocker reverberated "Whack, Whack!".

Chapter 6

Two bologna sandwiches and a mountain of Doritos piled onto a paper plate appeared as though it might topple at any moment. If it had, the crumbs would not be the first on Calvin's comforter. Since discovering Fountain, Gothica in particular, Calvin had quickly gone from sleeping at night to sleeping during the day. He and Maggie's bed was but eighteen inches from the card table that served as a computer stand. The mattress served as a dinner table, so that Cal could eat without missing the possibility of Vampyra's entrance. Creatures of the night, appropriately, seemed to come out only at night. McLeish unconsciously became one of them, changing his schedule to conform to theirs. Gothica was usually open during the day, but few of its subjects ever showed up until near dusk.

Less than a week had passed since Maggie left, yet the kitchen counter was already deep in unattended mail. McLeish rationalized that he would attend to that mundane business after his self-appointed sabbatical and recovery period from Maggie's treacherous mutiny. Powerful, commanding obsession became the driving force in his life, though he would never have admitted it, even to himself.

Eight o'clock Eastern Time. If Vampyra were to come, it would be in the next hour. She always showed up by nine and stayed until well past the witching hour. Anxiety and excitement filled him, as he impatiently drummed the card table.

Calvin barely paid attention to Stag, Loosifur, scabby porno elf, or any of the others as they conversed. His hand constantly clicked on the "Reload" button to see if any new vamps had entered the room, desperate for her arrival. Then, after repeated updates, there was her name.

"Sweet God, finally," he announced to the empty bedroom.

Concurrent with Vampyra's entrance was Calvin's transformation. When the nightress offered her usual greeting to the Prince, the change had already begun. The drooping right eyelid, the cocking of the head to the side, and the exuding expression of confidence that was the Timetravellar, revealed itself once more.

In the Room: Barbwire, Stag, Loosifur, scabby porno elf, Junket, Huge Rod, Timetravellar, Vampyra and **the Sorcerer.**

Vampyra: Bonsoir mon Prince...*deep French kiss*...

Stag: *cradling her waist, he returns her affection*...Well now, you ARE in a fit mood this evening ma chéri...and what brings such gaiety?...

Vampyra: I have hunted well...my dark heart...(and tummy...)...hehehe... are full...

Stag: Did you hunt as vampire...or as lupine?...

Vampyra: Non mon Prince, as vampire... this time I stalk in the city ... *gasp* ... Monsieur Timetravellar!... forgive please...I did not see you here...*kiss on the cheek*...

Calvin gulped, surging with excitement from her greeting. She not only noticed him, but indeed had kissed him on the cheek. It was an honor, and while not as flattering as a French kiss, it was a start. Mortal Calvin Ian McLeish was far too flustered, far too shaky, and far too nervous to reply. The Timetravellar, however, was not.

Timetravellar: *kisses her hand...still holding it...looks into the eyes of Gothica's most fair*...The moon has risen quickly above this realm...and looks jealously below to see the one that steals her light...and the attention of all creatures beneath her...she sees that it is Vampyra...and ducks behind a silvery cloud to...pout...

Vampyra: Séducteur!!!...*penetrating smile* ...you try to thaw this cold heart...no??...

the Sorcerer: Greetings Timetravellar...this realm and your ancestors...have long awaited your arrival...

Calvin looked at the message and wondered who the psycho named "Sorcerer" was.

Timetravellar: Vampyra, I only pay homage to the most exquisite of night's treasures...

Vampyra whispers to Timetravellar: It is not just my heart that you sweet words warm, Monsieur...*soft laugh*...
I receive you mail...you gift...I like it very much...the rose...it is my most favorite flower...*kiss*...

Timetravellar whispers to Vampyra: That flower...that you so admire...is coarse...offensive...when compared to thy sweet lips...

Panthera: *saunters into Gothica...a friendly wag of her tail to all Gothicans, as she bypasses the bar and curls her feline form up in front of the fireplace*...Well, HELLO...Sir Timetravellar...did you receive my mail?...

Vampyra: *glares at Panthera*...

Timetravellar: Why...uh...no...Panthera...I have not checked for any messages...I...did not expect any...have we met?...

Panthera: No...time knight...we have not met...*seductive gaze*...but do you not read your mail when notified that you have such?...*glares back at Vampyra...unconcerned by her stare*...

Timetravellar: *confused*...I have received no notification...

Panthera: *brushes up against the tall warrior's leg...purring*...Silly boy...see the rectangle in the upper left-hand corner of your screen?...it says "messages"...bet it's flashing isn't it?...

Timetravellar: *embarrassed*...Well...yes...

Panthera: Click on it...it'll take you to your mailbox and you can read any messages that you have...when you've finished...there will be a box in the upper left hand corner that says..."return to previous location"...that'll bring you back here...

Timetravellar: I shall return...momentarily...

Panthera: *giggle*...brb, Time...brb...that's cyber for..."be right back"...

*****

the Sorcerer: It is well that you are here Scot...our time has just begun...thy destiny calls...

Timetravellar had already left the room, but would quickly learn the customs of this new dimension, the acronyms, along with the alluring guile of some of its inhabitants.

Vampyra: *frowns*...You are new here yourself, Panthera...yet you speak, as though you were kindred...as though you were of Malkavian...or Torreador clans...

Stay away from Timetravellar...I am highest-ranking female in Gothica...I so command you!...

Panthera: *mocking, Glenda the Good Witch voice*...Oh rubbish...be gone...before someone drops a house on you!...
Vampyra: ??????...what do you say to me?!!...*eyes cold*...
Panthera: Huh?...oh yeah I forgot you're a supposed French speaking Canadian...phony...bitch...probably never heard of the Wizard of Oz...eh?......hmmm...let's see...maybe you can understand this......... ...P-I-S-S... ... ...O-F-F-!!!...

Chapter 7

Panthera's message boosted Calvin's spirit, but rather than respond to her mail, he would try romancing her upon his return to Gothica. Rising to take a bladder break, a small smile crept over his lips.

"Hmmm, this Panthera seems to be interested in the Timetravellar," he murmured. "Guess we'll see if she can resist Tt's smooth, southern style."

Zipping his pants, he headed back toward the computer, looking down as he approached the doorway common to the two rooms. A silly smirk remained on his face. Calvin basked in his own success and sensed that he might become a hot item within the vampire chat.

Breath would be snatched from him, however, and his stomach would grow cold, as his downward gaze locked upon something foreign in the bathroom doorway's threshold. Fear clutched his throat, and kept his head lowered, such that it would be an endlessly long moment before he could raise his eyes. Two large sandaled feet stood before him. Crisscrossing leather straps bound the massive calves up to the knee. That was as far as he could look. Someone must have broken into the house, as he relieved himself.

Eyes darting left and then right, his racing thought process groped for a proper course of action. With only the feet and calves to give him scale of the intruder, he could only surmise that the interloper was immense.

Finally, mustering his courage, he looked upward, higher and higher until his eyes met the stranger's. Inexplicably, his hysteria subsided. Why, he did not know. Before him stood a man, at least six feet, three inches. Donning a tattered dark blue kilt, a cloak, and an "X" of leather chest protection, the intruder looked placidly at Calvin McLeish. Yet, there was something eerily familiar about the tresspasser. His facial features were so similar to Calvin's own, that it bewildered the smaller man.

"I would not have come so rudely unannounced had it not been necessary," the tall one said calmly in a thick Scottish brogue. "But you divert from the vampiress, and fickly endeavor to pursue the feline one. Stalk her, romance her, tempt her if you wish. It is however, quite unfitting that you plan such a pursuit while the Dark Princess is in the room. Panthera is a quest better left to the daylight. When the sun is about, Vampyra shall be gone. Only then, would Panthera be proper amusement."

Calvin could not close his gaping mouth. His chin weighed a ton, and it seemed as though it might forever stay pinned to his chest.

Finally, after protracted silence, he asked, "Who are you?"

"I think you know who I am," replied the wayfarer. "After all you created me, released me from the dungeon of your mind. I am...Timetravellar."

Cal's knees buckled. He grasped the back of the chair for support and guided his collapsing body to the horizontal surface of the hardwood seat. What frightened him above all was the fact that the stranger's answer was known before it was spoken.

Raising his head to speak, McLeish began to question, "How can you...?" He stopped in mid-sentence.

Timetravellar was gone. Cal stood briskly and scanned the room.

"Hey!" he shouted.

There was no response, no trace of the intruder, and no way he could have exited without Calvin seeing him. Mentally traumatized, the writer searched his own mind to explain what had just happened. Lack of sleep? Whiskey? Stress? Could those things have created the hallucination? Perhaps he was simply going insane. His Aunt Mervis was as crazy as a brickbat, always had been as far as he knew. Maybe that inherited trait was just now surfacing. Maggie had rocked him emotionally, and he knew from growing up with an alcoholic father that delirium was possible from abusing the hard stuff. But, Calvin McLeish was mentally tough, and Jack Daniels had only been his roommate for a few days. Emotional stress and alcohol abuse did not seem plausible explanations. There were but two possibilities. Either he was insane or it had actually happened.

A series of screen blips grabbed his focus. Vampyra was calling, demanding his attention. Obediently, he returned to the keyboard. Her summons was irresistible, and the fantastic appearance and disappearance of the time warrior faded from the forefront of his concern.

Vampyra: Mon couer? Are you there? I see you name...

Timetravellar: Yes vampiress, I have returned... there are those who attempt to hinder me, as I make my way back to you...but their obstacles are paltry...I will not be detoured by my lessers...

Calvin's unblinking eyes froze on the computer screen. His hands seemed shackled to the keyboard. The facial expressions he took on, when he spoke as the Timetravellar, had returned.

Before, Calvin had made no distinction between

himself and the *other*, but now he understood that the Timetravellar had not left him at all. He had simply retreated into Calvin, back into his mind and back into his heart. In time, the would-be author would learn to share himself with his alter ego, but for the moment, he struggled with him, wrestling for dominance. It would be through that internal conflict that he would come to symbiosis with the Travellar. The Scottish titan would remain firm in his quest, faithful to his pursuit of the Dark Huntress,but gentle with the mortal he inhabited. Eventually, Timetravellar would lead Calvin to understand that they truly were two entities. While the human had created the character, only the character could navigate the two of them through the channel called cyberspace. Only the time knight could lead them to a different plane, a different playing field, and a different reality. Timetravellar too, would learn the skill of compromise, allowing Calvin freedom with many of the non-vampire characters.

Panthera: Welcome back, Timehunk...get my post?.........*snubs Vamp-whore-a*...

Timetravellar: Indeed, I have received your message, feline one...

Timetravellar whispers to Panthera: Meet me tomorrow, during the daylight if you can...I would be honored to come to know you...

Cathryn's face flushed, her breath becoming short and erratic. Excitement filled her, as she read Timetravellar's reply. She sensed a margin of victory over Gothica's tramp and replied quickly.

Panthera whispers to Timetravellar: I'm on all day beefcake...just look me up when you get here...*eg*...

Timetravellar: ...eg?

Panthera: *...shakes her head* ...eg is evil grin...you have so much to learn...

McLeish's alter ego recognized Cal's need to be a part of the new domain, and as a peace offering, relinquished Panthera to him, along with the daylight hours. But because the three situations had erupted simultaneously, Timetravellar maintained absolute control of the moment. Calvin's diversion to Panthera, Vampyra's impatience, and Panthera's forwardness had required quick, decisive action. Calvin was skilless in dealing with that sort of juggling act. When another distraction presented itself, Timetravellar predictably stepped forward.

Motionless and transfixed, the mortal sat, unable to answer the unrelenting doorbell.

"Maybe he's not here, Bit," Maggie postulated. "But his car is. I hate to use my key. What if he's got somebody with him?"

A measure of jealousy emerged.

"Piss on him, Bit. I'm getting our clothes."

Margaret McLeish keyed the lock and walked into a dimly lit kitchen with her next-door neighbor. Both figures stood stone still, unable to move, unable to speak, as the warrior's towering image emerged from the hallway darkness.

Timetravellar approached the gape-mouthed women and bowed slightly at the waist.

"Welcome ladies. May I be of service?"

Neither replied, astonished at his presence and locked in mutual silence. For a moment, Maggie thought she would faint. A shrinking tunnel of light and intense disorientation weakened her knees. The longhaired gladiator from the fourth dimension was dressed so oddly, and yet there was something so familiar about him. She saw Cal in him, and yet everything about him was larger and greater than the man she had shared her bed with for a decade and a half. But who the hell was he? Why would he be there with Calvin? Finally, she found the presence of mind to offer a response.

"Uh...uh...is Calvin home?" she asked reverently.

"He is...indisposed, I regret to say. May I offer some assistance?"

"No, no, no, no, that's perfectly all right. I'll just get with him tomorrow. Don't bother, we'll see ourselves out."

"As you wish, Milady," Timetravellar replied. "Do come back...in the daylight hours."

"Oh we will. You bet. No problem," Maggie replied. She grasped Bitsy's wrist and dragged her out the garage door.

Bitsy had not spoken during the entire encounter. Perhaps for the first time in her life, certainly for as long as Maggie had known her, she was speechless. Breaking through the pitch darkness of the garage, out to where the streetlight provided visibility, Bitsy remained silent. Finally, pursing her lips and squinting her eyes, she spoke.

"Girlfriend, I hate to tell you this, but your husband is a flamin', friggin', faggot!" she blurted. "He's nothing but a butt toy for that big FREAK in there. Did you hear what he said? Indisposed? Hmmph! I'll bet he was handcuffed to the bed or something like that. Why if I were you, I'd have my lawyer..."

Once more, Maggie's attention veered from Bitsy's soliloquy, as she tried to comprehend what she had just witnessed.

* * * * *

Calvin, rather Timetravellar, stayed online until two o'clock a.m., when Vampyra finally logged off. It was seven a.m., and he was so tired that he felt as though he were coming out of his body. He stepped out of the garage onto the driveway and walked toward the dew-covered newspaper on the front lawn.

A shrill voice screamed, so loud that the entire neighborhood could hear. "Freak!"

Calvin turned to face the abrasive clamor and beheld a bath-robed Bitsy McCall on her front porch wagging a finger at him. Narrowing eyes vented the anger and dislike that rose within him. Tolerance had been a monumental effort, when it came to Bitsy. For five years, he had put up with her mouth, her nosiness, and her stupid opinions. Maggie was gone, now, though, and there was absolutely no reason to continue the charade.

Calmly, without responding, Calvin bent over and finally spied what he was looking for. Picking it up, he stood erect and glared at Bitsy.

She challenged him a second time, jutting her pointed chin into the morning air. "Faggot!" she bellowed.

McLeish slung the quarter-sized rock at her from one hundred feet away, hitting the house siding next to where she stood. Shrieking an undecipherable threat, she bolted through the front door, slamming it behind her. Moments later, a bald-headed, beer-bellied Aaron McCall emerged from the same portal. McLeish felt his face flush, as the only McCall that he liked began to speak.

"You just throw a rock at my wife, McLeish?"

Calvin looked down at the grass, ashamed of himself, and then raised his head to respond. "Yeah, I did Aaron."

Still stoic in his demeanor, McCall countered, "If you're gonna throw at a target from that distance, your follow-through is real important."

Aaron swung his arm forward, as if hurling a baseball and then stopped with his throwing hand directly in front of his face.

"Right there, that's your release point. You probably came around sidearm. That's why you missed her. Just keep at it, you'll get her eventually," he said without cracking a smile.

Calvin could not contain himself and burst into a deep guffaw. Aaron waved at his neighbor and stepped back into the house.

Chapter 8

Multitudinous auburn ringlets draped the unused pillow next to the one where her head lay. Anger, resentfulness, indignation, and defeat each played Maggie their tune in a symphony that could only be titled *Bummer*. Breaking up was her doing. She had contemplated it for the past two years, and nothing would dissuade her from it now.

Still, seeing the costumed giant in her house dredged up feelings of jealousy. Was Calvin really a cake boy? Could he truly find more pleasure with that chiseled gargantuan than with her? This was not the way it was supposed to be at all. Her plans called for celebration, now that she had finally escaped. Control and persecution were hers to use and abuse as she saw fit. Yet now, she was losing her sense of dominance, and she became more disturbed than she would have ever thought possible.

Reconciliation was still out of the question, but where as she wielded power before, she now seemed a spectator to a drama created by her own handiwork. Why was that *thing* in her house? Bitsy's assessment that Calvin was a homosexual seemed logical, but intuition told her otherwise. After all, she had been married to the man for fifteen years. Surely, if he had those tendencies, his own wife would have seen evidence of it. Then again, emotional stress, rejection, and vengeance are powerful forces. Any one of them could cause a reeling spouse to align with strange bedfellows.

"Uh-uh," she thought. "That is just *too* strange."

Doubt checked her every postulation and frustrated her to near screaming. She barely slept, confounded by the events of the previous evening. Maggie groaned, as the alarm greeted her already opened eyes.

Normally, her thoughts would have been of Oliver, the new butcher. She had not told, nor did she want to tell Bitsy, that the very stud her neighbor spoke of was the one she was dating.

The affair had begun only two days after Oliver began work at McPhereson's grocery. What Maggie did not know was that he had left the neighboring town of Ridgeville because of an adulterous scandal there. His wife had given him a second chance, but insisted on a new start in a new town. Oliver promised faithfully never to stray again, but he was slime—the snot green kind.

Maggie was no nun herself, though, having done her son's football coach, a church deacon, and two of the city councilmen. The first time, she grieved nobly over her infidelity, but each progressive episode entertained less and less conscience. She justified her adultery by blaming Cal's inadequacies. Objective soul searching might have shown her that. Although Cal was lacking in many ways, it was her own wild hair that drove her to bounce.

Puffs of powder billowed in the small apartment's single bathroom. Face paint and lipstick applied, she employed the curling iron, the last touch of her daily masterpiece. Every morning was the same; and while few of the daycare workers dressed up for work, Maggie dressed up for everything.

Kids, other than her own, were annoying to her, but childcare was the only job she could find. She hoped the divorce would force Cal back to work so that he could make child support and alimony payments. If all fell into place as planned, working for Margaret Anne Preston McLeish was only a temporary condition.

Chapter 9

"Bobby Don, is that you?" Isaac asked.

Silence lurked.

"Bobby Don?"

"Yeah, it's me, buddy," Bobby Don whispered. "I didn't think I'd ever hear from you again. I called the Johnson City police department about six months after I left the force, to come up here. They said you had up and quit right after I left, right after the big blow up.

Listen Isaac, before you say anything, there's something I have to tell you. "I'm sorry. I was way out of line. I'm just a bigoted redneck. I was raised that way. I don't mean the things I say." A single tear rolled down his cheek, and his voice broke. "I love Michelle. I would never have said anything to hurt her...or you. I was jealous that you made detective before me. That's the long and short of it. When we argued that day, I wanted to...well it was just meanness and...envy. Your wife is the sweetest woman I've ever known. I'm sorry I called her a French...," his voice quaked, and he began sobbing uncontrollably.

"A French ni..." "I can't even say the word," Isaac said. "It's o.k. You're not the first person to vent your prejudice on us. Interracial couples develop thick skin. Either that, or they split up. But I must admit, I didn't expect it from my partner, a guy whose back I watched for six years.

"But Bobby Don, that's in the past. It's been almost five years. You were...are my best friend,' and I guess you always will be. Michelle was hurt when I told her what you said, but she forgives you. She's like that. I forgive you, too. I hope we can get together sometime. I'm not that far from you now, you know."

Bobby Don Baliss wiped the tears from his eyes, as a huge burden lifted from his shoulders. He seemed little concerned that several of New York's finest looked on, while he blubbered like a baby. The hatchet was buried—finally. If Isaac had asked him at that moment to leave the New York City Police Department and run naked through the city, he would have. He had always wanted peace, but was too ashamed to ask for it. Finally, the white man and black woman that he considered his greatest comrades, out of pure grace, forgave him.

"I've been keepin' up with you B. D.," Isaac said, diverting the conversation away from the past. "You're doing pretty well for yourself, at least if a person believes what the newspapers say. Detective already and credited with the collar on that Harlem prostitute serial killer. Not bad for a boy from Podunk, Tennessee."

"Wow, I don't know what to say," Bobby Don answered. "I'm impressed. I wish I could say that I know as much about how your career is going. Wait! You said you're not that far away from me. Where you at?"

"Haha! Some detective you are." Isaac laughed. "Well let's see, I married a French Canadian black girl who has *always* missed her mama and daddy back in Ottawa. I'm not that far from where you are...Gee, you're right. That *is* a tough one."

"Okay, smart guy. So you're in Ottawa," Bobby Don conceded. "What are you doin'?"

Hollander's face stilled and became serious as death.

"B. D., that's partly why I called. I need your help. I'm a detective for the Ottawa-Carleton P.D. Last night, the county coroner became the recipient of a body, the third in six weeks. Cause of death is identical to the previous two. All found near the party hub. All killed after midnight. It's shapin' up like a serial killer. Six weeks into it, I don't have the first clue," he said.

"So what is the M.O., Isaac."

Isaac hung his head, not wanting to say. Finally with a long sigh he replied. "Two puncture marks…carotid artery. Close to a half-gallon of blood missing from each body. Somebody's playing vampire games, but the thing that's so weird is they're trying to make it look as real as possible. Forensics is finding a quantity of saliva around the punctures. Don't get me wrong. I'm not suggesting anything more ghoulish than the fact that three young girls have been killed and drained of their body fluids. That, in itself, is spooky enough. But, this is a sick bastard, Bobby. I've put twelve and fourteen hours a day into this for a month and a half, and I have a big fat goose egg."

"Isaac, I have two weeks vacation and no plans. I think I could take it, now that the slasher is stuffed. Would your captain let me come up?" Bobby Don asked.

"Normally I'd say no, but this time he might. This is a tough one. The press knows about the murders, but we haven't released the cause of death on any of the three. It's getting harder and harder to hold them off. If we tell them we've got a freakin vampire on our hands, they'll ride the story to British Columbia and back.

I'll see about the clearance. You'll stay with us. I know Michelle is going to be excited to see you. She misses you. We both do."

Chapter 10

Flames surged from an animated dragon's mouth, as Calvin marveled. Beneath the cartoon, a caption read, "You Set My Heart Aflame." Valentine's Day had crept up without Calvin realizing it. The message was from Angelmyst, one of Gothica's regulars. He had only spoken to her briefly before, and this was a most unusual surprise. No romantic interest had ever presented itself with her, and almost certainly she was just being friendly.

"Now that was sweet," he thought, as he viewed the animation. "Hmmm, Valentine's Day. I should do something myself, but I don't have a clue how to send pictures or anything like that," he thought. "Well, I can at least thank Angelmyst. Maybe she can give me some ideas."

Activating the "Reply" icon, he sent his thank you note.

"Hey Angel...thanks a million. I just got separated from my wife...didn't even remember it was V-Day, anyway...it was nice that someone remembered me. Can you tell me where to find pictures?...and if so...how to attach them to a mail message?..."

Angelmyst was online as he sent his message. She answered immediately.

"That's a tall order Tt...I gotta jet right now...but I'll write up something for you to use later. It'll take a bit of explaining...If you want to send someone something right away without taking a short course on Windows or HTML...here's an address you can type in at the top of your screen where it says "URL" ...www.cyberflora.com... that'll take you to a Virtual Flower Shop...you can pick out a greeting card and a picture of a beautiful bouquet...type in your honey's address...and they'll send it to her e-mail addy...You'll be a big hit...guaranteed...C-YA..."

Cal's face shone. "This is so cool," he said aloud. A quick thank you note to Angelmyst and he was on his way. Realizing he did not know Vampyra's e-mail address, he went to her homepage, hoping she had listed it. He was relieved to find that, although her regular e-mail address was not provided, an address for a generic e-mail service, known as Lightningmail, was listed.

In all of his infatuation with Vampyra and in all of his sense of urgency to get to Gothica, he had never visited her homepage. A quick look below her name revealed a sensual picture of a large breasted woman wearing a low-cut dress. Reaching out from under the material covering the left breast was a small green scaly hand—bizarre yet intriguing. Everything about the enigmatic temptress seethed of dark sensuality. The virtual flower bouquet seemed trite when he thought about sending it to Gothica's reigning queen. But there was little time, and if he was to provide her with a remembrance, an unimaginative e-card would have to suffice.

Gnawing at his stomach, Timetravellar objected to the superficial offering. The immortal's instinct about romance left Calvin's awkward attempts in the dust. He knew that a few short lines of poetry were all that was necessary to capture the vamp's heart. And while she would appreciate Calvins offering, there would be countless other times when just a few words from the wayfaring immortal would warm her more than any pictorial sentiment could have.

Calvin was grateful the garbage truck had awakened him. Otherwise, he might have missed Angel's message and, then, been completely embarrassed when everyone talked about Valentine's Day that night in Gothica. Truly a nocturnal creature at that point, wooziness overcame him, as he returned from the kitchen with a glass of water.

Two more steps and he would have missed the red flashing message box. Curiosity overrode the pleas of a weary body, though, and he clicked. A message from Panthera had popped into his mailbox while he was in the kitchen.

"Yo, Timefox, you online?"

Calvin deliberated whether to answer. He had, after all, told her that he would talk to her during the day, at least Timetravellar had told her that. Now it was up to him to cash the check his alter ego had written. Something inherent in his nature, perhaps it was Timetravellar, would not allow him to ignore his seedling fan club. So, despite fatigue, he committed to stay with Panthera for as long as she wished. An exchange of mail messages followed.

Timetravellar: *bursts through the catwoman's door...rushes to her tempting body that lies horizontally on the rich Corinthian leather loveseat...grasps her satin cheeks between his open palms...and plants a juicy, fissioning kiss on her lips*...

Panthera: *gasps...not knowing what to say*... Uh...Travellar?...

Calvin smiled as he worked on a response.
Timetravellar: Yes,...your pussiness?...I mean your

felineness?...I mean most high of all cat creatures?...

Panthera: *still astonished*...Why Timetravellar...I just wasn't expecting such a warm greeting...your pussiness?...eh?...*purrrrrrr*...you take me by surprise Timestud...but I'm not complaining...it's just that...you seem different than when I've seen you before...in Gothica you're so...serious...so gallant...but this...this borders on...playfulness...I like to...*play*...*purrrrr*...

The ice, it seemed, had been broken. Whereas, Calvin felt enormous pressure when Timetravellar directed him with Vampyra, this exchange was more relaxed. Sexuality was just under the surface, but still, he was more comfortable when talking to Panthera. With her, it was Calvin writing the words, not his immense *closet* character. Panthera seemed real, not nearly as fantastic and overwhelming as the vampire. Clever, humorous exchange became easy with her, and just as Timetravellar suggested, daylight seemed a good place for the two to engage.

Timetravellar: What you see is what you get sweetlips...sometimes it's *him*...sometimes it's me...

Panthera: Him? Him who?...

Timetravellar: My alter ego, cat...I never know when he's gonna pop up...he's a smooth personality...speaks well...sometimes I'll be in mid-sentence and he just pops up...then again...sometimes it's just plain old me...*laugh*...

Panthera: *LOL*...I know what you mean... sometimes my feline side is more prominent than the other...

Timetravellar: Ubiquitous blackness falls over this ancient realm. In solitude, I turn, seeking the heart that was so long ago lost to me, seeking the mate-piece to this half heart...

The time traveler stands on the crest of a peak...in this...his new domain...His hair and cloak salute horizontally in a stiff wind...his massive form silhouetted by the generous amber light of the moon...Piercing cold assaults his immortal frame...and yet it pales in contrast to the frigidity of loneliness...

Here I stand...perhaps forevermore...a solitary traveler on night's lonely path...

Panthera: Be still my heart!...You confuse this feline, Timetravellar...you play with me...exciteme physically ... then you consume me as the flaming wick melts its candle's wax...Truly...you are a unique one...powerful with words ...seducing the heart...You shift so abruptly ... captivate me...beckon me to become a slave to your sweetness...

Timetravellar: Stop that you!...

Panthera: I have offended you?...

Timetravellar: No sweetie...not you...*HIM!*...I told you he pops up when I least expect it...never know what he's gonna do...he's quite a show off...*grin*...

Panthera: Mmmmm...I think I like both of you ... *giggle*...you both have a way with me...each a different way of getting me hot...

Timetravellar: I must bid you a fond farewell...sleep beckons...but may I...*kiss your hand*...wish you a happy Valentine's Day...

Panthera: Honey...if you were here...I'd show you a Valentine's Day like you have never seen...*purrrr*...stay in touch warrior...

The banter not only stimulated and amused Calvin, but it established a bond with Cathryn Meeks, a bond that came quickly. Yet, Timetravellar was the one whose romantic arrow speeded so quickly to Panthera's heart. It was Timetravellar's camaraderie with Calvin that spurred him to assist his real world counterpart.

The doorbell rang four times in a row.

"Jesus!" Calvin snorted. "Keep your damn pants on! I heard the first ring." Wearing nothing but boxers, he debated getting dressed. Five more rings convinced him to go ahead and answer. If they were that impatient, they would just have to see him in his underwear.

Halfway through the kitchen, he could see the obscured figure of a woman. At first, he did not recognize her. If he had, he likely would not have answered. Cracking the door open that lead to the garage, he beheld an unwelcome guest holding a covered tray.

"What do you want, Bitsy? You know Maggie doesn't live here anymore."

Bitsy McCall stood on the stoop, three steps up from the concrete floor. She had bleached her hair and wore a heavy mask of makeup. A light drizzle had begun and tiny rain droplets beaded up on the slicker she wore.

"My God, she looks like a skinny, ugly hooker," he thought.

"Well, I brought you something, Calvin. May I come in?" she asked, trying to soften her normal nasal tone.

"All I've got on is a pair of boxers, Bitsy. I'm not really dressed for company," he said scowling.

Bitsy pushed the door open, and walked in despite his objection. "Oh don't be silly, Calvin! We're both adults and have been neighbors forever. It's not like I've never seen a man in his boxers before."

She placed the covered dish on the kitchen counter, and followed by snapping her posture to erectness, almost as if she was standing at attention.

"So what's this?" he asked motioning to the dish.

Bitsy proudly removed the lid and revealed a sumptuous German chocolate cake. Still trying to feather her grating voice, she dropped her head slightly. She gazed intently at her neighbor and endeavored to show him her best bedroom eyes. "Why it's a peace offering, Calvin."

What followed, shocked Calvin McLeish to a plethora of emotions that left him dazed and disarmed.

"And this, Calvin, is a *piece* offering." Bitsy flung open the rain slicker to reveal her nakedness, covered only by a pair of red stockings, a matching garter, and a pair of spiked heels. Her tiny breasts appeared as two plums, each garnished by a single raisin. Erect nipples spoke of her intent, and for a brief moment, Calvin was speechless.

"Thought you and that Studley Doright you had over here last night might want to 'bury the hatchet,' so to speak," she said with a dopey wink.

As quickly as he had lost his composure, so did he regain it. He responded without his pursuer ever realizing the trauma she had inflicted. His right thumb slid inside the waistband of the plaid boxers; Bitsy's eyes locked on Calvin's crotch. An almost unnoticeable smile appeared on his lips, and his eyes shone, as he toyed with his prey.

"Well I certainly have something that you can get an eyeful of, Bitsy. It's something I've wanted to show you for a long time."

McLeish slowly, tediously eased the waistband down to a point where just the top of his pubic hair was visible. He stopped, watching Bitsy's immobile, bulging eyes. Impatient, she bade him continue. "C'mon big daddy. Don't tease me. I've been wanting to see it for a long time, too. Sweet God, show Bitsy what you've got!" she pleaded.

Calvin's eyes remained fixed on her downward gaze, waiting for her to look up at him. Finally, she did.

"Oh Bitsy, that's not what I wanted to show you," he said innocently.

"No?" she said in bewilderment.

"No honey," Calvin replied in mock sincerity. Grasping her arm just below the armpit, he firmly pulled her to the garage door, and opened it. He pushed her rudely out onto the stoop and said, "This is what I've been wanting to show you...the door!"

Slamming it behind her, he turned to see the German chocolate cake. "Shit."

Replacing the cover, he quickly swung the door back open. Bitsy was still standing there with her mouth opened, as wide as a train tunnel.

"You forgot your peace offering," he said plopping it back into her arms. "And the other PIECE offering— you can give that one to Aaron—if he can stomach it."

He fastened the lock, returned to the bedroom, and crawled back in bed. He needed rest. Valentine's Day in Gothica would probably mean a late night.

Chapter 11

In the Room: Trysta, scabby porno elf, Stag, Deathwalker, Angelmyst, quadrophobia, Vamprissy, RebelYell, Vampyra, Hostility, Queen Satania, Vampire Lestat01, stinky, Bloodbath, **the Sorcerer,** *and Fred*

scabby porno elf: Oh Vampyra, I have searched the world looking for just the perfect gift for you on this Valentine's Day...and at last...*hands Vampyra a box of Godiva chocolates*...for you...*starry eyed smile*...

Vampyra: That is most kind scabby...*frown*...

Stag: *laughs*...Well, so far during this evening of lust, you have received the bottle of Dom that I brought you...a harsh kiss from Hostility...a pint of "O" negative from Bloodbath...a fartrock from stinky ...and an invitation to have your breasts fondled followed by a complete body lick from Queen Satania...

scabby porno elf: Why do you frown Vampyra?...

Stag: Yes, truly with the abundance of gifts laid before you...what more could you wish for Vampie? ...*grin*...

scabby porno elf: Oh yes...please tell us dark one...has one of us done something to displease you? ...would you like to go to a private room to talk?...I am a very good listener...would you list me on your homepage as one of your friends?...PLEASE...*kneeling with hands folded*...

Hostility: *hands scabby porno elf a razor*...Here, slit your wrists...your groveling is pathetic...

Vampyra: *sighs*...

Queen Satania: Why not go with ME to a private room Vampie...I will say things to you that will stir your passion and take your mind from your troubles...and the incessant ramblings of that scabbed green cretin...

Vampyra: Non...you are all kind...but love for me is something that I may never have...the one that I did hope to see...well...*blood tear falls*...

scabby porno elf: I could be the one...you could pretend it is me...let's go to a private room...I'll say sweet things to you...

Hostility: Scabby?...

scabby porno elf: Why yes Hostility...what is it?...

Hostility: If you don't quit sniffing her like a pathetic dog...I'm going to cut your little green balls off...

Stag: NO VIOLENCE! I will not permit it...you know that it is forbidden here, Hostility!...above all rules here in Lacadia...above embracing a new kindred without my permission...above bowing before me upon first entering the room...above all things...NO VIOLENCE! ...you may speak freely, but ABSOLUTELY, no violence...

Hostility: *bows before Stag*...My humble apology...my Prince...

Vampyra: *blood tears cascade down face*...

Timetravellar: *the thud of heavy bootfalls reverberate throughout the room...as the immortal Timetravellar enters the dark chamber*...Greetings Stag...all...

The Sorcerer: Greetings Timetravellar...my son...do not forsake thy destiny...

Timetravellar: *looks curiously at the Sorcerer* ...Uh...yes...good evening Sorcerer...I shall...um... take heed of thy words...*turns to the Dark Princess* ...Ah!...what's this?...a tear?...*kneels to take the hand of night's most lovely of visions*...please do not cry Dark Princess...please do not frown...But for your smile...doth this room ever illuminate...but for your voice...doth music ever strike our ears...*sweet kiss*...

Vampyra: *beaming smile*...Oh Monsieur!...it was you that I long for on this night of love...I thought you would not come...it make me sad...but now my heart dance...

scabby porno elf: Quit groveling Timetravellar ... you're pathetic...

Timetravellar: * raises eyebrow and grasps hilt of his sword*

Vampyra: Shut up scabby...go away...

Timetravellar: I went to the great thinking rock...at the edge of the dark forest this eve...and upon it I climbed...what offering could I bring, I pondered?...what bounty to lay at the feet of darkness's most exalted fem?...what could this simple wayfaring traveler provide that is worthy of such an ethereal creature?...there is none, I thought...so I brought but this...*holds cupped hands to the Midnight's most fair*...Dark Princess...my heart...

Vampyra: oh, mon trésor...come with me to a private room...speak you silken words to me ... mmmmmm...

Timetravellar: I am at your command...it is you that makes this great chest rise and fall...you are the air that I breathe...

Vampyra: Oooh...Monsieur...you say the sweetest things...

Vampyra's and Timetravellar's names disappeared from those listed in the room.

scabby porno elf: Bitch...

Panthera: *strolls into the room...walks over to the bar*...A shot of Abosolut, bartender...*takes the clear jet fuel over to the fire and curls her feminine feline self up on the throw rug in front of the blaze...downs the shot glass of vodka in one gulp and throws the glass into the flames*...Happy V-Day everyone!...and for those of you who don't give a rip about Valentine's Day like me...consider Happy V-Day to mean...Happy Vampire's Day...or Happy Vegetable Day...or Happy Vasectomy Day...whatever floats your boat...

Hostility: *grins at Panthera*...My you're full of hostility cat...I like that in a feline...

Panthera: Anyone seen Timey?...

Stag: Who?...

Panthera: Timey...you know...Timetravellar...

Stag: Hmmm...yeah...he and Vampie just left...to be...............alone...

Panthera: Bitch...

scabby porno elf: I was just saying the same thing Panthera...what's so great about him anyway?...would you like to go to a private room and talk about your feelings?...I'm a good listener...you could pretend that I'm the one you dream of...

Panthera: Scabby?...

scabby porno elf: Why yes, Panthera...what is it?...

Panthera: Shut up!...

scabby porno elf: Bitch...

Panthera: *glares at scabby* .... Bitch...............

<u>The Cave</u>
Vampyra's private chat room

Vampyra: Mmmmm...my most sweet séducteur ...at last you have arrive...*kiss you cheek...lightly stroke you jawline*...you words...have stir in me... feelings ... feelings that I have not have in such a long time...

Timetravellar: No, dark orchid...it is you who hath unleashed this new creature that resides in me...I wander alone through the dense...lightless expanse of time...mingling for a moment with kind similar to me...but ultimately different...I come to places where the voices and the forms of others appear likened to my own...but I know that they are truly not like me at all...for there are few left in lastingness that bear my curse...I have fought the many of my true kind that wander eternia...many of them whose single purpose was to hunt me down...and vanquish me...but it is I who vanquished them...and now I truly do not know if there are any left that are...like me...

I have submitted to loneliness...and to the fact that I will forever stray through the millennia...left only to observe the plight of the fortunate...the mortals...

I have no beginning...and no end...and yet I was just created...I come from a time of five hundred years past...although I know not how I came to this time...my memories of the past...are dim patchy images...I know my source of origin...I know my own story...yet my memory of those things...seems to lie with the one who set me free...

And still, by some great phenomenon...by some wonderful chance...I cross your path...in the darkness ... and warmth...and light bathes my heart...

Vampyra: *hang head*...Non...non, Monsieur... you must not say that...I am not so...I radiate no light...I am of the darkness...sometimes I go into the light...but never stay...always return...always back to the shadows...There is an ugliness within me...that you cannot understand...you would hate it...hate me if you could see this vile beast that live inside me...it is only thing alive...within me...and the darkness feed it...make it stronger...When I go to the light...it is the beast that drive me back to shadow...the beast hate love...and keep it far from me...*tear roll down my face*...

Timetravellar: *presses tip of index finger to her separated lips silencing her anguish*...Shhh...I do not believe what you say...although I know that you believe it...But you have touched my heart with the tenderest of fingertips...*slowly steps toward his most precious desire, placing his hands on her tiny waist...he pulls her to him...and looks into the magic of her eyes...past those windows and into her heart...and there he sees... paradise...

He cups her face in his hands...pulling his cheek to hers...he smells the fragrance of night in her long, straight, hair...and a scent that is uniquely her...His heart pounds as a blacksmith's anvil, and he is awed by his great desire for her*...

Look into my eyes, Dark Princess...look deeply... there lies your home...I shall never leave you...nor shall any harm come to you...I swear it...

Vampyra: *a soft moan escape my lips*... Oh...mon trésor...*press my pelvis against you large male form...trace you jawline...stroke you cheek...feel my own femininity flood...and burning desire build within me*...

Timetravellar: *Intense passion rises...as my maleness unveils itself against you...slipping my hand from your waist to the roundness of your buttocks...I pull you closer...kissing your delicate neck and then your earlobes*...

Vampyra: *place my hand over my face so that you will not see the bloodtear rise into my eyes...I turn away...even though I am silent...my heart sobs*...

Timetravellar: Mistress...what have I done?...

Vampyra: It is not you, my sweet warrior...how do I explain?...

Timetravellar: Just tell me Vampyra...it cannot be so bad...

Vampyra: It IS so bad...as am I...I told you there is ugliness within me...there is another...another like me...a true vamp...to whom I owe my allegiance...

Timetravellar: What do you say?...

Vampyra: It is so hard to explain...Those in Gothica...many are vamp...vamp that pledge to live as vamp...those ones I bring to the darkness...they come because they think it is "chic" to be vamp...or because they lust...or because they desire to kill...Those vamp that I bring to this way of unlife...help stave off the pangs of hunger and the dark lust that live within me...but I am TRUE VAMP...I must have blood... eventually... always...I must feed...I am not a wannabe...*look down*...I don't want to be...this is just the way that it is...the way it has been for so very long...

Timetravellar: I do not mind my sweet desire...as I have told you...I too, have my own curse... everyone ...has their own curse...in some form...

Vampyra: But there is so much more...There is another...one to whom I am betrothed in cyberspace... we have not actually met...but I agree to be his cyber-wife ...he is like me...true vamp...there are not many of us in this cold world...we vow our devotion to each other, whenever one kindred soul comes across the other...
It is my vow to him...that make me turn from you...and yet it is you that I wish to run to... embrace...as always...this grim existence is full of sadness...

Timetravellar: *gently kissing your petal lips...I look deeply into your eyes*...If I cannot make love to your body then I will look into your eyes and make love to *them* with my own...I said that I would not leave you...ever...Honor and desire bind me to that promise...*picking you up...I cradle you at your waist and under your knees...you are weightless, as I carry you across the soft grass in the darkness...the moon's ethereal light showers us...I carry you under the boughs of a great elm and lie you down beside me...I stroke your hair and kiss your cheek...as we lie side by side...and marvel at night's lantern...obscured by the leaves of the great arbor*...

Vampyra: *I lay my head on your thick muscular chest...caressing it with my fingernails...then kissing it...I lie down there...as we drift into sweet sleep*...

The meeting ended and Calvin watched, as he, himself, transcribed the sweet emotion of his cyber-ego. "It is a sad thing," he thought.

Events beyond her control had stricken Vampyra with the curse, and yet her heart was so full of longing, sorrow, even despair. Timetravellar too, spoke such that his words implied a deep melancholy.

Immortality, handsomeness, bravery, and a profound sense of chivalry, were qualities that Calvin endowed upon his conjured creation. Now though, the character became reality. Timetravellar was complex deep and entangled. Those things that were the make-up of the time knight grew in intricacy, and were difficult for Calvin to understand. Just as one human being is puzzled by another, by his state of mind, by his state of heart, Calvin was forced to stand by and watch, as events unfolded.

In the beginning, Timetravellar was merely a reflection, a fantasy of McLeish. Now, he was a separate entity with his own troubled soul...and a great desire for one whom he had never seen.

Chapter 12

The following evening.

The Cave

Vampyra: My sweet Timey...you receive my message...I am so glad you came...

Timetravellar: *smile* You are my enchanted libation...my perfect addiction...as you call into the night...as you even think of me...my heart hears your calling and I bound across time and space...across all dimensions that separate us...the flight of my spirit...and my great desire for you...cannot be stopped...

Vampyra: *eyes hungry, as I move close to you...feel the bands of steel in your arm and your chest...never taking my gaze from the temptation of your throat*...

Within Calvin's mind, Timetravellar began to falter. Purity and honor were his mainstay, and the idea of submitting to vampirism did not appeal to him. He had seen many that willingly gave themselves to Vampyra, male and female alike. For them, the desire for acceptance was overwhelming, but for the immortal, no such need existed. He, very simply, was what he was. While his lover's nature required her to consume the blood of others, something in his being would not allow him to submit.

Timetravellar: *hangs head...unable to speak at first...fearful of the forthcoming moments*...I...I...do so deeply love you Vampyra...I would give you anything...I would fall into the pit of eternity again...even die...if you so asked...but...I cannot...I cannot...I cannot serve you as *undead*...please understand that I would slash my own wrist and drain my own life into a vessel so that you could be nourished...but I cannot become that which I am not...

As the river flows into the sea...so it is you flow into me...the great ocean does not become freshwater because of the river's gift...and yet its life, its fulfillment...its enormous raging passion...depend upon it...*grieves at his own words*...

Vampyra: *warm smile...sweet, soft laugh, from my heart*...Mon désireux chevalier...I do not wish to make you undead...non...I would never wish to harm you my love...I just want a taste...not to be filled...but to feel your hot, lustful, elixir trickle down my throat...

For vamp...it is as foreplay...sensual and erotic ... building passion to that long anticipated moment when your sweet maleness enters my anxious femininity ...that moment when your abundant fullness saves me...rescues me from my heated, flowing, emptiness...

Non, chérie...as you, I would give anything for your sweetness...I would rather have stake through my heart than for you to think I would hurt you...

Timetravellar: *smiles, as he looks into her celestial eyes*...Then, so be it my endless desire...*stands behind her and pulls her to him...his own arousal evident to her, as he presses against her buttocks...he moves his face close to her hair and inhales...her scent...the perfume of night that clings to her...is lush...inviting...his hands move from the hourglass of her waist and hips to the base of her wanting breasts...Excitement and arousal surge...as perfect maleness takes over...that primitive urging that is irrepressible, demands to be recognized*...

Vampyra: *my nipples harden with excitement ...almost hurting with desire...pleasure seize my belly as I feel you thick suggestion against my buttocks ... wild thought control my mind, as I anticipate what comes...and what may be...I turn to face you...to look into the magnificent blue that are your eyes*...It have been so long since I have felt a man...in some way...I feel guilty, for one I love from times long passed...but I have been faithful to his memory and he is dead...but you are much like him...strong...gentle...true of heart...you words...so much like his...

I long for you to take me...and wait for your next touch...

Timetravellar: *in the sublime isolation of the cavern...he lifts her and carries her to a feather mattress...the place where she sleeps when she comes to this place to be alone...a lantern burns on a rock shelf nearby and its yellow light compliments her perfect curves ...he kisses her dark wine lips and looks at that part of her breast that is exposed...

Delicately unbuttoning the front of her midnight blue silk dress...it falls on either side...and her small erect nipples cry out their urgency...he traces the curve of her breast with a light fingertip...and then outlines the distinctive flesh of her areola...and that which seemed completely attentive...became more erect still...

He removes the leather that protects his thick, hewn...carved chest...the clasp that holds his kilt together is fastened on his side...unleashing the garment it falls to the floor...and for the first time she is permitted to see his impressive erection...he lowers himself to her...wanting to feel her dark peaks against his chest...wanting to be bathed in her succulence...

Vampyra: *my legs separate without my command ...my knees rising to my chest...my heart pound so...that I think it will explode...your lips touch my nipples for a moment causing my hips to lunge for you...I feel your bluntness against my soft confluence...teasing me...not entering yet...I moan out my objection...and lurch again... begging to be taken...I hear...just barely...your gentle laugh...and then shudder as you immense, smooth, muscle invades my tiny chasm...you are so gentle at first...but I quickly accept you enormity...you find me...my center...and plunge into it and out of it more and more quickly...I rise to meet you each time...and it feels like your length comes all the way to my throbbing heart...

As I approach my own orgasm...I pray that you do not come yet...I grasp the back of you head...preparing for ecstasy... and then, riveting pleasure run uncontrolled through me and I scream the name of Timetravellar...as you dance in and out of me and my orgasm continue forever...I plunge my passionate fangs into your bulging neck...and you delicious éscarlate fill my mouth...trickle down my throat...you orgasm now come and you fill my deepness with you nectar*...

CHAPTER 13

Bobby Don shuddered. "Geez, Isaac. You gotta know I love you, to be walking the streets of Ottawa at freaking midnight in the middle of February, looking for a maniac."

"Yeah I know, it sucks. But, the three murders have come about two weeks apart. If another one happens at that interval, it should be soon. You saw the captain's map. All of them have happened in this area.

"Look at that poor bitch, Bobby Don. As many hookers as I've busted, you gotta feel sorry for them. Cheap fur coat and hot pants in this weather. Let's see if she knows anything."

"O.P.D, ma'am," Isaac said, as he approached the prostitute.

"Oh shit! Fuck you guys! I'm out here humpin the streets so I can feed my kids, and you're gonna roust me. Do you have any conscience at all? It's twenty stinkin' degrees, and I'm out here half-naked. Do you think I'd be here if I didn't have to be?"

Isaac looked down, almost ashamed of being a cop. He knew what she said was true. He also knew that it was a cop's duty to enforce the law, but that did not make it easier to hear her harsh words.

"We're not looking to bust you, honey," he continued. "Maybe another time. You've heard about the killings in this area. We're just trying to come up with something, anything. Have you seen anything unusual in the last month and a half? Anyone dressed unusually?"

The prostitute motioned to a passerby with a multi-colored Mohawk and full body leathers.

"You mean like him?" she scoffed.

"See your point," Isaac replied. "But listen, so far, all three murders have been young women. No hookers yet, but I don't think your profession is immune. Handing the brown-haired woman a business card, he continued. "Give me a call if you hear of anything. I promise, I'm not out to bust your ass. Right now I'm more concerned with saving your life."

"Yeah sure," she said dropping the card into a small plastic purse. "Look, I gotta work. See ya."

Clicking spiked heels became more and more faint, as her exaggerated hip-swaying walk carried her away from the detectives.

"If we're going to dress as homeless people, couldn't we at least wear gloves with fingers in them?" Bobby Don asked, blowing his warm breath into a fisted hand. "It's almost one a.m. How long we gonna hang out here?"

"I dunno," Isaac replied. "This is a wild goose chase. We've got zero to go on. Let's go get in the car and crank up the heat. We'll warm up, then maybe check out some of the side streets. Most of the clubs are closing. People are already beginning to thin out. Maybe even the psychos are staying in tonight."

* * * * *

Decreasing body temperature caused the undead female to shiver uncontrollably. Piercing gusts knifed through her clothing, stabbing at her already agonized body. Hunger drove her there, and the weather relentlessly attempted to drive her away.

Misery and discomfort were a way of unlife that vampires accepted. Each moment of existence bore some proportion of agony, depending on the circumstance. Already cold, the body was more severely affected by low temperatures than homeothermic creatures. Those few moments of comforting warmth that came from feeding were relished, reveled in, brief, though they were.

Standing just inside of the blackness of an elongate shadow, she patiently awaited for suitable prey. Cyber-conquests had been fewer of late, and her hunger stabbed deeply. Vampyra's hunting ground was but a block from her last kill, and finally one entered that looked promising. Another young female, in her mid-twenties, passed the long shadow cast by the building, unaware that she had walked within two feet of the vampiress. Athletic buttocks bounced rhythmically, as Pamela Fontaine hurried through the chilled night air. Admiration of her hindquarters was short lived, and the huntress' attention diverted back to the task-at-hand.

Perhaps it was a sixth sense. Perhaps it was the keenness that came from martial arts discipline that caused the stalked woman to react. Nevertheless, as Vampyra struck, her prey responded with a spinning back kick that connected with the predator's jaw. Unnatural strength, from a state of undeath and a compulsion to feed, kept the willowy vampire from unconsciousness, as she sprawled onto the pavement. Her jaw fractured and her senses dulled from the blow. The brown belt stood in a defensive posture, knees bent, and hands positioned as weapons in front of her.

Vampyra found her feet and stood, as pulses of nausea attacked her. Pain wracked her entire body, as she struggled to right herself. She had chosen poorly. This one was not like the one before. Her victim was strong and acute. She would not be so easily overtaken, as the last meal, and would defend herself to the death. But death indeed, would come quickly. The dark one collected her wits and mustered the strength for one all-or-nothing strike. She knew instinctively that the blow had done great damage and that she would not be able to engage in lengthy combat.

Thrusting forward, her accelerated lunge was almost imperceptible to the naked eye. Chiropractic popping emitted from the woman's neck, as the Dark Princess violently twisted her quarry's maw. Vampyra's grip relaxed from the point of the woman's chin and the back of her head. The body became limp. Twitching legs would be the last sign of life, as the attacker sunk her fangs into the soft surface of the woman's throat.

Nausea again flooded the vampiress. Pain from her broken jaw prevented Vampyra from feeding. The hunt had been a bust. A dead woman, whose beating heart was all but stopped, lay before her. At best, she could only have suckled a modest quantity of nourishment. Once the heart had stopped, blood pressure was gone and it was like trying to mouth-siphon a gas tank through a fifty-foot garden hose.

Despondency and agonizing pain were the only fruit reaped of the hunt. Many days of recovery and hunger would follow. Vampyra fully understood the consequences and cried out in despair.

A midget walked past the entrance to the alley, as she mournfully protested her plight.

"Hello! Is somebody there?" he asked.

There was no reply, as he stared into the multi-depth shadows of the corridor. Danger was imminent. He sensed that to enter was folly, and while he wished to help whoever had whimpered, he convinced himself that he was simply hearing things. He would not see the stalker in any form—and her form, at that moment, was not her own. Quickly resuming his pace, he continued walking.

The voice had startled Vampyra, and instinct shape-shifted her into wolf. Candace, the prostitute, now approached the alleyway on the adjacent sidewalk. A streak of silver-gray darted in front of her, as she nearly fell, trying to avoid the unexpected intruder.

Backpedaling, her body's momentum still tried to carry her forward. "Jesus! Help! Help!" she shrieked.

Isaac's hand was on the door handle of the unmarked police car when the plea struck his eardrums. Without discussion, he and Bobby Don broke from their course and ran in the direction whence they came. Four leather soles rapidly slapped the pavement, as they sprinted toward the streetwalker. Huffing and panting, they slowed and stopped, as they saw that she was all right.

"What is it? What's wrong?" Bobby Don asked, catching his breath.

"You guys wanted to know if I'd seen anything unusual, right?"

"Yeah. Of course," Isaac answered, still wheezing.

"Would you consider a wolf jumping out of an alleyway in downtown Ottawa unusual?"

"Well yeah, I guess," Isaac replied. "But I'm not sure that is the kind of unusual I was talking about. Anyway, wolves don't come into the city. It was probably a big dog."

"I was born and raised in the country outside Vancouver. I know the difference."

Isaac looked at Bobby Don and shrugged.

"You're okay, though?" Isaac asked.
"Sure, I'm fine." She smiled and continued her patrol down the sidewalk.

"C'mon B. D., let's go to the house. I guess even bloodsuckers stay in on nights like this."

* * * * *

A half mile from its isolated home on the ridgeside, a lone wolf trudged through dissected moonbeams on the forest floor. Its swollen head hung, favoring one side. Each step was laborious, and froth had built around its lips. Exhaustion and pain intensified with each negotiated footfall, but it had to move forward, as daylight was not far away.

"Concentrate," she kept telling herself. "You can't give in. You can rest when you get home."

She struggled for her very existence. If she fell to unconsciousness in a weakened state, daylight's harmful light would sap what was left of her. When healthy, she could stave off the unpleasantness of light, but she wondered if she would be able to continue this badly hurt. There was no option but to carry on. Falling to the injury before achieving the solitude of her dark chamber would take her existence from her, thus, she plodded forward, one step at a time.

Pushing the door open with her nose, she stepped in. Faint whimpers accentuated the pain of each step up the stairway to the second floor. Turning into the stone-walled bedchamber, one more commitment of strength was required before she could rest. The lupine figure stopped at the bedside long enough to summon what strength remained and finally leapt onto the mattress. She turned the uninjured side of her face to the red satin pillow and eased it to a state of rest. Hunger and pain were her only companions now, and she drifted into merciful slumber.

As she slipped into forgetfulness, the wolf body slowly transformed back to human-like form. Light from the computer monitor challenged absolute darkness. A small red rectangle flashed in the upper left-hand corner of the screen, but it would be noon the next day before her body would so much as move. Not until then would Stag's message receive a reply, and not until then that he would learn of Vampyra's misfortune.

* * * * *

Stag finished welding a stress crack in the frame of his 1970 Harley. Keeping the antique in mint condition was a challenge, but also a labor of love. Since overcoming heroin addiction in 1989, the high school dropout had become a successful small businessman. A throwback from the seventies, he sported a ponytail, boot-cut jeans, and black knee-high biker boots.To the thirty-something crowd, the college prep types, he was a loser, but in his own right, he was successful and had overcome the obstacles of a hard life.

Some roads are harder than others, and since early teenage years, Stag, Myron Arnot had seemed to always choose the absolute worst. The past decade or so, though, had seen him turn around. Diligence, hard work, and determination not to go back to prison, diverted him from self-destruction, and put him on a smoother and more productive path.

It was prison where he gained an appreciation for classic poetry and there that he became enthralled with vampirism. Bram Stoker's immortal piece along with the modern day, *Vampire the Masquerade*, stirred his interests such that upon discovering Fountain, he negotiated his way to sponsoring his own room. Gothica had been in existence for only nine months when Vampyra first became a part of his realm. Her knowledge of vampirism, and her intrinsic understanding of the *game* quickly gave her rank above all, except for Stag. When business was slow in the machine shop, Stag either kept a book on vampirism to his nose, or socialized in Gothica. If he was busy, only his lunch hour serred for those social or intellectual pursuits.

The weld was complete, but too hot to begin buffing, so he walked into the eight-by-eight office and hit the spacebar to obliterate the screen saver.

"Hmmm, message," he said aloud.

Activating the flashing red box, he transported to his mailbox. Vampyra's reply to Stag's last message was the first listed on a page of many.

Vampyra: Mon Prince...I am hurt...I need you help...I am alone...

Uncertain fingertips twitched above the keyboard. How did he respond? He was in Boca Raton. She was in Ottawa.

Vampyra had a flair for drama unequalled by anyone in Gothica. Using her femininity to get her way, to make a point, or to wriggle her way out of a sticky situation was something he had seen her do many times. She was a master at playing the game, or so he thought.

But something in the simple, brief plea for help rang of genuine despair. He jumped to her member page to see if she was online. She was not, so he answered in mail.

Monique, what is wrong? Please do not tease me if that is what you do. I take this seriously. Is there not someone who can stay with you? What happened?...

The message traveled through the telephone lines, over a thousand miles, in milliseconds. Still, it would be hours before he received a response. Unconsciousness had again overcome the wounded creature of night—and she slept.

Monique needed nourishment. The injury, too, demanded the healing power of healthy blood to repair the damage. Weakness prevented her from hunting. Blood meals would have to come from elsewhere, and yet there was no one to provide her with that which she needed. In all of her five hundred years, in all of the bad situations she had experienced, she had never asked for help. Now, there was no other choice.

Chapter 14

II

Seething sweat and blood profuse from every pore of his sinewy body. The rigors of interdimensional quest have left him haggard, depleted—starving for the Dark Princess. His mind knows boundary not, and his endless journey is just that—without end. It is a circle, represented by the bands of time. He may pass from one portal to the next, but there is no rest, nor is there peace, in this, his mission, his cold and unaccompanied journey. He seeks the one who set him free, imprisoning his heart, leaving him the willing incarcerate of her passion.

Twisting and thrashing in her bed sheets, Panthera's hips rocked gently in anticipation of her lover's kiss, his soft caress of her turgid nipples. His naked, chiseled form descended toward her. Waves of pleasure gripped her belly, igniting her center, liquefying her sexuality. Her breath deepened and labored, as she anticipated his maleness gliding into her.

    Cruelly, he would abandon her at , the moment of her intense heat. She lurched forward in the unlit bedroom—alone. Glistening perspiration trailed from her forehead and from the valley between her breasts.

Cursed, she rocketed back from the sedation of near-sleep. Blood pounded, raced through her vessels with such acceleration that she became deaf, save for the amplified drumming of her heartbeat.

Drafts from the buffeting ceiling fan poured over her saturated skin, but were ineffectual in cooling her unrequited passion. Sliding from its prone position, her hand glided between her thighs, journeying to the maddening fire, the pulsing throb that drove her to near-insanity. She found the source of her exquisite uneasiness. Intent on extinguishing the flame and quieting the riveting in her femininity, she stopped. Frustration overwhelmed her before she could relieve herself, and she slammed her fist into an innocent pillow.

Panthera had not slept in five days, each night the same as the night before. Timetravellar came to her in the land of dreams, romancing her to fits of ecstasy, only to evaporate a moment before his body and hers entangled and writhed in the dance of love. He captivated her and controlled her every moment. Distracted from her real world tasks, she repeated his sweet words in her mind, and continuously anticipated their next encounter.

Intelligence and sexual drive made for an interesting Internet personality, and Panthera was blessed with both. So too, was the competition—Vampyra. Every time the cat zeroed in on a new conquest, Vampyra was always there to lure him away. Even more infuriating was the fact that the vampiress did not intentionally attempt to spoil Panthera's fun. It was simply the enormity of the Dark Princess's persona that pulled worshippers from cat to vampire. Cathryn came in a distant second to Monique, and she knew it. Perhaps it was the ease with which the French Canadian drew followers to her, that so enraged Cathryn.

"C'mon Catty, you're a smart girl. Think! There has to be a way to keep her hooks out of Timey," she whispered.

Cathryn had come online only a few days before Calvin had, but her experience was already far greater than his. The male creatures, especially those in *Sexual Fantasies*, continuously pursued her. Still, it seemed the most intriguing characters resided in Gothica and it was there she made her nighttime playground. Even in Gothica, she developed a following, but Panthera always felt as though any boys left for her were Vampyra's table scraps.

Pecking order seemed ironclad in Gothica and moving up the ladder just did not happen. As long as the dark temptress was there, everyone else would rank below her. Cathryn and Monique Dubois Vampyra had, however, been posturing, circling, sizing each other up for a fight, and perhaps the time was right. Panthera would not so easily give up Timetravellar. She wanted him too badly.

If she challenged the black queen and lost, she would almost certainly be banned from Gothica. Friends and lovers were there, and to be exiled from the shrouded haunt would be a great loss. Sexual Fantasies was always just around the corner, and the guys that sniffed after her with their cyber-erections would, doubtless, always be there. The most intelligent, the most passionate, the most romantic in all of Fountain, though, seemed to congregate in Gothica. The Fantasies boys represented adequate entertainment during the day, but her passion and imagination were most excited by night. She had never been one to rock the boat, but Vampyra dredged up a jealousy such as she had never known.

All her life she had been something of a wallflower, never aggressive, even if it was something she desperately desired. Passion within her had grown and matured. Panthera was thirty-six-years-old and independent. Shyness had become an outdated quality that she could no longer afford. Before she would raise her hand to Vampyra, though, she would make sure she could win. For the moment, her plans were to do just that, win.

Rummaging through the medicine cabinet, she spied a large sap colored container. It was what she was looking at. Three Percodans rested at the bottom. She turned the bottle up, launched the acrid pills into her mouth and swallowed. As bitter as they were, they were sweet compared to the disdain she harbored for Vampyra.

* * * * *

Black leather chaps, black leather everything, helped repel the knifing Arctic blasts. Motorcycling from Florida to Canada in late February was insane, and Stag constantly cursed himself for lack of forethought. Vampyra was an icon to the reformed heroin addict, and he would have done anything in the world for her. She was his mentor, a siress of sorts, in the realm of vampirism. The Dark Princess seemed limitless in her knowledge and understanding of the undead, and although Gothica was Stag's room, she was its matriarch and his hero.

The worst was over now, as he crossed the St. Lawrence and headed toward Ottawa. Vampyra's two hundred-year-old stone house nestled in the solitude of the hill country near Algonquin Provincial Park, almost sixty-five miles west of the city. Stag could see light at the end of the tunnel, and lowered his body near the gas tank to enhance the bikes aerodynamics. An icy river of air poured over him as he exited the city on Canadian road 17. His numb and frozen fingers seemed permanently molded to the handlebars, and his moustache blanketed with a thick, heavy frost. In all his years as a biker, he had never worn a helmet and displayed all twenty-seven traffic tickets for that offense in a plush shadow box back at the garage. That day, though he would never have admitted it to another biker, he would have killed for the protection of a plastic skull and face shield.

Canadian motorists appeared unaffected by the asphalt's packed snow, but the subtropical cyclist could feel the back wheel spin and give, as he negotiated one turn after the next.

"This'd be great," he thought. "I'm finally going to meet her, Vampyra, mistress of darkness. She actually called on me to help *her*. So what does Stag do? He careens off a hairpin turn five miles from her house, dies in a snow-bank, and she never knows he was so close."

Determination seized him and courage became his copilot. She had summoned him, and he would not let her down. The portage had been painful and exhausting, but his mistress's call for help would not go unanswered. Dooley could handle the shop for a few days. Hell, he could handle it for a few weeks forever, if need be.

In those last few miles, he learned to master the slick road. Instinct and confidence guided him, and his mind wandered. What did she look like? Would her voice sound the way he imagined? Question after question popped into his mind, as he approached the unattended path that meandered through the hills to her highland dwelling. Pulling off on the shoulder of the road, he extracted the printed directions that she gave him. An unattended two-path road, just where she said it would be, snaked into the hills disappearing quickly behind a bend.

He stopped and deliberated the condition of the private road, wondering if he could make it on a bike.

There seemed no other choice, and aside from being anxious to see her, he desperately needed to warm his body. Nearly an hour later he spied the drive that led from the path to her perch on the hillside. It looked ancient and reminded him of something European, almost Bavarian. No lights could be seen and no smoke poured from the chimney.

Parking his hog on a slight incline, he carefully ascended the snow-covered steps. Three times, he knocked before trying the knob. It turned freely in his hand, and he leaned inside.

"Hello—Hello!" he greeted tentatively.

No one answered, so he kicked an accumulation of snow off his boots, and stepped inside. Perhaps this was not the right place, but it had to be. He followed her instructions to the letter. As he stepped in, he felt the cold of the unheated house.

Again, he heralded. "Hello?"

No answer. Heavy thuds echoed throughout the miniature fortress, and he marveled at the gothic atmosphere of the small stone castle. Candles and lamps adorned every wall and table. It was unquestionably the dark queen's residence, but where was she? Continued exploration took him quickly to her chamber. There, he found her motionless, ashen-skinned body lying still on a canopied four-post bed. Her face was distended, and for a moment, stag feared he was too late. Death and undeadness are cousins, and never having seen a real vampire before, his heart sank, fearing the worst.

"Monique," he said, nudging her shoulder. Her closed eyelids slowly separated, and a trace of a smile surfaced.

"Stag, I knew you would come."

The cyclist-vamp dropped to one knee and looked into the eyes of the one he had adored those last few months. Her eyes were a soft gray-blue and emitted a myriad of things he did not expect to see. Because she played the part of undead, irrespective of her personality in Gothica, Stag anticipated coldness in the portals to her soul. Instead, her gaze seethed with a gentle confidence, and possibly, as inconceivable as it might have been, a patient sweetness. The tresses of her hair changed from starlight to sable in the room's dim candlelight. He took her to be in her late thirties, but then again he would not have bet on her age. She seemed dated, yet timeless, and he was in awe of the immensity of who she was to him, and who she had always been.

"Monique, it is freezing in here. Let me build a fire," he said, motioning to the small bedchamber fireplace.

"Mmmm, that would be nice, mon Prince. You know us vampire never warm. But always yearn to be," she said smiling.

Perhaps, it was Myron's expression that revealed the truth to her. Monique Dubois had spoken candidly and the gentleness of her words had taken him off-guard.

"Mon Prince, you do not know, do you?" she asked looking into his bewildered eyes.

Myron Arnot could not speak. Reverence and awe filled him while her stare penetrated him and spoke to a nature deep inside that desperately wished to be vampire. Her simple comment about never being able to get warm, and the deflection in her voice unmistakably revealed that Monique Dubois, Vampyra, was the real thing. Knowing finally, after so much time, that there were indeed vampires, real honest-to-God vampires, shook him such that he slowly seated himself, never breaking eye contact with her. He had hoped it was true, would have willed it to be so, if it had been within his power. Still, somewhere in the center of his being, he did not truly think such existed. As ruler of Gothica and student of the myth, he somehow believed that he himself was the closest thing on earth to a card-carrying vampire.

Everything fell into place now within his exhilarated, confused mind. Of course, Vampyra was well versed in the legendary creatures of night. It all made sense. Small wonder that no matter how hard he studied the mythical creatures of night, she always stayed a bit more learned.

Adoring her all those months, he had also been secretly jealous of her. Supremacy in Gothica had never truly been his, even though she always saluted him as its monarch. Monique protected him in the hierarchy. To the others, it appeared that he was indeed the high magistrate. Inadequacy always hung over him, but he recognized Vampyra's great regard for him and was steadfast in his gratefulness.

"Holy shit," was all he could muster.

Looking down, the bedridden shape-shifter responded, "I am sorry, mon Prince. Do not misunderstand me. You are still, and will always be, 'mon Prince' to me. But I had so hoped that you were one like me. We are not many, and you know so much about us. Well, I just assumed, hoped that you were. Vamp like me, especially on the Internet, do not discuss the reality of our condition. It is dangerous. There are still those that hunt us. We are, around the world, devoted to each other. We know each other only by the words that we speak and the passion in our voice. You see, that is why I was so sure that you were vamp.Never have I known one so knowledgeable of our way. Never have one so perfectly emulate being one of us. You, mon Prince are truly remarkable," she smiled.

"So this is why you are alone?"

"Yes, I have been quite weak," she replied. "I contact the only one on this planet that I am sure will not desert me. Vamp or not, I know mon Prince will not forsake me."

A single bloodtear cascaded from the corner of her eye to her delicate lips. Monique squirmed in an attempt to make herself more comfortable. Wincing in the pain of her injury, Stag observed a glimmer off a protruded canine tooth.

It was so. The princess of darkness was a living fulfillment of his fantasy, and he was there to serve her, no matter what her need, no matter what her desire. At that moment, he would have abandoned his life in Boca Raton simply for the asking. To his dismay, though, her need of him would be short-lived.

Vampyra had suckled every meal for the last five hundred years, and while intelligent and technologically adept, she knew little of society, and little of how things worked in the real world. How and where to get what she so desperately needed was left to Stag, her rescuer, and he performed his task flawlessly.

Living on skid row in a cardboard box for a year had taught Myron how to survive and how to find what he needed. Whether it was the *heroin* that controlled him during that period of his life, or simply the need to eat, he knew how to acquire life's necessities.

Vampyra drifted back into sleep, weakened by the conversation. Myron stared at the needle scars between his forearms and tattooed biceps. Most of the shiny puncture wounds had come from shooting up, but some had come at the hands of Red Cross volunteers, the ones to whom he had sold his blood for cash.

"This should be easy enough," he thought. "Back to Ottawa, find out where the Cross is, and hit the blood bank tomorrow night."

* * * * *

Motionless eyes projected out the large picture window from the cottage dining room. A table-knife blade clinked, as its edge struck the rim of Michelle's wineglass.

"Bobby?" Michelle prodded softly. "Are you okay.?"

From deep within his own mind, Bobby Don Ballis forced himself back to the moment, returning from abstract thought.

"I'm sorry, Sweetie," he apologized. "After all this time, after all my regret, you welcome me back by preparing a feast, and all I can do is think about this case."

Smiling, the cinnamon-skinned hostess returned, "A good cop never leaves the beat. He *should*, but never does."

"Isaac, the fourth victim—she was within earshot of where we were last night, when we talked to that hooker. The coroner's report put the time of death at the very same time we were there. That poor child's neck was twisted so savagely. I can't get her out of my mind. The perp is a big guy, strong. But what has me confused is, when you compare the cause of death with the others, something doesn't ring true. Her autopsy showed that she actually died from the broken neck. Puncture marks, but no blood missing—so the autopsy says. And then, the Red Cross reports a break in at the blood vault. Twelve units of blood missing. Think this is a copycat?"

Isaac's dense black eyebrows fused at the bridge of his nose, as his forehead wrinkled and seriousness invaded his expression. "I don't think so B. D. If the media knew that we have a vampire psycho out there, I'd say, absolutely a copycat. But no one knows about these victims, not their cause of death anyway. I'm confused too. This last one…there are some answers in her death. I'm like you, somehow the blood bank burglary is related. It's almost as if they put up a fight, the attacker snapped her neck to end the altercation, popped a couple of holes in her, and then was scared off. So far, that sounds plausible. That would explain the difference in the cause of death and the abundance of blood still in the corpse. Logic would dictate that if this victim became too much trouble, the attacker would simply take another. So far though, there hasn't been another. Of course, they could just be biding their time, but how does the stolen blood fit into the picture? Or does it? I dunno. My gut tells me there's a big chunk of this story we haven't uncovered yet."

* * * * *

Stag secured a Nalgene bag to a wooden sphere that crowned one of the headboard posts on Vampyra's bed. She was unconscious, and had been for the last twenty-four hours. He had not been able to speak to her since their first conversation. Sunken, black eye sockets, and a deformed jaw were evidence that she was worsening physically. Myron's heart ascended into his throat, as he quickly plugged a length of eighth-inch Tygon tubing into a stoppered outlet valve on the bag of blood. Sliding a metal clasp onto the tube to control its flow, he was ready to begin nursing his goddess. He hoped it was not too late. Vampire legend dictated that she could not be killed by a simple physical injury, but the myth also implied that sunlight was deadly, and he was certain that was not true. As kind as Vampyra had been in praising him for his knowledge of her kind, Stag realized at that point how little he understood of what was truth, when it came to the undead. Conceivably, all that he held as truth was inaccurate.

Grave responsibility immersed him, as he controlled the trickle of dark liquid. The blood was cold, as was her fading body. Refrigeration was necessary to keep it viable and that which he had stolen remained iced in a large cooler. Body-temperature blood was what she really needed. Pale, ashen skin had begun to take on a purplish-blue hue, but he was afraid to warm her meal. Heating it might destroy its nourishment. Fear and feelings of inadequacy gripped him, with every action he took. He may as well have been performing brain surgery for the first time. There was no one who could help him make the decisions. For two days, he stayed at her side providing her with periodic sips of crimson nectar. Each subsequent hour filled him with more and more anxiety, and for nearly forty-eight hours, he attended to his charge, unrewarded by any change in her condition. At the end of the two days, weariness overcame the biker and he collapsed into abysmal sleep. During the time when he slept, the vampiress twitched occasionally and normal color crept back into her flesh.

Chapter 15

Nearly four days had passed since his dark love entered Gothica. Calvin paced the floor of his unkempt bedroom, frantic over her disappearance. Never had so much time lapsed from one of her visits to the next. Worry and anxiety clutched him. It was well past moonrise, and the Timetravellar's fretfulness gnawed at its human host.

Panthera kept Calvin, the mortal, occupied, and she pursued him relentlessly. Feline charm and hot-blooded femininity lured him to her cyber-bed day after day. Their passion for each other grew, as the vivid, carnal imagery she painted for him extruded the dormant, underlying talent that Calvin possessed as a writer. Sexually, she was stimulating. Intellectually she was fascinating. At times, Calvin wished his alter ego would simply cease to exist and allow him to pursue Panthera. He was keenly smitten by Vampyra, but knew she was out of his league. To pursue her as Calvin would have been a miserable disaster. Only his mind's character, the Timetravellar, could hold Vampyra's attention, as no other could. McLeish would have gladly relinquished any pursuit of the raven viper, but the immortal creature inhabiting his mind's eye would not allow it.

Nightly, as darkness fell, Calvin McLeish sat by and watched, as the tall one emerged from his cocoon. Infuriated at times, he would see Panthera there and would desperately want to engage her, but he could not. She, herself, was curious at his lack of attentiveness during the dark hours, but submissively accepted that it was a reality of their relationship.

Calvin psychotically grasped his forehead, mashing his scalp, as his hand stroked his head from front to back.

"I wish to hell you would leave me alone," he said to the time traveler.

A quarter moon hung directly over his house. Vampyra would occasionally come at dusk, but if not then, at least by midnight. More than half of the evening was over, and Cal sensed she would not show. His alter being would not yield though, and pressed him to remain attentive to the *friends online* screen.

"Give it up, damn it!" he screamed. "She's not coming. Get over it, will you?"

Then, as quiet as the still moment before a violent storm, he calmed. Eerily he looked around in confusion. Had Timetravellar given up? Calvin did not think so, and stayed alert for the next anxiety attack that certainly would come. He sensed someone was watching him, as a large, but gentle hand from behind folded around his right shoulder. Involuntarily, he gasped, as he spun to see exactly what had accosted him. Once again, the immortal stood before him, dwarfing McLeish in the dimly lit bedroom.

"Thou hast found disfavor with me, my friend. You think that my motivation is simply an obsession with the dark one. Your desire is for me to abandon her, and leave you to your own existence. But dear friend, how can I make you understand? She is not simply a source of entertainment for me, as you believe. She is life, my purpose, and the only reason that I exist at all. True it is that you created me, but my lifecycle ends if I cannot be with her, at least in the realm you call cyberspace. Can you illuminate the room?"

"Sure," Calvin answered, flipping on the light switch.

Possibly for the first time, McLeish understood the gravity of Timetravellar's dilemma. When the nobleman had come the first time, he was as real and as three-dimensional as any other being. Sadly, in the light of the present moment, Calvin could make out images directly behind the warrior, simply by looking through him. The shapes were not distinct, but Timetravellar's point was clear. The massive Scot had begun to fade. Just as blood nourished his dark love, so did her presence and melodious words nourish him. Vampyra was his life, his impetus to exist. And while he was only slightly diminished, Calvin understood that he could not go on indefinitely without being touched by her heart.

Sadness filled the mortal, as he began to understand how serious the situation became for his alternate identity. Poetry, chivalry, honor, passion—all of the things that he held sacred, resided within the champion that stood before him. Whether he could have expressed the sentiment with his lips, he understood now that if the gladiator evaporated, so too would those emotions and virtues that he held so dear. Then, as quickly as the giant had come, so did he depart.

* * * * *

Embittered and scorned, a wiry female figure peered from behind a juniper bush at McLeish's bedroom window. She had risked all to seduce Calvin, and vengeance was now to be hers. Hollow, determined eyes bespoke the poison that tainted her. Fear of whom he might tell, paired with a bruised ego, made Bitsy McCall a formidable adversary. She was certain he would tell Maggie of her attempt to lure him to sex.

Middle-age hormones found the skinny neighbor hot for adventure, ready for an affair. For years, she had been content with a husband that provided a living and security for the long term. When she met Aaron in college, he was an engineering technology major. Promise of a respectable income and material possessions made him a good choice. Passion, romance, and physical desire were all but nonexistent to her as a young co-ed. Now though, with the ripening of years, her juices flowed, and mating became an irrepressible drive. The phenomenon had emerged only in the last five years, and she had fantasized about Calvin more and more since they first became neighbors. Because Maggie was her friend, but mostly for fear of being caught, she had resisted the urge to come on to him.

Bitsy found Aaron physically repulsive. She had taken a separate bed just a few years after they married. Times arose when she desired something, usually expensive, that would find her in her husband's bed bouncing for his pleasure. Yet, even those infrequent conjugations were ghastly, and she avoided them as much as she could. Looking back on her choice of a partner, she mentally kicked herself in the ass.

How could she have known that copulation would become such a driving force in her life? If she had even suspected that her loins could feel such yearning, she would have put more effort into snaring a man that was at least physically adequate. She could not have known that her feelings could change in this way, though, and therefore rationalized that it was not her fault. Adultery was inevitable for Bitsy McCall, at least she hoped it was. Unfortunately, divorce was out of the question. Bitsy figured she had invested too much time and effort in Aaron. She had the house she wanted, the car she wanted, and a zillion credit cards. Cooking his meals, wiping his kids's butts, keeping the house straight, and letting him poke her every now and then were her labor. Rewards for her toil were the possessions she had accumulated and she would not throw them away for a one-night stand. If good fortune did smile on her, and she did find a rich, breeding animal that could satisfy all of her needs, then she might consider leaving the slob. For now though, getting her pipes cleaned would have to be done discreetly. No one could find out.

Bitsy had badly miscalculated when she bared herself to Calvin, and anxiety twisted her core. If Calvin did expose her to Maggie, she would deny it and direct her friend's attention to the fact that Cal had another man in the house. She would also describe him throwing rocks at her, and point out his bizarre and irresponsible behavior. She was relatively certain that Maggie would buy it, but still, she needed to cover her trail with a barrage of evidence that implicated Calvin.

Photography was not Bitsy's area of expertise, but Elsa knew a lot about it and had told her for poor lighting to use a faster speed film. The brightness of a strobe would have given her away, so she propped the camera lens on the windowsill, and held it as still as possible. Waiting, hoping that Calvin's giant kilted roommate would disrobe and engage the smaller man in disgusting homosexuality, Bitsy was disappointed. No physical exchange seemed eminent, so she took three pictures of the two, as they conversed in the bedroom. The photos were not as damning as she would have liked, but they were something, and would have to do in starting a file with which to blackmail Calvin.

* * * * *

McLeish could only manage a blank stare, as he sat sentinel at the Gateway monitor. Two days had passed since Timetravellar had come, and even longer since Vampyra had written or surfaced in Gothica's dim room. Calvin remained satisfied since his last encounter with the great one. Panthera was a limitless source of steamy, erotica and, for the mortal, life in the cyber was good. But his heart sank, as he groped for something to write on the traveler's behalf. Frustration overwhelmed him, as he scoured his mind for words to lure the vampire out of her seclusion. Midnight passed, as did one o'clock and then two o'clock. The author-role-player had a mission and it was to bring Timetravellar and Vampyra together.

Selfish encounters with Panthera, and others that he had come to attract, were his passion. In his own way, he learned to write romantically, but his purpose was to filter through the mundane, and find the ones impressed by his limited talent. Those citizens of Fountain were the targets he seduced into cybersex, the ones who gratified his ego. Yet, in the midst of trying to maintain his fantasy life, the relentless haunting of the wayfarer accosted him.

"C'mon Cal, you know how he writes. Just put something gushy down. She'll see it, start things back with *him* and I can get on with my relationships. This ought to work."

McLeish fumbled to serve as Timetravellar's proxy. He had sent a few poor attempts to Vampyra over the past week, but they were quickly composed—unworthy. The messages lacked heart, class, or the immortal's incomparable flair. Trashy innuendoes scribed to pacify the champion that dwelled in his mind reeked of amateurism. Until now, he had all but ignored, turned a deaf ear to the suffering of the voyager. An occasional soft-porn nuance seemed adequate compensation for the fantasy figure. This time though, he would try a little harder, yet even this seduction was paltry compared to his alter-ego's mastery of the written word.

I stand alone waiting for you. My maleness aches to be inside of you. Your hot breasts stay in my mind night and day, and I think of how wonderful it would be to be inside of you. Your wet depths would drive me crazy, as I pushed myself inside you.

"Not bad," he thought. "That's as good as he writes.

She ought to at least get juiced, rush back to his arms and maybe satisfy the big lug."

Calvin launched the message from his mailbox. A tiny nagging voice, perhaps it was the Timetravellar, called his bluff. Deep within his own heart, he knew that what he created for the wanderer was cheap, without sincerity, and vulgar. But his own selfishness again masked the remorse that tugged at his gut and he continued.

Hopping from one homepage to another, he searched for a lonely heart. Three a.m. and the pickings were slim. He wished that Panthera were on. The short prose he had written, as Timetravellar's proxy, stoked his fire and he wanted to engage another—a hot woman looking for cybersex. Only one hundred twelve people inhabited Fountain, at the moment, and scanning the *online* list was looking like a wasted effort. Most of the time, Calvin was particular about homepages that he would visit. The alias had to be either imaginative or sexual in tone. That night was desperately boring, and he finally spotted an alias that piqued his interest enough to visit.

"Hmmm...Blakkvelvett," he said aloud. "Brown sugar. I've always had a thing for black women, even though it's not accepted in the Land of Rednecks." Calvin hammered out a short note.

"He stares at the ebony queen with a lustful heart. Her full lips and protruding round buttocks give "rise" to feelings that pale women cannot bring...*kiss the back of your neck*..."

Few black women came to Fountain, and his intermittent attempts to engage those that did had been miserable failures. Logic told him, however, that if he was attracted to the black femme, then surely there were some that might be attracted to whites. Timetravellar, and the bait that his creative homepage represented, surely must be intriguing to at least some of them.

Conceivably, he would one day find a dark chocolate mistress, but harbored no hope for that particular night. Yet, as he moved his cursor to the logout icon, an instant before he terminated his renewable existence, the message box began to flash. Calvin was tired and parried with himself, as to whether he should even retrieve the note. Nothing waited for him in the bed that he would soon occupy, though, and no mission waited for him at dawn's light. Unenthusiastically, he zipped to Blakkvelvett's message.

Blakkvelvett: How beautiful!...do you always write such things to those you know nothing of?...*smile*

Calvin managed a weary smile, paused to think of a clever reply, then returned her volley.

Timetravellar: I often write...and I often admire...the promise...of beauty...

If he had stimulated her, so be it. If not, that would be okay too, but now he must lie down. Weariness would have its rest, and this time, he logged off for a few short hours of sleep.

* * * * *

Normal color of lifelessness slowly seeped back into the huntress's crippled body, and each subsequent day found her improved from the previous. Stag had been her ever-attentive nurse and rarely slept. Vampyra's needs, however, required his constant vigilance, and he had resorted to amphetamines, as a way to remain conscious.

As he witnessed her transform from emaciated patient back to the sultry seductress, his heart yearned deeply for her. The crisis neared its end, and he had come to her as a hero would. All those many months he had clung to her, admired her, and loved her. She was even more thrilling than he had imagined, and his fondness and loyalty transformed to love.

Vampyra was, always had been, his idol, his supreme heroine. Lack of sleep, exhilaration from the yellow jackets, and genuine feelings for her finally gave him courage to speak his heart.

"Monique, there is something I must tell you, and something that I must ask."

"What is it mon Prince?" she asked smiling. "You look so serious."

"This is difficult for me. Everything is difficult for me. You and I have shared something very special for a long time. I cannot be certain of your heart, only my own. I am in love with you, Dark One. I wish to join you forever in this bed. You are truth. You are true vampire...eternal."

Unbuttoning his sleeve at the wrist, he bared it for her to bite and suckle.

"You shall be my siress, my mate, my lover. And I shall be here with you forever. Never again shall you lie here destitute. I shall protect you from all harm, and I shall give you the love that you so richly deserve. I know in Gothica, you speak of Vasquez and your cyber-bond to him. But this is reality and a real woman needs a real man, a real vampire needs a real vampire."

He smiled with the hope that she would gratefully accept his proposal. Instead, he was surprised and ultimately dejected by her reply. The princess of shadows turned her head on the pillow, as crimson tears poured from her crystal eyes. After a lengthy silence, she turned and looked back into his weary, sagging face.

"It is so complicated, mon Prince. Yes, there is Vasquez. But there are two others too. One is my own sire. He haunt me, pursue me through time. Vermin like that leave not peace for creature like me. He come here, unwelcome. He take me, rape me, laugh at me. I am strong fem, but he is most powerful vamp on this wretched planet. He make me undead so many years ago, and now, he own me. Lazare is his name. He is most hideous thing I have ever known. I beg him leave me alone, but I am his property. He come here when he want sex, or simply just to defile me. He force me. If he hungry, he come in my sleep, pin me to my bed and suck blood from me. Sometime I have just hunted, just filled my belly and he come and take it from me.

"Then there is Vasquez. He need me and is very good to me. My feeling for him are feeling of allegiance, warm love, but not hot love. Mon Prince, there is yet another in my unlife, another whom I have not met. That one, he melt my heart, know the depth of my soul. You see him in the room. His name is Timetravellar.

"I never lie to you, mon Stag, and will not start now. Love always escape me and it will no doubt this time, too. But it is the Timetravellar that I lie in this bed and dream of, and his heart that I long for. Please forgive me, mon Prince. I do not wish to hurt you wonderful heart, but I cannot lie. You too special to me.

"As for me…bite you wrist, you wish to become vamp. Again, I cannot grant you what you wish." Tears again plummeted from her hypnotic eyes to the satin pillowcase. Sobbing, she continued. "Vampire are les misérables, most cursed of all creature. I cannot do that to my sweet Prince. You do not know what it is that you ask. I feel so bad. You come to rescue me, and I give nothing of what you desire in return. But, please know this. The thing you ask, I refuse because I love you Stag."

Stag looked down, as her soliloquy of rejection and refusal concluded. "But you do not love me, as I love you?"

Sorrow flowed from her eyes, as she slowly moved her head from side to side.

Chapter 16

Almost two weeks had passed since Vampyra's disappearance from Gothica. Initially, Calvin seized the opportunity to explore the pseudo-reality that Fountain provided. Panthera, Blakkvelvett, and others became his love slaves. He was their master and they willingly submitted to his domination. Nevertheless, after a week, the mourning of Timetravellar could not be ignored. Calvin had tapped out a few more notes in his stead, but they were inferior to the time stalker's words, and for whatever reason, had not drawn Vampyra back from her hiding place. Travellar's maddening cries haunted Calvins every waking minute. Sleepless dreams became frequent, as the time warrior desperately tried to create a reality for himself and his dark love. Without Vampyra's presence and intoxicating words, his attempts were futile.

    Calvin found himself sitting at the computer, or on the toilet, wakening from a dream-state where his alter ego had taken him. Sometimes, hours passed as he was projected into a reality where the Scot and the vampiress would sit together under a tree by a stream and talk or hold hands, or make love. Other dream-states were brief, and only consisted of the warrior and his mate riding Chronos, the Timetravellar's steed, through an open meadow.

The mortal felt empathy for his counterpart, and did attempt to connect him with the shrouded vixen. He was an ordinary mortal, and his own obsession with the Internet was his primary motivation.

Timetravellar's despondency began to affect Calvin, the mortal. Literary writing was something McLeish had given up, and cyber-romance had taken its place. Irritability and anxiety chewed so sharply at his intestines that he could not enjoy the rendezvous with Fountain's heated vixens. Now, each time he rushed to meet one and began to cajole her, the unmerciful prodding of his Celtic conscience needled him such that his focus and concentration evaporated.

Deep, leathery pouches hung underneath Calvin's eyes. The little sleep he garnered diminished even more as time went on. Message after message from Panthera and the others poured into his mailbox, but he could not answer. His soul was tortured by the agony of his mind's creation and Calvin McLeish feared he might go insane.

"It's four a.m. for God's sake! What the hell do you want from me? I write her, tell her how hot I...uh...you are." He stopped, and began again. "That's the damned problem! I don't know where you end and I begin! This is driving me crazy! Look Scot, she's just some lonely bitch that is playing with you. Do you think you're the love of her life? Look at her homepage! There are a *million* guys on there that she plays with regularly. This is *fantasy* Timetravellar! Look at me. I find new ones everyday, talk dirty to them, get them hot and for all I know they're playing with themselves while I'm doing it. Look at how many people are online. Just find another one, for God's sake. This Vampyra is probably three hundred pounds, fifty years old and is missing her front teeth. Get a grip! You're driving yourself insane, and me too. Dammit, if you want me to do something to make it easier for you, I will, but stop punishing both of us. If you want to wither up and die over some fantasy character, be my guest, but don't take me down with you." Calvin caught himself looking at the ceiling, as if speaking to someone in outer space. "Shit." He snorted, as he walked into the bathroom to blow his nose.

"So why don't you show your face?" he bellowed from the tiled bathroom. "You don't seem to have any problem showing up when it's convenient for you. Damn!"

Once more, as it was the first time, he stepped across the bathroom threshold to be shaken by the figure before him. It was Timetravellar, lying on his mattress. More transparent now, he had faded much from their last encounter. What color could be seen was washed out, dim. Shame and remorse flooded Calvin, as he beheld a creature that was surely not far from death.

"Look, I'm sorry," he said. "Just tell me what to do."

The mass of perfectly shaped muscle lay perfectly still, his words almost inaudible.

"Calvin McLeish, it is I who asks forgiveness. 'Twas you that gave me life, at least existence. I have tortured not only myself with my grief, but I have eaten at your insides, as a maggot would its carrion.

"Truly, there is nothing that you can do. You have written in my stead. Perhaps, despite your efforts, she has lost interest in me. Perhaps she is simply gone from this realm, the one in which I exist. My heart is torn with pain, and without her, I shall meet my end."

"Yet you, kind sir, have been more than my vehicle to cyberspace. You have also been my friend. I know not where imagined immortals go when they no longer continue to exist. Likely, they disappear into the reaches of darkness, as though they had never been. But if there is a world beyond cyberspace, and beyond your mind, my birthplace, then I shall think of you with warmest regards."

A single tear fell from Calvin McLeish's eyelash, while he watched his creation become increasingly more faint. Guilt haunted the writer, as he realized his selfishness and disregard for Timetravellar's plight.

"Bullshit," he said finally.

Timetravellar's left eyebrow raised in astonishment, as he listened to Calvin's strange response. "My friend, I fail to see the connection with bovine excrement and the fading of a great warrior."

A broad smile darted across the mortal's lips. "Never mind that, I've got a plan. First off, this Vampyra has been online for months, almost a year. She's hooked on cyberspace, Gothica in particular. No way she's just going to disappear. She has too many followers that fill her needs. My guess is she's playing some sort of game by not coming to Fountain, or maybe she's just out of town or something. The Dark Princess will return, and you will still be around. She'll return because it's that silver tongue of yours that will bring her back. Now get back inside my head and help me write something that'll blow her skirt up."

"It would be unbecoming to lift the vampiress' dress without her consent!" the Travellar gasped.

"Jesus, you're such a rube. It's just an expression, Timey. Now get your washed-out self in my brain and let's get down to business."

The Scottish swordsman's head bowed, as he began to speak. "I have not the strength to pilot your hands. I am indeed in dire straits," he confessed.

"Bullshit."

"That word, again. Why is it that you are so captivated with that which fertilizes the moor?"

Calvin shook his head. "Forget it. You can talk can't you?"

The reclined cavalier again raised his eyebrow, and with obvious sarcasm said, "It would appear that I can."

"Then you talk and I'll write."

"I am not sure that for even that, I have the strength."

"Geez, don't be such a pussy!" the human barked.

Scotland's descendant looked again in absolute astonishment. "You call me a cat?"

"Shuddup and talk," Calvin continued.

"Be silent and yet speak at the same time?"

"Speak to me, as if she were here in the room with you, o.k.?"

The time knight, weary and wasted, closed his eyes and imagined his dark queen there in the solitude of the bedchamber. To Calvin's amazement, he was taken again into a dream-state where the vibrant immortal, on bended knee, took the hand of his willowy gothic female. He gazed fervently into the seductress's pale blue-gray eyes.

Moon pours her amber oil over the most precious and exotic of night's treasures...the heart that beats within this great chest aches for your touch and the melody of your voice...indeed it is your magic, your charisma that make this chest rise and fall...it is all that is your being that enraptures this simple wayfarer...and you that brings meaning to my existence...it is thy heart to which I shall forever be bound...

And if I must be sentenced to roam the dark and barren wastelands of time, that cold and empty expanse...if I must do this in cursed solitude...then let me re-begin my pilgrimage with the sweet wine of thy lips...fresh upon my own...let me one last time feel thy soft breast...pressed against mine...let me smell the midnight in thy hair...so that I shall never forget my black orchid, the princess of darkness...the princess of my heart...

Returning from his trance, the words etched in Calvin's mind, and forever would be. He turned to address the timeless one, but was not surprised to find himself, as he so frequently was—alone. Quickly scribbling the heart-song onto a napkin, he lay down, not intending to sleep, but sleep he did.

Chapter 17

Devastated, Stag stayed in a separate chamber from Vampyra. She grew stronger and her face was nearly back to normal. A shattered heart remained hidden behind a cheerful face, as he would never let his mistress see the pain she had caused him. It was not her fault. Without question, it was beyond her control. Life had always been difficult, and while her rejection hurt him deeply, it was not a great surprise.

Serving her was an honor, and he would stay by her side for as long as she needed him. The one thing that grieved him above all things was her request for him to print off her mail. Vampyra pretended to be concerned that her followers had missed her, but Stag knew in his heart that Timetravellar's contact was what she needed. One hundred six correspondences waited for replies, and she smiled when Myron brought her the thick stack of printouts. She quickly scoured each page looking for the Travellar's name, frantic to read his sweet words.

Indeed, the undead fem found seven total messages from her knight, but her forehead knitted into furrows and a scowl crossed her face, as she read. "I do not understand," she said finally.

"What is it, my dark queen?"

She did not respond at first, choosing to stare at the printouts instead. "How can this be?"

She teetered between sadness and anger.

"What? What is it, Monique?"

"These notes. They all say they from Timetravellar. But, this writing is that of an imposter! These words are shallow, cold. They do not come from the beautiful heart that has warmed my own cold heart. How can this be?"

Vampyra wept, and Stag again became comforter, counselor, and confidant.

"Will you write for me?" she pleaded. "I must know what has happened to my sweet Timey, and I must know who this imposter is."

"Sure Monique, just tell me what to write."

Stag swallowed bitterly and faced the light of the monitor.

Vampyra: You come to me with crass words of lust...tell me you want to put it in me...tell me how hot you are for me...and how you can almost smell my wetness?!...WHO ARE YOU LIAR?!!!! What have you done with my beloved immortal...TELL ME!...For I know you are not him...you who uses the name of the timeless one...if he has come to harm from you or anyone else...I will hunt you to the darkest reaches of this cold planet...and suck the life out of you, as you whimper yourself...to death...

Do not underestimate me Imposter...I wield great power and the sword of the knight who has begun to capture my heart is dull and sweet, when compared to the savagery that I shall impose upon you...I shall bring all hell's forces upon you in a single instant...and your eternity shall be a cold emptiness filled with anguish such as you cannot imagine...*fire rages from my eyes and my heart*...bring him back...or prepare yourself for doom...

Calvin's eyes gawked, as he read the vixen's ultimatum. Panic supplanted logic, and the threat filled him with inexplicable fear. Travellar's magic words fled his mind, as he groped to reply. She was on at that very moment, or so it seemed. Indeed Stag transcribed her heart, but it was Monique Dubois who commanded his fingers, and she demanded restitution for the impersonation of the her lover.

Timetravellar: Hey honey! What has gotten into you? Are you on the rag or something? I've been writing you all week...and not a word from you...all of a sudden you're back in cyber-world, ready to cut my balls off...don't you know how much I've missed you?...

No sooner than he had launched the message, his heart sank. She would never buy that. It was even worse than the other notes he had sent her. What to do? If he wrote the satin words that the Scot had forged in his mind, she would become even more suspicious. Worse than that, if he did not send the sonnet, the timeless one would haunt him, punish him, and drive him mad with his grieving.

Vampyra: Again you mock my intelligence charlatan!...Do you not think I see your worldliness...do you think that I believe that you are my precious immortal...my Timetravellar?...I lie bedridden for a time...but when I rise...it will be to take wing, as a creature of the night...and come to where you are...The days when hot blood warms your body are few left...I warn you...do not sleep...do not take your eyes from that which lurks behind you...for it is there whence I shall come...it is from there that I shall strike...swiftly ...savagely...unmercifully...

His eyes narrowed, as he read the baneful warning. Now, it was he, who was suspicious of the threat's originator. Vampyra, especially when passion or emotion fueled her prose, butchered English. Although she was bright, and understood much of the language, her writing was technically off the mark. Aside from the dot, dot, dots, this writing was done fairly well. Everything that was plural was expressed as plural and everything that was singular was expressed as singular. Verb tenses were not confused. Possessiveness was not sporadic. Yet, in this heated conversation, she seemed to have managed syntax efficiently and precisely.

Timetravellar: *one eye droops to near closure, as the ample cavalier places his hand on the hilt of his broadsword*...It is you who are the imposter I think...it is Vampyra's name that is stolen by another...the French siren that has forever commandeered this warrior's heart...speaks to me in a different way...whoever you are...bring your savage intent...Taste my blade...Transform from undead...to eternal silence!...

McLeish had forged the words almost immediately. His message was clear, without fear, and without reservation. Instinctive retaliation was the reply of an intrepid combatant, whose temper lashed back, changing his posture from defensive, to offensive. Cal watched in near amusement, as the two resolute wills clashed for dominance. Neither Timetravellar, nor Vampyra were convinced that their words were judicious, but both cyber-nobles were quick of temper, and took shit off no one.

Vampyra's eyes darted back and forth, as Stag read Tt's last rebuttal. This most recent counter seemed more familiar, but still, she was not persuaded.

Vampyra: I have been ill...I do speak to you through a surrogate...The words are my own, but the one who transposes my message is adept in this language ...Now...explain YOURSELF...

Timetravellar: And what convinces thee...that I do not speak through another?...

Vampyra: Your attempts to quell my ire become weak...and cheap...you have no agent that transcribes your words, as I do...you attempt to deceive me...perhaps the immortal for which I had found favor...is simply another cyber-serpent in a twisted mass of ten thousand others...you are not the first deceiver that has lured me...but you are certainly the most adept...never has one warmed this cold heart so completely...never has one created such surrender within me...never has one...given me such hope...

And now...my tiny hope is scattered to the universe by the barbarous wind of your perfect deception...and this heart that once lay dormant...now becomes barren once again...

Well done, Timetravellar...undoubtedly...another trophy for you...I take my leave...

Timetravellar: Wait!...

Vampyra: There is nothing to keep me here...let me retreat to the shadows...away from the light that I thought was you...allow me to bleed...in peace...

Indignant magma that coursed through the knight from Vampyra's harsh words now cooled. Tenderness, compassion, and affection transformed his fury. In the way that Calvin and Timetravellar communicated, not in words but in exchange of emotion, Calvin understood it was time to write the words embossed in his heart and soul.

Timetravellar: *moon pours her amber oil over the most precious and exotic of night's treasures*...The heart that beats within this great chest aches for your touch and the melody of your voice...indeed it is your magic, your charisma that make this chest rise and fall...it is all that is your being that enraptures this simple wayfarer...and you that brings meaning to my existence...it is thy heart to which I shall forever be bound...

And if I must be sentenced to roam the dark and barren wastelands of time, that cold and empty expanse...if I must do this in cursed solitude...then let me re-begin my pilgrimage with the sweet wine of thy lips...fresh upon my own...let me smell the midnight in thy hair...so that I shall never forget my black orchid...the princess of darkness...the princess of my heart....

She ordered Stag to shut down the computer, when he had completed reading the final message of the Travellar. For Stag's sake, she pretended to be still angry and displeased. But those last words fanned her embers, and a spark of hope and desire, once again became a small, but growing flame.

Vampyra's italicized name disappeared from Cal's screen. She was offline and Timetravellar's medium wondered if she had even received his last post. Amusement became concern. The literary serenade that Timey had put in his mind seemed powerful enough to the human. As he had witnessed his own fingers fashion the bouquet of emotion, he presumptuously assumed that it would melt the heart of the fanged diva.

Calvin came to respect and admire what he considered Timetravellar's great talent. Eventually, he would understand that it was not a skill, nor was it an expertise. It was merely the transcription of the great warrior's heart. Nevertheless, he and the knight had put forth considerable effort to make amends, and she callously snubbed him—them.

"Bitch," Calvin muttered. "Who the fuck does she think she is. Old Timey hands her his heart on a platter and she slices it up like roast beef. Then she just leaves."

Quickly, he typed her name in the top of the message box and composed but one word.

"Chickenshit!"

Firing the message with his mouse, he crossed his arms in defiance of her insensitivity. But as quickly as it had happened, a plea for tolerance came from within. It could not have been clearer if someone had screamed it in his ear.

"No!...please," the voice implored.

Calvin watched, as the dim, obscured figure struggled to separate from his body. Before, his alter ego possessed such strength and resiliency that he detached himself from Calvin instantaneously, deceptively. Weakened from his grief, he now labored to enter the real world. He grappled his way out of McLeish's body, much the same way a butterfly fights to be free from its chrysalis.

Shamed by his weakened state, he looked into his host's eyes. Light that had brilliantly emitted from his own eyes in the beginning was all but gone. Grave consequences befell him from the absence of his dark love. Yet, on the brink of his own extinction, his only thoughts were of her. He had come to ask for Calvin's forbearance and patience with her.

"It is not within my being to beg, mortal, but, beg I shall. I beseech thee to treat her respectfully. She is the love of my heart, and I am the creation of thine own mind. If you have such disregard for her, then so be it. But as a part of you, I ask that you be forgiving of her. Never I have seen her, and never I shall. My days in the realm of your mind are truly numbered. She trusts me not, and I fade, as the light at the setting of the sun. But, in as much as I do still exist, the only thing that keeps me from complete dissolution is the memory of her words.

She is most precious, most unique of all night's creatures. Vampyra is a delicate flower, a gem under night's umbrella. If I must cease to be, then please let me leave knowing that she has been treated well. The message that you allowed me to send her is inadequate to show her my heart. But, at least I want my last words to be kind, sweet. I can disappear into the universe easier, knowing that one day she may look back on the one called Timetravellar, and her heart warm from that memory."

Calvin gazed somberly at the phantasm that was his inner self, his ideal, his psyche. McLeish's self-centeredness and adventurous lust had won its battle over the voyager finally, and in surrender, Timetravellar merely beseeched Calvin's forbearance.

McLeish was free to play and partake of whatever, and whomever he chose at that point. Celebration seemed in order, so why was he so completely and dismally depressed? Possibly, he had missed an opportunity to connect with destiny, and perhaps somewhere inside his thick carnal skull he comprehended the sadness of what might have been. Like Scarlet O'Hara though, he would think about that tomorrow, and begin his lustful hunt for fresh meat. In that way, Calvin was something of a vampire himself, feeding off the loneliness, the emotion, and the horniness of Internet femme. While he did not leave them undead, he did leave them, and most would feel drained, used, and void when he was gone.

* * * * *

Despite her feigned dissatisfaction with Timetravellar's message, Stag knew. He sensed that her heart danced. Exuberance radiated from her eyes, as she barked her dictation. Her deception had failed. In his own heart, he had submitted to the fact that she would never be his. Somehow, though, it was all right. Myron idolized Vampyra, and as much as he loved her, he was content to be her servant and her friend. When he offered to be her lover, and protector, it was out of concern for her well being, as well as his own passion. More important than his own needs, were hers. If she was truly happy, if her heart found joy in this immortal Scot, then he could be content.

CHAPTER 18

Sweet drowsiness supplicated the mortal to enter the land of dreams, and leave the harshness of reality behind. An eternity of nothingness yielded to an awakening within, that domain where nonsense is logic, and the imagination of the dreamer becomes his pilot.

Walking briskly with two companions, a large figure entered the gates of a magnificent palace where centurions took their posts in France's night air. Moonless and an intense, deep blue, the ceiling of the universe spoke to the heart of the knight. The infinity and romance of a midnight indigo canvas was the warrior's home, his love, the only place in which he truly flourished.

Once inside, the three travelers stopped in an immense foyer. It was, as was every other part of the castle, monitored by a skilled swordsman, an elite of the Marquis Lazare's royal guard.

"M'lord MacTavish, I shall inform the master of your return."

The massive Scot admired the ruby sphere that was the butt of his sword hilt. The handle was a gold eagle claw that grasped the large, deep-red orb. By chance, a graceful movement reflected in the dark red ball and caused him to look up. Descending the stairs was a chambermaid, perhaps the most exquisite creature upon which he had ever gazed Locked in his stare, she would look at him but for a moment. To engage the watch of a nobleman, even a Scottish knight, was forbidden. Returning his attentiveness even for a fleeting second would be considered impudent and brazen for one of her class. Yet, as did his heart race the instant he beheld her, so did hers erupt in kind.

Stepping onto the marble floor from the curvature of the staircase, she looked away and hurriedly ventured toward a corridor adjacent to the vast anteroom. As she reached the darkened recesses of the hallway, she stopped and turned to look upon Glynn MacTavish...the Timetravellar.

"Move your ass, wench!" the sentry bellowed. "Do not look upon this warrior. Do you wish me to stripe your back with my lash?"

The sable-haired servant stepped forward to bolt from the hell-storm that rained upon her, but from her peripheral vision, as she turned, she beheld an image. That image so astonished her that her stomach became cold with fear. The centurion gasped and gurgled, as his feet dangled and kicked in panic. Bulging biceps and triceps appeared as massive rocks bursting on the Celtic warrior's arms as he clutched the cruel guard's throat and suspended him above the floor.

"Never let me hear you speak such bile to one so fair. You hold yourself above her, and I hold you...by your neck."

Timetravellar's sneer eased, as he looked upon the grateful and awestruck face of the maid. She curtsied quickly and then disappeared into the darkness of the hallway. Easing the sentinel back to the floor, Glynn MacTavish's eyes remained fixed on the penetrating darkness of the narrow passageway.

"Who is that?" the Scot asked.

"A trollop," he replied between gagging coughs.

The guard was embarrassed. He was one of the Marquis' elite, and the rough-cut Celt had manhandled him, as he would have a length of rope. Still grasping the guard's tunic, MacTavish pulled the sentinel's face to within a breath of his own.

"You, of course could not have known this. I myself did not know before I entered the mezzanine. But, that enchanting creature will be the love of my life, and I shall follow her to rainbow's end. It is that fair and gentle fem to whom I shall give my heart. It is her honor that I shall defend for all time. So you see, your life hangs in the balance of my hands and it would serve you well to treat her, and speak of her, as the treasure that she is. I am willing to cross sword, nay, even die for her. Can you say the same?"

A burly Quenton MacTavish laughed deeply at his younger brother's chivalry.

"Always rescuin a damsel in distress aren't ya, Glynn. Boy, she's a wench like any other. Let the fellow be. He's just doin his duty. Let him go now. We're guests here."

The younger MacTavish abided by his elder's instructions, but his eyes kept their fire.

A quiet mage that traveled everywhere with the two noblemen held his tongue. He always did. He was there, keeping a promise to Lachlan MacTavish, their father. Lachlan had been his student and like a son before he died in the Battle of Dunbarton. At death's door, Lachlan grasped the old sorcerer by the wrist and entreated the old one to look after his sons. Motherless for years and now fatherless, the young men were capable of looking after themselves and the MacTavish castle. Wisdom however, comes with years, and Lachlan's boys had but a few between them.

* * * * *

Calvin's eyes burst open in the desolation of his bedroom. This dream, it was confounding. He would have sworn to all he held sacred that it was not a dream, at all. No, he had *been* there. His palm wiped beaded perspiration from his top lip, and his senses alarmed from something pungent. Contorted in the darkness, his face revealed his own confusion. That odor, what was it? Bringing his fingertips to his nostrils, he inhaled shallowly. "Oh my God," he whispered. The pungent scent so prevalent on the tips of his digits was the body odor of the guard that Travellar had admonished. McLeish stumbled to the bathroom sink, splashed cold water on his face, and toweled off. The cursed smell reeked, clung to his skin like the juice of an onion. Squirting a full tablespoon of liquid soap into his cupped hands, he scrubbed briskly and rinsed. It was still there, not even slightly diminished. Calvin looked at his swollen sleep-deprived eyes in the mirror. His entire existence had become so bizarre, and with each passing day, it seemed that Timetravellar became more a part of it.

Chapter 13

III

The freshness and promise of night brings forth its creatures, scurrying from their iniquitous dens to hunt, those seeking filled bellies and those seeking carnal pleasure. And for some of nocturnum's fold, they are one in the same. Whether it be the taste of flesh in their mouths, or the taste of it in their loins, it is the flesh that brings them out. That unique scent, the fragrance of flesh... is the aphrodisiac of moon's children.

The gentle, pendulous sway of her hips gives rise to his maleness. Watching her, lurking in dense shadow, he is a shadow himself. He watches, stalks, as she floats along the illuminated path at lake's edge. Deep cover of the forest Ténèbres hangs at the very brink of that walkway, and as she passes, she journeys within a whisper of where he stands.

Quietly, undisclosed, his eyes devour her, as night's lantern penetrates the sheerness of her gown. Her nakedness underneath is completely revealed to him, so much so, that he can make out the down of her love nest. Had she paused on the path adjacent to where he lie in ambush, even for a moment, she might have felt his moist, rapid, shallow breath. She might have been forewarned of the predator that lay in wait—but she did not.

In that darkness, under shrouded cover, the whites of his eyes, alone, shone from the infinite pitch of his blind. But she would not detect him, as she passed, not until his steel hands clutched her tiny waist.

She had come to the forest and to the lake because it was here that there was absolute solitude, infinite quiet. It was here that she was free, here that Lazare could lay no claim to her, or force his depravity upon her. In this place, in dark of night, her dreams became reality. Her fantasy replaced the heartbreak of the real world.

Yet, in that marvelous seclusion was danger, and there was no rescue from it. If one was so unfortunate as to encounter its peril, there was no intercession, no deliverance. And so it would be that clear summer's night, when she opened her mouth to scream, when she filled her lungs to plea for salvation, that no one would have heard. Even if his hungry lips had not sealed her own, even if his tongue had not forcefully intertwined with hers to mute her desperate bleat.

Writhing in his steel grip, she was as a fawn in the clutches of a great cat—and fall she surely must. Twisting, struggling, she found the immense attacker on top of her, and she feared that her heart would burst from fear and exertion. Clasping his upper arm, she could feel the chiseled rock of his biceps, and she knew that she would succumb to his treachery. That, just as with Lazare, if this was not the Marquis himself, she would be taken by a man-beast once again, as she had so many times with her lecherous master—Edouard Emilien Lazare.

Perhaps it was a glint of moonlight striking the assailant's eyes that first allowed her to peer into his soul. Or, perhaps it was the second time his lips touched hers, this time softly, tenderly, without the savagery she dreaded. And as his approach turned from one of brutal assault to delicate entreaty, her fearful emotion ebbed and turned, as the great ocean's tide. Although she could not make out his form in that transient moment when starlight struck his softening eyes, her mind inexplicably reeled back, back to the night when he had liberated her from the guard's cruel scolding. She knew at that moment the eyes capturing night's sparse glimmer, were the same she had gazed upon from the palace's darkened corridor.

Tensed muscles relaxed, eased from relief that her predator was not a vile ravager. The icy-cold in the pit of her stomach warmed at his gentle kiss—his mouth's sweet touch. Each stroke of her cheek cajoled her to his amorous intent.

Melting at each continued affection, she sighed as his lips moved from hers to her willowy neck, and then to her ear, and then lower and lower to the perfect mounds that protruded from the neckline of her transparent gown.

Unbuttoning her garment, his journey moved him down her body. She shivered as his lips and flicking tongue stopped to admire her feminine breast. She felt him ease the lapel of her dress to the side, as he exposed her peaking desire. Encircling the darker outer flesh that defined her exquisite nipple, the chambermaid shuddered, as the Scot's warm lips and wet tongue entombed her beckoning breasts.

Continuing his erotic journey, he paused at her belly to sample its silken texture and to admiringly probe her adorable navel. Still, his destination called, and he continued his pilgrimage, until finally he arrived at the asylum of her passion. Tantalizing flicks of his whip-like tongue on the satin of her inner thighs caused her to lurch and softly giggle, as she knew that soon he would pay homage to the flower that was blossoming for him. Teasing her loins a bit more, momentarily ignoring her rising flood, he, at long last separated her impassioned lips with his skillful approach.

Tasting her wine and finding the pearl of her ecstasy brought him to full manhood and the beast that lay within him howled to be released from its cage.

Being probed and petted with the tip of his mouth's masterful serpent, she pitched, moaned, and recoiled from each continued affection. Timetravellar was now beyond his own ability to control the primal drive that urged him to her center. Hands placed on either side of her head, he looked deeply into her eyes, peering through the windows that breached to let him see the passion within her soul. But there, it was his own reflection that he beheld. There in her eyes, he was as a god. It was there he saw that she desired him with a power beyond his comprehension.

The warmth of her nectar and the delicacy of her flesh enveloping his tightening girth now caused him to moan with rapture. Her hips rose to meet his own, and her gentle cries escalated, as his thrusts became unbridled—frenzied.

Instinctively, her heels mounted his buttocks and she pulled him into her fervid depths. Wave after wave of irrepressible pleasure mounted within her, and her own rising thrusts now gripped him, as he moved in and out of her. Carnal hysteria rose, as each bucked and lunged for the other, with uncontrolled desire. His hands now moved from their prone position to the small of her back, and she raised her hips, lifting his overwhelming weight so that he could clutch her bouncing buttocks. Thrusting savagely now, she affirmed his efforts and screamed *desperately into the night, and finally his own voice echoed throughout the forest—across the lake, and up to the moon, as their song climaxed and rose into the boundless night sky.*

Exploding into her eruption their blazing rivers of bliss united, bursting into a cascading waterfall of passion, mixing deep within her center. The furious dance of love slowed to a gentle waltz. His eyes again softly affixed to hers, and she became hypnotized by the magic of his gaze.

Tender, loving lips united to consecrate the union, and the Timetravellar, who was then, the mortal Glynn MacTavish, drifted into pleasant oblivion in the arms of a chambermaid who—five hundred years later—would be simply known as—Vampyra.

Darkness fed his energy and was the medium in which he existed. Marquis Edouard Emilien Lazare represented the best and worst of France. He descended from high nobility, but was now, at the start of the sixteenth century, the last remaining male of the family line.

One hundred years earlier, his great, great grandfather commanded the loyalty and respect of all France, but no class prized him more than the peasants of the realm. Fabian Lazare had been the right-hand man, the moral advisor of King Charles VI, also known as "The Deranged." Fabian was not only a nobleman, but also a philanthropist and served as the crown's conscience and as its soul.

The world-renowned Lazare vineyards, even in that ancient time, merited praise as being among the finest in the entire world. Still, Fabian Lazare was a simple man at heart, and despite obscene wealth, likened himself to the hardworking and poverty stricken of the French kingdom. For, they were the true spirit of France. They defined its culture, its past, its present, and its future. The commoners of the countryside embodied fifteenth century France and the aging Lazare served as their guardian angel.

Countless times, he ordered his driver to halt the mahogany and gold inlaid chariot, as Fabian journeyed to a political council meeting or caucus. A burdened traveler or vagabond would often find himself in awe and amazement, as the Lazare carriage pulled away. And he, the downtrodden, was left on the roadside, mouth gaping, and holding a sack of gold equal to twenty years of labor. Fabian Lazare's face would remain stoic, but his heart would dance as his carriage left the vagrant shrieking in joy and praising the name of Fabian Lazare.

Not one, neither pauper nor king, would have guessed that a mere hundred years later, the Lazare name would be synonymous with evil. His great, great grandson, blinded by wealth and a tarnished soul, would seek the power of darkness and become one of its greatest archangels.

* * * * *

Succumbing to grief, Monique Dubois' father died months after the Marquis had requisitioned his daughter. The old goat herder was without wealth or influence and his mournful cries of anguish fell upon deaf ears when Lazare's black army abducted his innocent child. The Marquis' sinister reign paralyzed the land, and Philipe Dubois knew full well what was in store for his precious Monique. Each time the ignoble legion had come to the hamlet, Philipe had managed to conceal his attractive daughter.

But that one dark day, just after her fifteenth birthday, they came. Philipe had trudged beyond the facing hill to search for a young kid that had disappeared in the night. Just as wild dogs had apprehended the young goat, so had the black guard taken his innocent daughter. Philipe, himself, had gone to the palace to appeal to Lazare, but was heartlessly turned away.

Neighbors and the pittance of family that Philipe had were of little comfort. No one spoke of the abominations that certainly befell Monique, but Philipe knew. He had heard the stories that everyone else heard. Young girls forced into the black nobleman's service were raped and defiled.

They worked from sunup until long after dark, toiling as slaves of the barbaric demon. By night, he came to them, and savagely forced his wickedness upon their innocence.

Subjected to a myriad of perversions, Lazare's flowers wilted, but it was the *bite* that Monique found so debilitating. She hated feeling him force himself into her, tearing her tenderness with his savage sexual weapon. The repeated rapes crushed and infuriated her, but that rage kept her will keen. The bite was most damaging, though. She could cope with sexual molestation, but each time he sucked life's blood from her delicate throat, she seemed to lose a little of herself. Every minute of every day was a struggle to remain strong, but each time the vampire fed upon her, she felt a piece of her soul drift away. Fortunately, for Monique, the Marquis owned many young women. He liked variety, and her turn as concubine and blood meal was only once every two weeks. The puncture wounds never healed, though, and the flesh around each of the two openings remained red and swollen.

Most of the incubus's flock became aged women before their twentieth year, but Monique refused to completely submit. Though she could not repel him, she focused her hate and her hope on the future. Then, that one magical night, she beheld her knight, her desire—her salvation. Without a word spoken between them, she knew he was the one, the one to whom she would give her heart. His simple act of chivalry, and velvet soft eyes could see her through a thousand abuses. Glynn MacTavish, she discovered his name to be, would be the candle in her darkness, and her hope for all eternity. She would cling to the image of him, and he would give her strength, simply by thinking of him. Despite her longing and her determination to remain defiant against the evil that befell her, she grew troubled at her own craving for...blood.

Chapter 20

Cathryn yawned, as she perused one home page after another. Gothica was closed and Sexual Fantasies fell to domination by the lesbians that had become the ruling daytime occupants of the room. She had *cybersexed* with a few of the more creative lesbians of the realm, and while homosexuality was a provocative notion, men were still her great passion.

Just before leaving Titty-man's page, Timetravellar's name appeared at the top of her screen, notifying her that Calvin had just logged on.

Panthera whispers to Timetravellar: Hey there Timestud...you've been giving your attention to someone else lately, I think (pout)...I haven't heard from you in a couple of days...I know you're a hot item with the ladies, but don't forget about me...I doubt if anyone appreciates you more than I do...and God knows...I literally dream about you every night...and wake up soaking "wet...*eg*...

Timetravellar whispers to Panthera: *groan* ...Cat...you can't imagine what my cyber-life has been like lately...it is so bizarre that I won't even "go there"...but, please don't think I'm not interested ...Truly, ...above all I interact with here...you are the one that is the most stimulating to me...

Panthera whispers to Timetravellar: Oh my sweet Time-"piece"...you do tell the sweetest lies...but right now...can you spend some time with me?...

Timetravellar whispers to Panthera: Yes...I have time...nothing would please me more than to frolic with you this fine morning...'twas an unrestful night...filled with strange dreams that left me...troubled...exhausted...

Panthera whispers to Timetravellar: *strokes her sweet desire's head*...My poor time knight...*presses her lips to his neck...plucking...nipping at his flesh with her teeth...her naked breasts lightly brush his firm, muscular back*...yes...let us frolic...tell me a story...let me hear the honey drip from your lips...it is that sweetness I so hunger for...

The dark troubled waters of his alter ego faded to the recesses of Calvin's mind. Panthera brought a sweet, unpretentious sexuality to him and filled his need.

Timetravellar whispers to Panthera: Ah, yes...a story...indeed...I shall tell you of a dream that I have very recently had of you...I shall create a private room called "Penetration"...meet me there...

Panthera whispers to Timetravellar: Oh, God, honey ...I'm already hot...be there in a flash...

Each of the two would-be cyber-lovers clicked on the private room icon and found each other. The room allowed a better format to view each other's words and allowed for complete privacy.

Timetravellar: She stands at the massive oaken

doors that are the nearly impenetrable barricade to the castle...rain stings her face, as a fierce wind flings its liquid daggers...She knows now that she should not have left the village with the storm approaching...but her sister in the country had beckoned her...The baby would come soon...and Panthera was to be the mid-wife...But now in this sea of darkness...not even the path could be seen...

She had lived in the village all of her life and knew every inch of the countryside in a ten mile radius...And here she found herself completely lost...with no sense of direction...In the distance she saw, through an endless darkness, a single tiny yellow light...It most certainly was someone's dwelling...but whose?...

The woman, named after the goddess of the feline, had traveled this path a thousand times...and although lost...she knew of no residence near the path that led to her sister's...In fact, there was no residence at all between the village and her sister's cottage in the country...So how could this be?...It were as though it had appeared from another dimension...from a dream...but she was not dreaming...Clearly, she was aware...and yet somehow...the night and the storm...presented this castle...

Grasping the wrought iron ring that served as a great door knocker...she lifted it to bang a metal plate affixed to the oak, but a moment before she could strike...the massive gate swung inward...yet there was no one there...Fear clutched her heart, as she gazed upon the castle interior...Torches reflected off a polished stone floor...Save for their light...the inside was dark...ominous...

Panthera stepped across the threshold and beheld eerie images created by undulating shadows cast by the torch flames...No one had let her in...yet the doors seemed to have sensed her presence...Scanning the bowels of the great stone mansion...her eyes grew accustomed to the sparse light...To her left, a great staircase built of rough igneous rock rose upward into the castle, its banister a highly polished cherry wood...Her eyes followed the curvature of the ascension and her heart began to flutter...Instinct told her that at the top...she would look upon something...something that was fearful...and yet exciting...

When her eyes completed their journey to the top of the stairs...they locked...paralyzed by what she saw...In the half-darkness of the second level...stood a bare-chested figure...His mane hung below his shoulders, and his glacier-blue eyes knifed through the darkness to hers...Fearful and yet somehow placid...she felt herself climbing the stone risers, one step at a time...When she achieved the summit...her still unblinking eyes remained on his, as if hypnotized by their hue and their intensity...She stood so close to him that she could feel the heat of his breath upon her...His hands found each side of her narrow waist...and he pulled her to him so that one pelvis pressed firmly against the other...No words were spoken...He lowered his lips to hers separated ever so slightly, they kissed...Panthera wondered if the exquisite figure could hear the rapid thunder of her heart, as their lips fused...as their tongues intertwined...and as their bodies entangled in a desperate embrace...

The great Scot, one hand still on her waist and the other cradling the bend of her knees, lifted her as effortlessly as he would a pillow...Like passionate ghosts, the lovers glided down the dim corridor to the bed chamber...He carried her across an arched stone threshold...Candlelight danced erotically off the irregular surface of the stone walls, as she scanned the enormous room...On the opposite side of the great room an alcove lay partitioned away from the main chamber...There in the middle of the recess was a grand bed, its headboard and footboard made of ornately carved walnut...Its crimson, satin shimmered in the candle's dim glow.

Lowering her to the mattress...his eyes never

broke with hers...Propriety demanded she object, ordering at least a feigned resistance...but passion urged her to submit to his intent, and passion became her great master.

The carved torso nestled beside her, and she felt her arms grasp his rippling back, as he once again kissed her fevered lips...Her will had long since faded and her only semblance of self-control was the fact that she did not grasp and tear apart the buttons of his trousers...And then...she felt his sweet fingertips ferreting the neckline of her dress, finding her desirous peaks...Each touch...each light provocative twist of her nipples caused her belly to shudder with delight...She wanted to feel herself tightly envelope his length, and allow him to find the extent of her depth...Relief came, as he began unbuttoning the row of clasps that held together her gossamer dress...She sighed, grateful that the warrior undressed her...for she was very close to ripping off her own garment...

His strong, muscular hands explored each curve...each of her soft mounds...His touch communicated his worship of her sensual shape...Spasms of pleasure gripped her center...as his hands explained to her satin flesh...his desire...The Scot's lips pressed against her throat, while the tip of his hot, wet tongue flicked against her earlobes. Placing her hands on his waist...she attempted to pull him to her—into her.

Calvin typed feverishly, creating the story as he went. When first he entered the realm of cyberspace, this sort of impromptu writing would have flustered him, immersed him in terrible anxiety. By that point, though, he had become a master of spontaneous creativity and such encounters became second nature.

McLeish's mouth gaped. He had paused to collect his thoughts, when suddenly the story continued. Panthera became interactive in the storytelling and picked up where Calvin had just left off. In one sense, Cal wanted to maintain control of the erotica, but in another, her intercession excited him.

Panthera: Desperate passion overwhelms the feline one, as his caresses drive her mad with want ...She craves his hot flesh inside her and rolls to her side, then to her knees...spreading them to shoulder width...Arching her back, she presents her offering to him...Finally, after what seems an eternity...she feels his hands grip her waist...he strokes his rigidness up and down the valley of her buttocks...teasing her before entering her melting nest...The hair of his stomach and his groin, the heat of his flesh against her round buttocks, extract a soft moan from her lips, and she can no longer cope with emptiness...She must be filled...and rocks back against him...her body demanding him at her core...Finally...she feels his blunt sweetness... Lubricated by her love oils, her succulent lips separate as he pentetrates her...He is so thick and so long...that she cries out in painful ecstasy, as he passionately lances her wellspring of lust...Panthera's belly spasms and she cries out...her love knot dragging methodically against his muscle ...Her chasm floods with passion's hot elixir and she pays homage to the beast that takes her willing blossom...His thrusts become savage...and she thinks she can feel him growing inside her...Her thighs tremble, as she approaches her own orgasm...Eyes rolling back...head hanging...she screams out as she releases... Consonant with her own gripping pleasure...his deep voice screams, as he too explodes into her... Finally...the erotic dance slows...and the two perspiring lovers collapse...he on top of her...The stranger rolls to his back...Pressed against the satin sheets...she looks deeply into the infinity of his azure eyes...and there she thinks she could remain...for all eternity...

Calvin was amazed at her conclusion to the story. He could not have written it better himself. Unfortunately, she had excited him to the point that he realized that it had been too long since he had last made love. In one way, virtual sex had brought him pleasure. In another way, he found himself saddened by his own loneliness.

Timetravellar: God, Panthera...you are so good...I only wish I could be with you in real life...I would pleasure you beyond your wildest imagination...

Panthera: Sweetie...if you can come to where I am...I'll rock your world...nothing would give me more pleasure than to spend hour after hour of being everything you ever fantasized about...

Timetravellar: *eg*...Even if my fantasy included ....tying you to the headboard?...in front of a mirror...?...

A pause followed, and for a moment, Calvin thought she had gone off line.

Timetravellar: Panthera?...you still there, Sweetie?...

Panthera: Mmmmm...oh yes, I'm back darlin'...I just sent my address to your Lightningmail account. You be here Friday night...and I will treat you like a god...

Astonished, Calvin smiled. She was just what the doctor ordered.

Timetravellar: I hope you're serious Cat...I'll be there if, you are...

Panthera: Oh...I am deadly serious, sweet Time knight...what would you like me to be wearing when you get here?...

Timetravellar: *wicked grin*...Just perfume...

* * * * *

A taut, vengeful face revealed Bitsy's bitter intent. She watched through separated Venetian blinds, as Calvin stepped into the town of Candler's only airport shuttle van. The airport was used more by crop dusters than it was by commercial airlines, but there were a few puddle jumper flights each day. One flew to Atlanta for connecting flights, one was a pick-up on the way to Savannah, and the other was a flight that terminated in Jacksonville.

"Hell hath no fury like a woman scorned...Calvin McLeish," she muttered under her breath. Bitsy proceeded to a pine entertainment center and reached behind the television. From there, she removed an auto-focus/auto-zoom 35 mm camera.

"I'm gonna stick it in you and break it off," she seethed.

She walked outside and quickly passed through the chain-link gate that led to the McLeish's backyard. She methodically removed window screens on the back of the house. Tugging on one window sash after another, she finally found one that was open. And that simply, she entered Calvin's lair.

* * * * *

Calvin's heart pounded as he thought about what he was doing and what he was going to do. There was no question, as to the reason for the rendezvous. They were to make wild, passionate love, purely because they excited each other. It occurred to Calvin that she might not be physically attractive to him, but what scared him more, was that she might not be taken by *his* physical appearance.

He was in excellent condition, and if there was anything in life that he had followed through on, it was exercise. Not an ounce of fat existed on his five foot nine inch body. A washboard stomach testified to the thousands of sit-ups and crunches he had done. Thick, longer than average hair resembled a lion's mane, and had he been a bit more confident, he would have realized that he was nice looking.

His heart raced, as he tapped on the condominium door. The taxicab that brought him from the airport pulled away, and panic replaced excitement. What if she were a thousand pounds with no teeth and hairy armpits? He considered that perhaps he was thinking shallowly, but after all, he *was* there for sex and not platonic conversation. Darkness momentarily obliterated the pinpoint light that shone through the door's peephole. He knew she was looking at him.

"Who is it?" came a voice from within.

Smiling sheepishly, he responded, "Timetravellar."

A security chain rattled, as it slid from its track. The door eased open. There before him, was the woman he had flirted with, cybersexed, and impressed with his writing. She peered at him with bedroom eyes and finally spoke.

"Damn, come on in honey. You're better looking than I hoped."

Calvin could not speak for a moment. She stood unashamedly in front of him, with little more on than a smile. She wore heels, peek-a-boo stockings, a garter belt, and an underwire bra that pushed her breasts up such that they nearly exploded from their cups. Tiny panties barely covered what would have been pubic hair, had it not been shaved. She looked to be in her late thirties, and had light brown hair.

Cathryn Meeks was not a centerfold out of Playboy, but she was, indeed, sensual. Her hips were only slightly larger than they should have been, but everything else was perfect. Twenty years in the past, Calvin would have found that one slight flaw, damning. Age, though, had changed his perspective, when it came to appreciation of the female form. At one time, a woman had to be slender, perfectly proportioned, with a near concave belly, to meet his standards. Now, a slight pudge could be a turn-on, and he found himself relieved and grateful that he found her so attractive.

He stepped into the living area of the beautifully decorated condominium. American Indian motif seemed to be the theme, as evidenced by an afghan on the couch, which was itself, covered with material of aboriginal design. Several paintings of bareback-riding Comanches, along with other western scenes hung from the apartment walls.

A pair of candles burned on a quaint glass table with dinner settings for two. She had told him to be prepared to eat when he arrived in Wilmington. Concentrating on the meal would be difficult, given the way she was dressed, but the pasta she had prepared along with the chilled champagne turned out to be the perfect prelude to an evening of fantastic coitus. Panthera farmed her kids out to her parents under the pretense that she needed to study for exams.

There would be no distractions, no Timetravellar, no telephone calls, just an evening of pure pleasure. As it turned out, Cathryn came through as promised, fulfilling his every fantasy. Her bed was pre-staged with braided wrist restraints, a full-length mirror on the wall next to the bed, and a tripod mounted camcorder. She was perhaps the most uninhibited woman he had ever been with, and somehow, she helped his tangled mind unravel.

Cal would never cease to find Panthera sensual and alluring, but one thing came of their relationship that he had never considered. She would grow to become one of his most cherished memories. Had his time in this world lasted longer, they may have even ended up together.

The morning after the sex-fest, Cathryn filled a Thermos with coffee and drove Calvin to Myrtle Beach.

Cold, biting wind blew off the ocean, but their arm-in-arm walk along the sandy shore rejuvenated a deteriorating McLeish. Sitting on the jetties, Panthera listened to the unfathomable story of the Timetravellar and how McLeish's alter ego had emerged and so completely complicated his life. He questioned his own sanity for divulging what sounded like absolute bullshit to his newfound sex kitten. To his amazement though, she simply listened with soft eyes and a warm heart. Her comprehension and willingness to believe him endeared her to him. Her acceptance of his tale bound him to her for the rest of his time—that short period remaining, when he could still be called...mortal.

With but a twenty-seat-capacity, the twin-engine commuter raced down the Wilmington runway and lifted from the airstrip. The flight terminated in Jacksonville, and time in the air was just over one hour. Small though it was, the subsidiary of Cloudland Airways maintained a staff of flight attendants that offered big airline amenities. Calvin sipped a Jack and coke and laid his head back on the seat-rest. Peaceful exuberance warmed the traveler. The weekend of only before-imagined passion loomed in his every thought. Cat confessed she was married, but for a day and a half, she had been his willing love slave and had hopped to obey his every perversion. The promiscuous vixen treated him as a god, just as she promised. She was fabulous and he wondered how soon she might be willing to romp again.

He drifted in placid solitude, on the brink of slumber. His hatred of Maggie dissipated. The tangled mess represented by the Timetravellar did not cross his mind. Feelings of failure, as a husband and as a writer, seemed to belong to someone else now. Perhaps writing was not his calling, although Cat and some of his other cyber-concubine might have disagreed. Nothing seemed to matter at the moment, just the peace that had been granted him. In his mind, Calvin knew that his restoration, his re-vitalization would not last, but at least he had been able to experience it. Maybe it would be a turning point for him, a new leaf. The droning of the twin-engine propellers seduced McLeish to that other dimension, the one like sleep, where he dabbled in another reality.

* * * * *

Confused by his own physical stature, he stared at his hands. The Calvin in him did not understand the metamorphosis, but the immortal did.

Timetravellar found himself transported to a place and time that became increasingly familiar. As always, it was night. He appeared from nowhere in a back courtyard outside of Lazare's palace. The massive Scot gazed at a window on the third floor, and instinctively knew that the fourth window from the end was his destination. A vine-covered trellis served as a ladder. He climbed. At the top, he anchored himself to an immense stone gargoyle and swung to an eight-inch ledge traversing the length of the palace's third level. Tentatively inching his way, he maintained a handhold on the rough, vertical, stone walls. An overwhelming blast of wind snatched his cloak over his head and nearly jerked him from his perch. MacTavish, the dream-world equivalent of Timetravellar, hurriedly unsnapped the epaulets of his cape and watched, as his cloak, caught by yet another gust, flung twenty meters across the courtyard. His heart slowed, as he achieved the fourth window. Wiping condensation from its panes, he peered inside to behold Monique Dubois, a captive maidservant, brushing her hair.

In that world, even the unlikely made perfect sense. The dream-state presented bizarre and unnatural circumstances, as would a normal dream, yet those events, without detail or explanation, seemed plausible. Calvin never questioned how and why his character behaved as he did. He was, at least within the bounds of absurd dream-state logic, simply a spectator.

Monique pulled her brush, one velvet stroke after another, through her sable tresses. Her visage struck him with awe and enchantment. She was, without question, the most angelic creature upon which his eyes had ever rested. MacTavish looked on her in her bustierre and cotton pantaloons, and his heart ached for her.

To be certain, his attempt to see her was brazen. She might scream for the palace guards. If she did, he could not mount an escape from the third floor. If he chose to fight his way out through the castle's interior, it would be disastrous.

Still, he could not stand to be without her. He had watched her and even encountered her in the cover of Ténèbres late at night only a week before. He had taken her and made passionate love to her in the shrouded ecstasy of darkness. He was almost certain she knew it was he, at least, he hoped she knew. If she had made such passionate, riveting love to one she thought to be another, his heart would be broken. Yet, even in the darkness of the forest, even though his face remained masked by pitch, she *had* looked into his starlit eyes. There, in an intertwined embrace, she had shown him where he belonged. His home was her heart, and his purpose was to be at her side.

The burglar of her heart rapped the window with his bare, battle hardened knuckles. Monique gasped, jumped from her chair, and folded her arms across the part of her breasts that were exposed. Again, fear clutched her, as the crouching, unrecognizable silhouette perched like a predator preparing to pounce upon its prey.

Then, to her exhilarated relief, as if illuminated by candlelight, those marvelous, soulful eyes shone through the obscurity of night. Monique's eyes burst wide, as she realized it was him, and her delicate lips spread, conveying the message of her heart. Her father had reared her to be proper, though, and the girl from the French countryside hid her eagerness. Dropping her head so that her eyes peaked out from underneath her tilted brow, she tried to look angry. MacTavish placed his palms together as if praying, or begging, and she could not contain her own laughter. She ran to the window, and swung it open. The kilted giant hopped from the ledge to the chamber floor.

"You assume much, highness," Monique said.

"I assume nothing," MacTavish returned, as he dropped to one knee.

Gently taking her hand, he brought the back of it to his lips.

"I only come to pay homage to my queen."

"Sir, please. You embarrass me. I am not a noble, as you are. You know that I am but a peasant, an indentured servant, a pitiful slave of...Satan himself. It is not fitting that you bow before the likes of me."

Her eyes darkened and her head dropped, as she admitted her plight to the Scottish knight.

"Ah, but you are wrong, Milady. You...*are* the queen of my heart. Forever, I shall be bound to you...and I shall be your incarcerated servant, your willing...slave."

"You do not understand, my knight. I may never be yours, nor you mine, even though it is my heart's greatest desire. I am the owned concubine of the son of all evil. I am not chaste. I am a pariah whose only salvation is death. Yet, even that escapes me, as I become one of the undead. I can feel it growing within me, as a cancer grows. Would that I could, I would plunge a stake into my own heart, so that I may never infect another with this pestilence. Somehow, though, taking my own life, or unlife as it becomes, is beyond what I can do."

Monique's expression of joy transformed to one of agony, as she confessed her quandary, her curse. A single blood tear cascaded from her cheek onto that of the kneeling admirer. Removing his dagger from its scabbard, he lanced the tip of his forefinger such that a pearl of blood rose. He touched the blood-laden finger to the blood tear that had fallen on his face, and the two separate droplets became one. Pressing the forefinger of each hand together, he rubbed them circularly so that the mixture of blood would be forced into the laceration.

"So that you may forever be in me, our blood is mixed. And at least within me, your blood along with mine, shall nourish my heart, and I shall never abandon thee."

Calvin could hear the words, "...and I shall never abandon thee," spring from his own lips, as the stewardess gently shook him. She was embarrassed for him, as he came back to consciousness, and her face flushed.

"Sir, you are talking in your sleep—and very strangely I might add."

Calvin looked around the plane to see a number of passengers gawking at him, some even snickering. He smiled, still lifted by his adventure with Panthera.

"It's just a dream," he thought. "I'll never see these people again, anyway. Let em' laugh."

Chapter 21

Tender kisses on each cheek warmed Myron's heart, as he zipped the closure of his black leather jacket. Vampyra was well, and while he would have stayed with her forever, he sensed she needed her privacy. The Harley thundered its report, and he turned the handlebars toward the gravel drive. He and the vampiress exchanged glances of affection, and, finally, he blew her a kiss. The two-wheeled stallion disappeared quickly with a bend in the path, and he was gone.

Vampyra stepped back into the chilled stone fortress and immediately proceeded to the computer. Pulling up Fountain, she scanned her messages. For Stag's sake, she had avoided getting online the previous few days, but her heart yearned for the Timetravellar. She had cuffed him around pretty hard the last time they spoke, the encounter when Stag transcribed her harsh words. But her great admirer and nurse was gone, and she could resume her routine. Her belly was well-filled thanks to Stag, and it would be a while before she would have to hunt. Hundreds of messages from her followers awaited a reply, but her only thoughts were of the immortal one.

When she logged on, she did not expect to see Timetravellar's name, but was disappointed all the same. Her dilemma became one of whether to pursue her heart's desire or to continue to play cat and mouse. The crass messages she had received from Calvin, writing as the Timetravellar, still disturbed her. Just as she required blood, though, it seemed she also required the majesty of the immortal's words.

    Had she been less prideful, she might have dropped him a line. Timetravellar had stiffened once when she accused him of masquerading as another, and she humbly submitted, but her turn had come to stand proud and not succumb to the temptation to run to him. She needed him, but respect was important. The vulgarity, with which Calvin had written her, smote her honor and showed a lack of respect. Words of the true time warrior, words that spoke of *moon's amber oil* made her knees weak, her heart swoon, and her femininity rise. This time though, she would remain steadfast, requiring him to beg *her* forgiveness. Love is after all, give and take. As she had given in before, now he must come to her. Her stomach pitched, as she embraced the possibility that he may never return, never again anoint her heart with his special magic. Vampyra sensed a mystical bond between the immortal and her, but a shred of doubt remained. Staring at the screen, desperately wishing to abandon honor and write him, she powered it off. Unyielding stubbornness could be reversed, in the future. Submitting this soon could not.

* * * * *

    Night fell and candles ignited throughout the stone tenement. A wolf bayed at the rising moon. Countless Canadian nights she had reveled in the wolf's song, as it worshipped the silver sphere of night. That night was different, though. Cries of her lupine brother howled shriller than normal, almost panicky—as if warning of danger. The timber wolf that lamented on a ridge two miles away understood not why fear set in, but somehow did understand that unmistakable evil approached. So he howled, wailing a warning to the temptress of night, a warning she could not understand.

Reaching into a vault that lay within the stone walls of her bedchamber, she removed a bottle of deep red wine. The coolness of the interior walls remained constant nearly year round and made for a perfect wine cask. Burgundy was her weakness, aside from Timetravellar, and she seated herself in a plush leather seat that faced the bedroom window. No sooner than she sat down and began to marvel at the silver light of earth's orbiting lover, a sheet of frigidity passed over her. Horror gripped her heart. She knew whence the cold had come.

Twelve years had passed, the twinkling of an eye in vampire years, since he brought forth his evil. Vampyra boiled in anger and fright, as she sensed his presence. Yet, she would not let him see the alarm in her. For five hundred years, with unpredictable frequency, he chased her, even now that she was vampire.

Emilien, as he demanded she call him, came to Monique, as he did all of the once-chambermaids. Five centuries since their transformation to undead, he hunted each of them down, while they scurried across the planet, fleeing his depravity. He always found them, though, and when he did, he forced his exploitation upon them, both sexually and as a vampire. And when he left, he left his girls hollow and drained, their souls even further diminished. The world was filled with living beings from which Lazare could pick and choose, and take them he did, in every country and in every century. The chambermaids he once imprisoned in his palace, though, were simply sport, and he punished them with his meanness, whenever the mood struck him.

Despite sipping wine only moments before, her lips became dry. Determined resolve bristled within her. This time she would fight as she had never fought in all her five hundred years. Before, when Lazare had come, her existence had no meaning, no purpose, and her will had weakened. Now, though, there was Timetravellar. If one were to take her, it would be her gladiator, not a vermin from five hundred years passed.

Rising slowly, she turned to face the sunken eyes and gaunt face of her nemesis. Lazare instantly found the blaze in her eyes, eyes that spoke of an inimitable will. He was a bully like any other, only persecuting the weak. Though he would not show his fear, it was there. Never had one of his unwilling flock so silently defied him. He would cut his losses and feign another reason for the visit.

"Do not touch me you vile bastard! I will not allow you to take blood that has been given me, nor shall I allow you to again pluck the fruit of my loins, not now, not ever!"

Walking through the archway of the bedroom, Lazare faked smugness. "Oh, indeed!" he scoffed

"Indeed," she countered.

"Hmmm, to take you or not to take you, that is the question. I have not come to suckle your neck this time, nor to plunge into your depths, but your arrogance challenges me to do both, just to show you who your master is. Ah...it is no matter. I have only hours ago plucked a virgin. Not only did I tap her tight girlhood, so did I drink from the fountain of her life. So you see my sweet Monique, I do not require the aging and paltry offerings that your decrepit body can provide me, at least not this night. Moreover, I have come because we are linked, you and I, and I feel the presence of one that is not undead. This one is neither human, nor like us. You know of whom I speak. You have challenged me this moment, and it is because you have taken up with this mongrel. Do understand that you are still my whore and that I shall have you, whenever I choose. You are lucky that my belly is full and my testicles drained. Otherwise, it would be you who lay whimpering at this moment, instead of that tender young girl. Rebellion is an ugly thing, Monique. It is as offensive as an unfitting garment. Shed yourself of it, or ...suffer."

With unblinking eyes, Vampyra returned, "You are correct in what you have felt through the power of night. The one that you speak of will come for me soon, and soon after that, he will come for you."

"Damn you, wench! Do not threaten me. I am powerful above all vampires. I shall peel the flesh from your suitor, as an angler filets a fish. Whomever he is, he is no match for Edouardo Emilien Lazare!"

Monique stood her ground. "He will find you and defile you, just as you have me, and the rest. Restitution and revenge come soon, you baneful pig. Leave me before you worsen your plight."

Lazare grasped the edge of his cape, snapping it like a bullwhip in front of his face, and in the beat of a hummingbird's wing, shape-shifted into a nighthawk and fled through the open window.

Vampyra's heart grew cold and her knees quaked with fear. "Oh God, what have I done."

She turned to the opened window and scanned the moonlit horizon. Five hundred years of torture and hatred had culminated in that one moment. Monique Dubois stood tall against her relentless tormenter of centuries past, and she had threatened him, threatened him with an imaginary immortal. Hope, and loathing had taken control of her when Lazare, The Wicked, had arrived. Her weapon was an enigma she knew only as Timetravellar. It was the faith and passion of her heart that fought back against Lazare's evil intent. The raging fire in her eyes had caused Emilien, at least for the moment, to falter.

The gauntlet was thrown down before her unholy master, and she must be prepared to make good on her threat. Hatred alone could not give her strength to challenge the evil one. She desperately needed a champion to battle in her stead. When she lashed out at the ancient vampire, she fantasized that Timetravellar truly was her champion and would chivalrously come to her aid.

Pride had caused her to bristle at Calvin's disrespectful passes. Still, even in the midst of her indignity, her heart glowed for the cyber-warrior like coals in the center of a fire. But, how would she approach him? Coyness had transformed to insult and she had accused him of vulgarity and deception. Would she now kneel before him in humility, beg his forgiveness, and ask for his protection?

Eyes fixed on a dark horizon, her stare moved to the floor at her feet. She was in great peril. Day-to-day existence was difficult, but especially so when cursed with deathlessness. Projecting her mind into the future, the countless centuries of defilement that surely lay before her caused her to weep.

A fictional character she had only just met loomed large in her plight. Monique feared that Timetravellar might be a bald-headed, overweight car salesman. Perhaps, he had simply learned, cultivated his adeptness of the written word. To truly believe he was immortal was folly. Gothica's inhabitants, for the most part, were role-players. True, a few old-world vampires existed in that realm, and true, a number of neo-vampires had come into the ranks. But, if she were to be honest with herself, she had to admit that he was just a fantasy, an illusion.

Having contemplated the reality of her circumstance, and the foolishness of her actions toward Lazare, she stared blankly at a dwindling candle. Through five hundred years she had never called upon anyone for help, but twice, in just a few weeks, she looked to another for rescue.

Centuries before, she used peasants, servants, and suitors to deliver messages, but in modern day, no one could deliver a message to Timetravellar as quickly as her Pentium. Only a few days had passed since she sparred with Calvin, and she could not have known that her lover's mortal host had flown to North Carolina to pursue his own passion. When she did not receive a prompt reply, she believed that the timeless one had turned away from her.

* * * * *

    Calvin returned on a Sunday afternoon. Although physically weary from the journey, his mind and heart surged with vitality.
    "Now, I know what people mean when they say, 'screwed up.' I actually feel like I have been unscrewed. I'm as relaxed as an old sock." He laughed at his own paradox. It took an entire weekend of boundless screwing to help him finally get unscrewed. Perhaps, after all that he had been through, the pleasure of a woman was the only remedy he needed.
    Sunday evening went quietly. He unpacked, nursed a Jack and Coke, and watched a welterweight fight between two guys he had never heard of. He sat in the recliner, his favorite perch while the pugilistic battle raged, his attention drifted to thoughts of Panthera. Replaying the fabulous moments of ecstasy over and over was more entertaining than the fight. His perspective had changed, he thought. Maybe he should go about trying to be more responsible, as Maggie had preached. Perhaps writing and cyberspace were worthless pursuits. Reunion with his estranged wife was unlikely, but this seemed a pivotal point in his life. It was a shame that Cathryn was married. He would have liked to pursue her. If she could make him feel like a king for one blissful weekend, what would a long-term relationship be like? Then again, the magic could not last forever, so he would be content to relive

his Wilmington weekend in his mind. Maybe she would invite him again. Her husband would be gone for three more months. Surely, she would come to yearn for him, as he knew that he would for her. A smile spread over his lips and he melted into deep, satisfying sleep.

Chapter 22

Aaron McCall unfolded an aluminum stepladder into position. "Damn sorry excuse for a cable company," he snorted. "I bet if we were in Atlanta, they'd put the co-ax underground."

Disgruntled at the distortion of the television picture, he assumed the coaxial cable insulation had worn through. Vanishing Point Cable Company ran their cable overhead utilizing existing telephone and power poles. About every two years, Aaron had to repair the cable at the point it entered the attic through an outside wall. Constant movement from the wind caused the cable to wallow in the drilled hole, eventually wearing the plastic sleeving. It had been just about two years since McCall performed the surgery, and he figured the repair would take care of the problem.

"Hmmmph, looks fine to me," he said, as he examined the cable. He descended from the fourth rung, folded the ladder, and placed it back in the carport utility room.

"Maybe it's at the television itself," he thought.

Aaron opened the doors to the entertainment center and turned the TV to its side. A loud "clunk" echoed from the back of the cabinet. His eyebrows knitted, as curiosity rose. Reaching around behind the television, his fingers found the fallen object. It was a camera, one he had never seen before. What was it doing behind the television? Aaron reached to the rear and disconnected the cable and power cord. Lowering the bulky set to the floor, he was surprised to find two more objects at the back of the shelf when he stood back up. One was a legal-size envelope, the other, a logbook. "What the...?" he muttered.

He pulled the closure flap to the envelope and removed its contents, a dozen photographs, and their negatives. Bewilderment spread over his face. Cocking his head, he held a photo so that he could view it through his bifocals. "What in the *hell* is this?" he said aloud.

It was next door neighbor Calvin talking to a *mountain* wearing a skirt. He hurried through the rest of the pictures, all were of Calvin and the longhair. Aaron shook his head rapidly from side to side. Who took these shots, and why are they in my house?" Examination of the logbook, which turned out to be a diary, revealed answers to all his questions.

February 5, 1997

Yesss! Maggie left Calvin today. I don't blame her. He's a sorry excuse for a husband...but I must admit he's got a fine body. I wouldn't really be disloyal to Mags if I did the "wild thing" with him. Mmmmm! He does have a cute ass.

February sixth through the tenth chronicled the plight of Bitsy's soap opera stars, which Aaron found amusing in a bizarre, pathetic way.

February 11, 1997

Mags called me up and wants me to go with her to the house to get some things tonight. I'm so excited. Part of me is delighted that she is putting the screws to that piece of shit. Still, something about that piece of shit gets me hotter than the pits of a black mammy's arms in mid July...I must admit that I am myself confused at my feelings for Cal...I guess it's one of those love/hate things...

Aaron speeded through the next couple of days' entries until he reached February 14.

February 14, 1997

yippee...Valentine's Day. I yearn to be taken by a man...a real man...I want to feel like I've had a python in me. I want to be tied to the bed and taken savagely by a young, tall, breeding machine with a penis the size of a salami...but NOOOOO! Separate bedrooms or not...the disgusting pig that I live with is going to want to poke me with that vestigial stump that he calls a cock...Oh God, how can I get out of it...every time I see him naked, I want to puke.

(Late Entry)

Big mistake. Tried to give Calvin and that animal that's been hanging around their house some pussy. That son-of-a-bitch threw me out! He had a chance to fuck me and turned me down. I would have sucked him till the back of his head caved in. I would have treated him like a god. Now I'm going to...<u>FUCK</u> him. "Hell hath no fury like a woman scorned,"...Mr. McLeish. Those words shall be my banner, as I dedicate myself to...revenge!

Aaron's eyes narrowed, as he read the words of her heart, words that he had known to be true for most of their marriage. A small, but diabolical smile spread over his face. Further inspection of the diary revealed her plans to find Calvin in a compromised position with the big Scot. If the opportunity never presented itself, she would fabricate enough evidence to make it look as though Calvin were a flaming homosexual. Being shunned by her neighbor was more insult than she could take. As she had said in her diary, part of her hated him anyway. Once he turned her down, all of her hated him.

Aaron smirked and nodded his head. "Oh yeah, I should have tossed your dried up ass outta here a long time ago."

He paused, as he viewed the pictures Bitsy had taken while Calvin was in Wilmington. Most of them were simply pictures of an untidy house, close-ups of liquor bottles and a sink full of dirty dishes. One photo caught his eye, though. It almost appeared as a double exposure.

Bitsy's intent was to photograph the unmade bed, but closer inspection of the picture revealed a faint image. It appeared as an almost ghost-like visage of the great Scot, lying still as death. As faint as the apparition was, Aaron thought that the color of his skin and the blueness of his lips, unmistakably resembled that of...a corpse.

* * * * *

Almost two weeks passed before Aaron approached Calvin. He took the opportunity to pick at Bitsy, asking pointed questions which vaguely implied he might know something of her escapades. Finally, after thirteen days of continued, subliminal harassment, she broke.

"Why you son-of-a-bitch!" she shrieked. "You've been reading my diary. That is private!"

Without taking his eyes from the morning paper, Aaron responded, "Not anymore."

Bitsy sneered and jutted out her chin, as was her way when she grew angry. "Aaron Oleander McCall, if you ever delve into my private life again, you will find yourself *cut off*. That is, if I don't leave you."

Turning to the sports page, Aaron tried to concentrate on the college scoreboard.

"Looks like the Tarheels might have a shot at a conference title," he thought privately.

"Aaron! Did you hear what I said?"

"Yes, I did Bitch...er, uh, I mean Bitsy. In a way your words are quite prophetic, my dear."

Bitsy's lips pursed and her stare turned venomous. "What do you mean by that, you big tub of guts?"

That diabolical grin, again, slowly crept over the engineer's face. He continued scanning the newspaper.

"What I mean is, I won't *ever* again have to poke that cold clammy thing you call a...well, whatever you call it. And you *will* be leaving me...just as soon as you get your shit packed."

Bitsy gasped.

"Don't let the door hit you in the ass, Bitsy," he celebrated, turning to the stock market page.

* * * * *

Calvin's eyes bulged, as he read the diary. His face reddened when he came to the part about Bitsy offering him some.

"Aaron, I'm sorry. I couldn't imagine how to bring it up to you, so I didn't."

"It's o.k. Cal, don't look so mortified. Geez, you feel worse about this than I do. But, there is one other thing. These pictures don't mean much, but look closely at this one."

He tilted the photograph to the light so that Calvin could see the image.

"This one looks double exposed, yet there's not another negative that shows *your friend* stretched out like he is here. You can barely see him I know, but he looks..."

Calvin looked at Aaron and finished the sentence.

"He looks dead," Cal concluded. "When do you think she got these pictures of the inside of my house?" he asked, trying to change the subject. "I can pretty well figure when she got the ones of Timett ...... uh ... Tom...my friend Tom Terrific." Calvin smiled sheepishly.

"That's what I call him, anyway, Tom Terrific."

Aaron's eyebrows arched.

"I'm not even going to ask why you call him that," Aaron replied. "What two people do in the privacy of their own bedroom is their business."

McLeish's expression fell to one of surrender. He would not even attempt to rebuke Aaron. He hoped his neighbor was kidding.

"Anyway," Aaron continued. "My guess would be that Bitsy took the pictures when you were out of town a couple of weeks ago. She's a world class snoop. She probably knew you were going out of town before you yourself knew. But...what about the photo?"

"Truth is Aaron, I do know something about this one photograph," he said pointing at the ghost picture. "Don't worry though. There's no foul play or anything like that, o.k.? Just trust me."

Aaron pulled his hands back to his chest, palms facing Calvin.

"Hey partner, this is for your information. That's all. I'm not on a need to know basis."

"Thanks," Calvin said. "You're a good friend."

* * * * *

Calvin locked the garage door after Aaron left. It was getting late and he wanted to "surf" a bit before he hit the sack. Clicking to his mailbox in Fountain, he was reminded of a message that he had received from Vampyra upon returning from Cathryn's. There it sat in the box with a number of other messages. He had not answered it, and yet could not bring himself to discard it. Opening it up, he read again her dramatic plea for help.

Vampyra: Oh Timey...I am in grave danger...one come from my past to destroy me...I have no one to turn to but you...please...if you care for me...at all...please help...

Calvin smirked. "I guess I'm supposed to think that since she didn't write again, that this *one* from her past has done her in," he surmised. "She does have a flair for theatrics, but I've seen her operate like this in Gothica before. She's great at pulling a sucker in with crocodile tears, only to play him like a cheap ukulele. But not Calvin McLeish, not on your life.

"I do sort of hate it for Timetravellar, but he's left me alone for quite a while and that's fine with me. Maybe Panthera will somehow set me free. I do know that I feel better. If Aaron hadn't brought this picture, I would probably be convinced that I was just going crazy, and that Timetravellar was just a figment, a specter that my stressed and twisted mind created. But no, Aaron had to bring the picture over, and now I start feeling sorry for him again. Uh, uh. Not this boy, not this time.

"Things are going to be the best they have since Maggie left, and I'm not going to get back into this role-play thing again, not unless it's with Panthera. Speaking of Cathryn, let's see if she's left anything for me today."

Cathryn's latest message began with deliberate promiscuity.

Panthera: Oooh Timepiece, I have tasted your delicious flesh...and I long for more...long to be filled with your exquisiteness...

The message went on for two pages. When Calvin finished, he filled the oval garden tub with water as cold as the spigot could produce. Screaming softly as he sat into it, he shivered and reached for the cordless telephone. Cathryn answered and purred, as he began to speak.

"Baby, if you're going to keep sending me stuff like that, you're going to have to adopt me cause I'm gonna end up on your doorstep for good."

Cathryn laughed. "So when are you coming back to the Wilmington Love-Palace?"

Chapter 23

Vampyra curled within the cocoon of an angora blanket. The fire she built raged, and yet, despite the blanket, the blaze, and a bottle of cognac, she shivered from unmerciful cold. Her state of existence was in shambles, and she wept silently. Only weeks before, she owned her unlife—mostly owned it, anyway. That was before Lazare had come, before her jaw had been broken—before Timetravellar.

The thought of a wooden spike piercing her heart seemed more appealing, as the days passed. She could not do it herself, but there were plenty who would gladly send her to hell. Even in Fountain, there was one called "Vampire-Stalker." She had heard from Stag, and Pristen, a true vampire, that the Stalker was no role-player. He knew that vampires existed, and knew that there were real vamps in Fountain. The Stalker had one kill to his credit, a vampire known as Estefan, who hailed from the city of Chicago. Estefan had been a member of Fountain, but had been "staked" just a few weeks after Vampyra had come online. She had met him briefly on the net, and while he seemed sweet enough for a vamp, he lacked the necessary staunchness to stir her interest. When she heard of his demise, she grieved, not because of her closeness to him, but from sadness at the dwindling of her kind. Few remained with which she could commune, few that could relate to the agony of her plight.

"Is this to be what I must experience for all time?" she pondered. "Will there be no end to the cold, to the loneliness?" Her belly growled with displeasure. Like it or not, the hunt would soon begin. She mourned the fact that she must go kill another human. It seemed so barbaric to take a life so that her lack of it could continue.

Self-pity overwhelmed her, as she looked into the night sky through the back door window. Monique Dubois had been a simple peasant girl who brought harm to no one. If anything, she had been a kind and gentle creature.

"How...why has this happened to me?" Monique slapped her upper thigh, scolding herself for wallowing in her own misfortune. Trying to stiffen and be courageous, she told herself to extract what she could from her existence, or to simply end it. After all, those were her choices. She could fret and moan for the next two hundred years, but when it all came down to it, there were only the two choices.

Displacing self-depravation with more pleasant thoughts, she gently caressed the mane of her imagined lover. Though it seemed like an eternity since she last spoke to him, she held fast to the image that she had of Timetravellar. She smiled at the curiosity of her own feelings. Many had pursued her before. Many had thrown themselves at her feet. Beyond his silver tongue, she wondered what was so magical about him.

Suddenly, she gasped. Not until that very moment, had it occurred to her. Perhaps that was why she was so taken with the timeless one. Yes, of course, that was it! Timetravellar was so much like one from her distant past.

It was the way he spoke, that had attracted her. The splendor of his words flowed from his sweet lips, as a crystal stream cascades from its mountain peak. Timetravellar was so much like the Scottish knight she met in France, so much like the cavalier that had peered at her through the palace window. She had not thought of Glynn MacTavish in ages. Her eyes smiled, as she remembered the first time he rescued her from the bullying guard. The night when he apprehended her in the dark forest was the sweetest of all recollections, though.

It started out as a simple walk. In the darkness of Ténèbres, she found solace, a place her mind escaped the brutality of the real world. Sometimes, as she walked the moonlit path, she fantasized about just running away from the barbarism of her haughty master. He would find her though, and her punishment would be excruciating, worse even, than the torment she endured. At least she could go to the woodlands and pretend—pretend to be free and happy.

When she first felt the Scots powerful grip on her waist, fear gripped her such that she thought she would faint. Then, a twinkle of starlight became the sparkle of his eye, and she quietly rejoiced, as tumultuous desire replaced panic.

"Ah, the memory, the ecstasy of that perfect romantic moment," she whispered. It was a beautiful coincidence, the similarity between MacTavish and Timetravellar, but it was just a coincidence, she decided. MacTavish had been her lover some five hundred years earlier. Timetravellar was a romantic illusion of the present, who, for the most part, she had inflated to god-like status in her own mind.

Growling angrily again, an empty stomach snatched her daydreaming mind back to cold reality. Time to hunt, but, only a half moon presented itself.

"Travel will be more difficult, but c'est la vie." Monique Dubois stepped out onto the slate patio. A stiff breeze contemptuously slapped her body, while a whippoorwill echoed a song of solitude and loneliness. Monique let her head fall back, and focused, concentrated on a single star. In that instant between "whip" and "poorwill" of the night bird's song, Vampyra transformed. Fluttering awkwardly above the patio, she righted herself as vampire bat, and flew in the direction of the moon—and in the direction of downtown Ottawa.

* * * * *

Two weeks passed after Bobby Don returned to New York. His vacation expired and the Isaac's vampire hunt had still produced nothing. Just as Isaac called in reinforcements, the attacks had stopped. Frustration, disappointment, and a sense of defeat shackled the Ottawa detective. Isaac would continue his pursuit, at least until the captain called him off. What were the chances that just as soon as he brought in a ringer like Bobby Don, the attacks would stop? It seemed to Isaac as though the killer sensed his every move. In truth, the timing of Vampyra's injury and her disappearance from the streets was simply Isaac's bad luck.

Monique assumed local authorities would investigate the corpses she left in the alleyways, but their pursuit did not worry her. She was cleverer and far more powerful than the likes of any local police force. Being hunted was expected. It was part of being a vamp. Almost always, someone endeavored to track her down. Most often, it was the police, but sometimes it was a vampire hunter. Over the course of the centuries, she had slain a number of each, not out of viciousness, but out of self-defense.

On the night she fell to the kick-boxer, Monique sensed that danger was nearby. It was almost as if she could smell the hunters from where they lay-in-wait. Hunger drove her there, however, and she would return to stalk her prey, without fear of those who tracked her. Vampyra avoided encounters with her would-be captors, but if backed in a corner, she would lash out with a wicked vengeance.

As she entered the core of the city from two hundred feet above, neon lights and the bustle of people served as a beacon that drew her. Fluttering once again in the dark path of a back street, she hovered five feet off the ground. Looking left and then right, she determined the alley to be deserted. Then, as if a dark curtain dropped, she transformed to human-like form.

Isaac Hollander paced back and forth in front of his unmarked car, this time, without Bobby Don's companionship. Early March nights still dropped below freezing and he questioned his own sanity. If he got in the car, he might as well go home. He would be able to see little from inside the vehicle, much less hear anything. Nineteen times he had staked out the strip, and nineteen times he had gone home disappointed and half frozen. The most exciting thing he ever saw were the hookers that strode up and down the avenue. But on that night, even the whores were scarce. If anyone knew about the killings they sure weren't talking, at least the people he had questioned weren't talking.

"Give it up," he told himself. "You're on a wild goose chase…and the goose is probably at home in a warm bed." He paused, blew warm breath into his fists, and came to a decision. "One more hour, and I'm gonna throw in the towel for good. Either the killer is on to us, or he's just stopped. I'd be as well off to wait until it happens again…*if* it happens again."

No sooner than he surrendered, a shadow from half a block away caught his eye. Isaac rubbed his eyes and shook his head in disbelief, a wolf? No way, it couldn't be, not in the city. He remembered what the prostitute told him a month earlier, one street over from where he stood right then. His eyes squinted, and he walked rapidly toward the trotting lupine figure.

Vampyra was warmed from the blood she had just taken. Her belly was full and though the journey back home would be long, it had been a successful hunt.

Traveling as bat or nighthawk would have been quicker, but the lethargy of post feeding made flight difficult, if not impossible. When she had attacked the strong young martial artist the month before, the debilitation of the injury caused her to travel as wolf. That night she had been too weak to maintain sustained flight, despite the fact that she had never fed. At one point on her way home, she had shifted to nighthawk and flown for a few miles, but she felt as though she may faint and returned to the ground, finishing the journey as a wolf.

That night, as so many before, she had taken a healthy, but weak young woman who offered little resistance. As she trotted, she smiled introspectively, unaware of her surroundings. A few more blocks of travel through the deserted alleyways, and she would be near the city limit. As troubled and depressed as she had been, feeding brought a brief exuberance that was a bright spot in her otherwise dark existence. Three more blocks and she could cross the highway into a field that led to miles of forest. The forest was safe, and she always breathed a sigh of relief when she achieved the protection of its shadows.

Then to her dismay, her keen wolfen ears detected footsteps from behind. Without breaking her stride, she craned her head backward to see what followed.

"Damn! Who is that?"

Isaac broke into a run, as he lost sight of the wolf. The sprint warmed him to the point of sweating and he peeled off his parka, dropping it on the pavement.

"Shit! Where'd that wolf go?" he wondered, as he labored to keep the pace.

Isaac had just passed under one of only a few alleyway streetlights and was creeping back into the darkness. When he reached the intersection of his alleyway with that of another, something from behind the corner of a building burst forth, clutching him by his throat. Before he realized what was happening, he found himself in the grip of an entity so forceful, that death seemed almost certain. His eyes bulged, as blood pooled, backing up in the constricted arteries of his neck and head. Lightheadedness came quickly, and his vision blurred. Something clutched him forcefully, with supernatural strength. It pulled him close to its face, and it was the face of a pale, but lovely female. His mind reeled in chaos, as it tried to understand how such a petite woman could have rendered him so defenseless.

Her expression remained as calm as a September morning, and she held him above the asphalt. Carefully studying his face, she finally spoke. "You are a constable, a police, oui?"

Rasping a response, he muttered, "Yes...detective."

Vampyra pulled him close, while still keeping him suspended above the ground. She sniffed his clothes, then flicked her tongue in the air the way a viper would when sensing its environment. "You hunt the huntress, oui?"

The five foot, two inch vampiress lowered him to the ground so that he could speak. His head had turned scarlet from her hold, and she feared that he might pass out. Normal color returned to his face, as his feet made contact with the alley floor. She did not relinquish her grasp, but loosened it enough for him to speak.

"I hunt the one who has killed so many. I hunt the depraved killer of innocent young women, women whose lives are cut short by the insanity of bloodsucking."

"Hmmm, you think me insane?"

Confused by the strength and power of the one that held him at bay with such little effort, Isaac answered after a lengthy pause. "I am here to bring to justice to the one that slays the innocent. I followed a wolf into this alley. It is the second time in a month that I know of a wolf being here, in the center of Ottawa. The first time a wolf was here was the last time one of these murders took place. I do not come for you. I follow the wolf."

"But Monsieur," she said smilingly. "I am the wolf. I *am* the one that you seek. I am the night huntress that take the life of those you say are...innocent. I do not kill for sport, nor do I kill out of hatred. I simply kill so that I may eat."

Isaac looked into the endlessness of her eyes. There he saw the essence of her being, that which was dark, that which was vampire. Fear swept him, as the rising tide floods a marsh, and he felt the warmth of his own urine release and travel the length of his leg.

"Do not hunt the huntress constable, lest ye become the hunted."

The mistress of night loosened her grip on Ottawa's finest, never breaking eye contact. The dim light darted from her elongate incisors, as she spoke. Vampyra turned and walked hurriedly into the darkness.

Isaac Hollander stood in fear's grip and he watched her blend into the pitch of the alleyway. Then when he was prepared to turn, he saw her image reappear in a far streetlight, her cape dancing behind her. That which had been a brisk walk transformed to a full run, and that which had commanded human form metamorphosed to the figure of a wolf.

Cold horror seized Isaac. He would indeed fill out the reports as required, but there would be no mention of the wolf, or Vampyra. How could he possibly relate the events that had just transpired? He would be thought a madman. His superiors already considered him obsessed with the case. Certainly, the truth would find him removed from it, if not sent for psychoanalysis. The following morning he was informed that another victim had fallen—cause of death, the same as the others. But he knew that without being told. When he dangled in the clutches of the creature, he knew beyond all doubt, that he had encountered the perpetrator of the murders.

Days passed before he told Michelle and even longer before he gathered himself enough to call Bobby Don. The whole thing was insane. He had just witnessed, just been manhandled by what appeared to be an honest-to-God, shape-shifting vampire.

Chapter 24

In the Room: quadrophobia, scabby porno elf, Hostility, Queen Satania, Lustybustybitch, Vampire Lestat01, stinky, Blakkvelvett, Gargoyle, Punishment Park, Panthera, Timetravellar, **the Sorcerer,** and Stag.

scabby porno elf: Welcome Lusty...I don't believe we've met...as you can see my name is scabby...I'm considered...one of Gothica's highest ranking males...I am one most sought after by the juiciest females in this realm...would you like to go to a private room?...

Lustybustybitch: No offense scab boy, but I don't know you...and I'm not sure I want to know you...if you're one of the most desired males in this room...this is NOT the place for me...

Hostility: Don't pay any attention to him my large breasted friend...he's like a dog...have you ever seen a dog that constantly wanted to keep his nose right in your crotch?...well...that's scabby...he'd probably have an orgasm if anyone ever DID go to a room with him...just ignore him...he'll leave you alone after a while...

scabby porno elf: Well!...that's it!...I don't know why I even come here...EVERYONE treats me like dirt...

Hostility: We don't know why you come here either scab-head...everyone treats you like dirt, because NO ONE can stand you!...

scabby porno elf: *poof*...GONE!!!!!!!!!!!!...

Hostility: Good riddance...ya little maggot...

Queen Satania: It is because there are males like scabby that make me grateful to be lesbian...*grin*...

Panthera: Gosh Hostile...you were a little rough on the cretin...don't ya think?...

Hostility: Shuddup pussy...you're one to be talking...you treat him as bad as I do...if not worse...

Calvin bristled at Hostility's hostility.

Timetravellar: Watch your tongue with the lady asshole!...

Hostility: Oh...like I'm gonna take orders from you...time dick...you move in on every female in Gothica...and expect everyone else to bow before you like you were Stag or something...Panthera's a slut...everybody knows that...every vamp in Gothica has had a cyber-piece of her...if you think you're defending her honor...she HAS none...so PISS OFF!...Besides, word has it that you're the one that ran Vampyra off..."love em' and leave em' Timey"...that's what everyone calls you now...Vampyra was a goddess to us all...but now she's gone...and everyone knows that it has something to do with YOU!...

Calvin's blood boiled, as he read the impudent words. Anger and guilt swirled within him like two streams uniting in confluence. Hostility had attacked

Panthera and his instinct was to rise up and defend her. Still, the accusations held some truth. He did not know that others in Gothica were talking about him. The cyber-romancer thought that this whole role-playing behavior bore no rules to speak of, and that his relationship with Vampyra was private. Now, he was being told that his real world lover, Panthera was everybody's baby and that he, apparently, was a villain of the dark realm.

Calvin glanced at a photograph that lay on the computer table. It was the one Aaron had given him, the one showing the faint image of his Scottish alter being. Now his heart weighed heavy. Remorse grew in him like a climbing vine that would eventually surround and squeeze his heart. Timetravellar had been selflessly stalwart, if not heroic. Hostility's venom-filled words stung, but there was also an element of wisdom in them.

Calvin pushed aside the pangs of Timetravellar's fading existence and prepared to fire back at Hostility.

Stag: Hostility!...You have been warned time and again about your threats and your nastiness toward other Gothicans...While I would agree that scabby is a nuisance, he is still one of us...and while I have no great love for the Timetravellar, he has broken none of Gothica's laws, as have you...Vampyra's heart DOES break...and Timetravellar DOES share responsibility in her grief...but there is far more than you or anyone else knows about Vampyra's disappearance...she has been ill...and I have been with her...whether or not she shall return to Gothica remains to be seen...I myself...since caring for her...have taken a sabbatical from Gothica to compose myself and my feelings...It has been two weeks since I left the dark one...and five weeks since I have been here to my palace...But to return and find you...Hostility...attacking my subjects again...as I have warned you not to...infuriates me...

Hostility,...YOU ARE FOREVER BANISHED FROM THE HALLS OF GOTHICA!...LEAVE NOW OR BEAR MY WRATH!...

Hostility: But my lord Stag...I did not know you were here...I have not seen you in so long...I thought you had left forever...please forgive my behavior...I do not wish to be excommunicated...

Stag: GO I SAID...AND GO I MEAN...BE GONE!!!!!!...

Hostility's name disappeared from those listed as present in the room. A barrage of greetings followed from all Gothicans at Stag's return. No one had noticed that he had entered the room, just as no one was aware that he monitored the conversation.

Timetravellar: That's tellin' him Stag...*broad smile*...

Stag: *glares at Timetravellar*...Do not attempt to align yourself with me Travellar...I am not your friend and I did not just then come to your aid...I enforced the laws of Gothica, as I am so sworn...I have recently spent weeks with the queen of this realm, nursing her in her pain...but above the physical calamity that she suffered, the greatest agony that she bore...was inflicted by you...

I would give her everything...my all,...my eternity ...simply to be at her side...yet it is you that she yearns for...your black heart that she desires above all else in this world...I was the one who transcribed her words, as she spoke to you that day long gone by...but I too saw the words that you spoke to her...some sweet... some disrespectful...You...I believe, toy with her...play with her heart...If you ever hurt her again, as you have...I will hunt you down and kill you...You are no friend of mine...nor are you friend of any Gothican worth his salt...

For, anyone who smites the queen of Gothica...must be considered vermin...and must be shunned by the faithful here...

All ye of Gothica...while he shall not be banned...as he has broken no law...I do command that all faithful Gothicans shun the vagrant Timetravellar...until such time as I reverse this command...

quadrophobia: *shun*...

Queen Satania: *shun*...

Lustybustybitch: *shun*...

Vampire Lestat01: *shun*...

Stinky: *shun*...

Blakkvelvett: Oooh...I'm sorry sweetie...but I must do what the Prince says...*kiss...pout*...............*shun*...

Gargoyle: *shun*...

Punishment Park: *shun*...

the Sorcerer: The time draws nigh great knight...reach deep inside and find within yourself, who you truly are...Atrocities of the past are left to you to right...Do not forsake thy father's, father's, father's, father's, father...

Calvin glared at the Sorcerer's message and shook his head.

"You'd think there'd be some kind of psychological test required to get in here," he thought.

Panthera: Well...I guess this is where I make my break with all you bloodsuckers...I'd rather spend five minutes between the sheets with Timetravellar, in cyberville or the real world, than spend ten thousand lonely virtual nights with you freaks...*she thumbs her nose at the crowd*... this shun's for you...............*shun*...

Timetravellar: Wait a minute people...uh...Stag...you don't understand...there are sort of two of us that use this name...the name of Timetravellar...it's hard to explain...but I'm not the bad guy you're making me out to be...I mean I know I haven't exactly been warm to Vampy...but I'm not the Timetravellar that she wants...it's the other entity...the one that emerges at the oddest of times...I've sort of played the field...at least until recently...Panthera's my main squeeze now...but you gotta believe me...

Yeah...I'm the one that acts like an asshole to her...but I'm NOT the one that melts her heart...I'm NOT the one whose existence fades into nothingness because she doesn't write...I could care less...Does any of this make sense to you?...

Stag: *shun*...

Timetravellar: Well...I don't know what to say to all of you except...KISS MY ASS!...

Panthera: Come on sweet meat...let's blow this freak show...I'll set up a private room and we can get each other lathered up...

Calvin stared incredulously at his monitor. A sense of emptiness invaded, as he tried to cope with the fact that he was an outcast. How could this have happened? Timetravellar had been a respected and desired member of Gothica at one time, but now he was an exile? Perhaps he had not been ousted the way that Hostility had, but he was a blight upon the inhabitants of the Dark Room, just the same.

Finally, the truth struck him sharply. All of those things had been true. *Timetravellar* had indeed been held in the highest esteem. It was *Calvin* that marred the character. It was *Calvin* that had shown disdain for Vampyra, and it was *Calvin* that had come to be known as a cad, a womanizer.

Panthera coaxed and tugged at her lover to come to the privacy of a secret chamber. She sensed that he was hurt and betrayed. Had he gone with her, perhaps she could have taken his mind off the punishment just handed him. He did not go, though. Devastation from the shunning and the realization that he was no longer welcome in Gothica left him numb.

Timetravellar whispers to Panthera: Thanks sweetie...I guess I'm not much in the mood...Damn if that wasn't a kick in the pants...even Blakkvelvett shunned me...I thought she was completely engrossed in the Timetravellar...

Panthera whispers to Timetravellar: *giggle*...You mean *turned on* by the Timetravellar don't you?...You do know that Blakk is well...a guy don't you?...I mean... Vampyra may be "the Queen," but he is "A Queen."...

No sooner than she sent the whisper, she regretted it. The amusement over Blakkvelvett's homosexuality was intended as a diversion, a lighthearted counter to what had just happened. Calvin did not, however, find any amusement in it. He had cybersexed with Blakk countless times late at night when no one else was about. His stomach pitched and rolled, as he recounted the embarrassing things he had said to the cyber drag queen. His whole existence, it seemed, was coming apart. Panthera was his only bastion of comfort left, but he knew that even she would not be enough. For the first time, he truly understood the enormity of his compassionless disregard for the warrior. What had been an untarnished reputation, in the beginning, now drew loathsome disdain from Gothicans. Timetravellar didn't deserve this. His honor was as pure as any that had ever walked the halls of Fountain, yet he, Calvin McLeish, had ruined the reputation of his valiant alter ego.

Timetravellar whispers to Panthera: I guess not Cat...I'm not much in the mood...thanks anyway...I wish you were here...I feel sick to my stomach...

Panthera whispers to Timetravellar: Oh come on honeybun...this is just cyberspace...all that crap doesn't mean anything...besides...there are all kinds of other rooms...we'll go there...we'll make new friends...you'll see...

Timetravellar whispers to Panthera: New friends...sure...I don't even seem to know the value of the one true friend I ever had...I've let him fade away...evaporate into thin air...and never lifted a finger to save him.........Oh Cat...I'm a mess...
You've stood by me...made love to me...and been everything that I wanted from a woman in the real world...Next to Timetravellar...you ARE my best friend...*disbelieving smile*...Listen to me...my whole existence is here...and in my own mind...
I'm gonna go for now...I need some time to try and sort out what is happening inside of me...*kiss*...talk to you soon...

Chapter 25

Just as night vision was important to a wolf of the forest, so it was important to Vampyra. Adrenaline from the encounter with Isaac had worn off and she became sleepy, as she ventured deeper into the woodland.

She preferred her bed to the damp, cold cave, but a filled belly made her eyelids droop. She would retain her wolfen form and scamper up the rocks to the chasm that she had utilized so many times before. Steam trailed from her canine nostrils. She bounded past the trunks of two thick spruce trees guarding its entrance. There was a spot inside where dead, deciduous leaves had blown in and accumulated.

"A fitting bed for any animal," she thought, as she curled up on the soft pile.

Had Monique been in human form, she might have actually frozen solid from the cold. A thick winter coat, however, repelled the elements, and she floated in the pleasantness of near sleep. Just before entering the final abyss of nocturnum's trance, a face lurched at her through the darkness. Springing to her feet, she recoiled baring her teeth.

No one was there. It was a dream. The face of her hated master haunted her even there, while she existed as wolf. Emilien spoiled everything. He always had. Even the pleasant warmth she extracted from her victim now escaped her, as the chilling image of Lazare persecuted her troubled mind.

Monique awoke after restless slumber, two hours before dawn. The thrill of the hunt was a memory, as was the encounter with Isaac. The wolf that she was still, leapt from the mouth of the cave to the forest floor a few feet below. She had to hurry. Daylight approached and she was still eight miles from home. If the sun caught her near her home, it would not be so bad. Daylight was offensive, but not the end-all of her kind that legend foretells. Sunlight upon vampire flesh felt like a severe case of sunburn, at first contact. Hours of prolonged exposure, though, would lead to sickness, especially if the vamp was not healthy. Recovery from a small exposure was instantaneous, once the creature had returned to darkness. Thus, it was the unpleasantness of coming dawn from which she ran, and the security of her stone fortress to which she ran.

No matter where she went, Lazare's image loomed just over her shoulder. Existence, life if you will, held no purpose for her anymore. Love escaped her at every turn; it had for centuries. Long had it been since she had allowed her dark heart to be stirred. Forever had it been since she felt the warmth of a man. Yearning for love and lusting for blood in a world of mortals seemed the ultimate contradiction—the final damnation. Perhaps she would give herself up to a hunter of the undead. It would end her agony. Part of her was a survivor, while the other part of her was willing to surrender to the infinity of death.

There were vampires relatively happy with their existence. Those of the more carnal nature worried little about feeding on someone else's blood, yet vampirism was a fate Monique had come to against her will. Perchance, that was the difference. Those who had willingly chosen the way of the vamp were secure in its abominations. Those forced into it loathed its destiny.

Then, there was the accursed Timetravellar, the one that plagued her mind and soul, both day and night, the enigma that had, thus far, kept her from dementia. Dubois surmised that it might be a love-hate relationship. She loved the imagined character that he could have been, but hated his flaws, his imperfection, the crudeness of his human side. The Princess of Darkness would soon discover that the humanity she found so repelling was simply that of Calvin McLeish, the mortal. The essence of the one called Timetravellar, truly embodied all she fantasized.

    A glint of blinding light scorched the horizon, as she trotted over the cold, brown moss of the forest surrounding the miniature castle. Curling her wolfen lip, she scoffed at her enemy, the dreaded sun. She had again foiled its attack. Her den was but a few steps away now, and she knew she had succeeded. She had survived another rising day.

    Nosing the wooden door open, she looked back at the rising brilliant orb. Perhaps she had not won at all. Surviving the onslaught of dawn only meant preserving herself for Lazare to, again, debase her. A hopeless romantic, she closed her eyes and dreamed of a rescuer, one that would vanquish the evil one. As always, in her mind's eye, desperation drove her back into the arms of the time wanderer. Why was she so taken with him? What was it about him that so reminded her of that Scottish nobleman that she had loved so long ago? Glynn MacTavish had disappeared from her life soon after they met. He was strong, tender, and courageous. Lo, those many centuries she dreamed of him, and lo those many centuries she grieved over her loss.

    Guilt gnawed at her, as she thought back on the night when he came to her window. Bittersweet, resplendent memories filled her mind, in the same way that a beautiful woman's perfume fills a room. He had mixed their blood together, into an incision on his forefinger. That, in and of itself, was the single most noble, romantic thing that she had ever seen. It was the second most endearing thing that he had done for her. She thought back on that night, and remembered all of it, his words, his touch...and his sacrifice.

"And at least within me, your blood along with mine, shall nourish my heart, and I shall never abandon thee," he said. Rising and looking into the placidness of her eyes, he had taken the brush from her hand.

Her sweet, supple breasts burst from the cups of her bustier. Eyes, as infinite as the sky, held him spellbound for a moment, and without forethought, he found himself lowering his lips to hers. The small, delicate hollow at the base of her throat pulsated, revealing the savage, rhythmic, surges of her heart.

Lips fusing in human passion, each lover's blood blazed with desire for the other. Power above all powers, they were driven to unite, to become one.

As he pulled her to him, she became immersed with immeasurable desire. Before MacTavish, she believed that she could never want a man in such a way. Repeated molestation had tainted her imagery of men, and a despondent heart had surrendered to never knowing love. Yet, from somewhere in the vastness of the universe, perhaps the only man that could have made her barren heart blossom came to her there, in her very prison.

Gently lifting her into his arms, he strode to the modest bed that lay in a corner of the tiny, unadorned, stone room. She felt as though she had been laid in a field of flowers, and as though a symphony played for just the two of them. Travellar stood and extinguished all but one candle. Darkness was blissful, but he was so desirous of her, and so anxious to see her exquisite form. Monique sighed, as the beautiful sculpture lowered toward her. In his eyes were safety, passion—adoration. Quickly, their garments slid from their bodies, falling limply to the bedside floor. Indescribable beauty was theirs for a moment. Longing flesh touched longing flesh and passion effused from her to him, and back again. The heat of their bodies uniting, and the rhapsody of two becoming one, played out the inexplicable magic of...love.

Monique floated in another plane, as he moved deliciously in and then out. Her sweet elixir too, intoxicated him and their cries rang from the chamber. That part of Monique's mind, where a small remaining portion of logic and sense still existed, beckoned her to silence her mouth and his, as they danced. Eagerness and desire became their drug though, and fear of being heard faded from their minds. As the two impassioned lovers shouted out their eternal promise, each to the other, multiple footfalls stampeded the hallway.

A legion of Lazare's men stormed the bedchamber, torches in hand. Glynn MacTavish leapt from his lover, and grasped the hilt of his broadsword. Sparks burst from his blade and that of his first opponent. The initial clash was brief. A bone-chilling "thwump" echoed through the room, and the first Lazare henchman was liberated from his head.

Two more took his place and the horrible clanking of metal on metal again resounded. To the left, a sentinel's eyes bulged, as he gurgled and spewed from the four-inch wide blade thrust through his throat. The guard to the right quickly pressed to take advantage of MacTavish's vulnerability; the underdog's sword still hung in the neck of the second soldier. Savagely swinging his sword overhead, the third attacker brought his blade down with vengeance. The blow would have chopped the Scot in half like a piece of cordwood, had the defender not wheeled. Spinning from left to right, Glynn MacTavish's mighty weapon found its mark halfway through the ribcage of his third victim. The sword sucked the flesh and grated the bone of the defeated one, as Monique's lover prepared for another assailant. But, there would be no more attackers. The knight would be frozen, paralyzed at what he beheld.

Dark-haired and ominous, another conscript knelt on the bed, the point of his blade under Monique's chin.

"Wield thy blade once more Scot, and it will be your slut that is separated from her head."

His arms dropped limply to his sides, and the ornate, blood covered sword that had just slain three rang out its abrasive surrender, as it fell on the cold stone floor. "Dark and ominous" motioned to yet another of Lazare's disciples, who seized Glynn MacTavish and bound his hands in front of him.

"No, I beg you!" Monique pleaded. "Take me. 'Twas I that lured him, hither. 'Twas I that betrayed my master. He is innocent. Punish me."

"You shall indeed be punished," the Dark guard smirked. "Were it I that was to be punished, I would choose your lover's fate. His shall be quick compared to yours. The executioner's axe will drop, and then darkness, nothingness. You on the other hand, will never adequately pay for your indiscretion, and the master shall take his measure against you, forever."

The noble Scot looked mournfully over his shoulder at his sweet Monique, as the guards brutally forced him through the arched threshold of the room.

The chambermaid, once a peasant girl, shrieked out her anguish. "No!" Sadly, the only man she had ever loved was ripped from her. She begged pitifully, as they poured from her room. Grasping the cape of a sentinel, she doubled over when his boot fiercely buried into her stomach. In all of her grief and in all of her defilement, she had never known such despair.

The naked nobleman was pushed and prodded down the corridor of the upper floor. At the foot of the stairs, a livid Edouard Emilien Lazare stood in wait. The captive descended the terraced path until he reached the bottom. There at ground level, Lazare approached the proud, unashamed knight.

"Yes, she is quite good, is she not?" he taunted. "Whereas you have had your last taste of her, I shall enjoy her moist prize...endlessly."

MacTavish's expression did not alter. Then, like a bull bursting from its corral, the warrior lunged forth grasping the vampire by the neck. Turning him as one would turn a lamb, he smashed Lazare's head into the cold granite wall of the antechamber. Just above Emilien's left eyebrow, blood flowed from a spider shaped split in his flesh. A palace guard smashed the hilt of his sword into the base of the nobleman's head. MacTavish slumped, unconscious, to the floor.

Monique Dubois would never again be able to speak to her paramour, and she always wondered if he knew how much she loved him. For years, Lazare wickedly described MacTavish's end, while he raped her. Physical humiliation it seemed was not enough for him, and he wallowed in her grief and in her sense of loss.

* * * * *

The gothic woman, still a wolf, stood in the foyer of her house. Throwing her head back, she elongated and was again of human form. A tiny smile occupied her face, as she remembered. He had said that he would never abandon her. Ah, it would have been so sweet had he not. He had yielded to Lazare's men to save her, but all the same, he was gone. Would that she could, she would go back in time, back to that night in the small bed. And before they took him, she would tell him of her love for him.

Thinking about Glynn's death, troubled her. She gracefully floated down the corridor to her bedchamber. There, perhaps, she could distract herself from the past and from the present. Sitting down at the Pentium, she powered it up and logged into Fountain.

At first, she did not notice the curtains billow, there in her sealed tomb. A breeze stirred from within the enclosed sarcophagus, and then she knew. It was him, again—Lazare. A moth fluttered to the center of the room and then exploded into human form. Indeed, the vile predator of her centuries, Emilien Lazare had returned. He paced the floor of her room, his face wracked with anguish. Fingertips placed on his forehead above his left eyebrow, he massaged, as if nursing a terrible headache.

Vampyra glared in hatred and in fear. Had he come to fulfill his promise? Panic gripped her soul, but she would not let him see. Something was wrong with him. How peculiar. Never had she seen anything but arrogance, hatred, and contempt in his eyes. She perked at his show of weakness.

"What is it? What *has* this demon frightened?" she wondered.

"Who is the one you spoke of?" Emilien asked quietly.

"I do not understand," she replied.

"Oh, I am certain that you do. Do not play games with me. You are in grievous peril, as it stands, now." Lazare endeavored to maintain his advantage over her, his persecuting dominance.

She looked into his eyes and saw something that she had not seen in all of the five centuries that he had bullied her—terror.

"Who is this BASTARD that you threaten me with?" he bellowed.

"He is a great knight, a valiant Scot of great strength. He comes for me, I think, although he is not here yet, and he will come for you, Emilien."

"Then it is true. I have felt it. When I was here with you last, I felt it. When I become still, in the darkness, though I do not sleep, I dream."

"And what is it that you dream of, you evil lech."

Lazare's head snapped sharply so that he faced her.

"You know full well what it is that comes to me in wakening dreams. Do not play me for a fool, Monique."

She had no clue of what he was talking about. It was evident, though, that he was convinced she knew.

"Then let me hear you say it. Let me hear the words that tell of your haunting," she probed.

"The kilted one, the one who courted me as an ally against the English, the one whose head I displayed on a spike in front of my palace, the one for whom you spread your legs."

"Why do you speak of Glynn MacTavish? How is it that he troubles you so, five hundred years after you murdered him?" she asked caustically.

"Bitch from hell! You know why I speak of him!" Lazare's eyes flooded with horror.

"He is here, in this time, and I know that he is the one with whom you threaten me!"

Vampyra laughed bitterly. "You truly are insane, Son of Satan. You fear a dead man from the past? Why he would have to rise from the dead and travel through ti..."

She stopped before completing the word *time* and then whispered in her own mind, "Timetravellar!"

Lazare's face seemed almost paralyzed with pain, as he continued rubbing his brow. Never before had Monique Dubois sensed any sort of dominance over the wicked one, but no—something had change—something was different. The all-powerful ruler of those who roam the night was crippled, somehow. Vampyra saw a chink in his armor. The question was only how to drive a weapon into it, and bring him finally to his knees.

"Each day it burns more than the previous day," Lazare complained.

"What burns, Demon?" she asked coldly.

"This," he replied pointing to an asterisk shaped scar above his eyebrow.

Chapter 26

1508 A.D., Strasbourg, France.

The temperature loomed just above freezing, and a dense fog clung to the Lazare palace. Dusk came early that day hurried by gray, overcast skies and the evil mist that blanketed the countryside. The cloud that hung just above the ground was dismal, foreboding. It was the chariot of the grim reaper. Death's messenger had come for his prize, and would not wait long before he took his charge across the River Styx.

Two hooded figures emerged from the misty darkness and walked hastily in the shadow cast by the great palace wall. Approaching a barred portal just above the ground, Quenton MacTavish and the trusted sorcerer knelt.

In a loud whisper, Quenton beckoned, "Glynn-boy!"
No response.
"Glynn, it's Quen and Ian!"
Finally, a wretched figure came to the iron bars. Quenton opened his mouth to ask the prisoner where Glynn MacTavish was, but then realized to his great sadness that the prisoner *was* his younger brother. Eyes filled with tears of compassion, the elder MacTavish looked upon the stringy hair and scarred face of his younger sibling.

"Glynn-boy, I told you about them damsels," he said mustering a smile. "They'll bring you nothing, but trouble." Quenton sniffed, trying to maintain an optimistic air for his brother's sake. Glynn's face was covered with three months growth of hair and an eternity of pain. Floggings, the rack, and mutilation had brought the young nobleman to agedness in but ninety days. The inextinguishable glint in his eye was gone, and his gaze was that of a ghost.

"We've been banned from this place, brother," Quenton continued. "But not to worry, we'll get you out of here. We made a big mistake aligning ourselves with the likes of this French madman. Ian and I have camped in the woods since they put you in here. We've tried negotiating with this bastard, but we've had no success. Truth is, Lazare has ordered his guards to kill us if we showed ourselves. That's why you haven't heard from us.

Actually, that's why we've come here tonight. On the morrow, we return to Scotland. We'll gather some of our boys, the Colquhouns, the McEwens, and the Lairsey's. We'll return in a month and turn this place into a heap of rubble, little brother," he said confidently.

"No, you won't," Glynn replied.

He reached his pitiful hand through the bars. The first joint was missing from his fore and middle fingers. His little finger was completely gone.

"Please, hold my hand," he implored. His eyes fell on his older brother, as a sorrowful rain.

"On the morrow..." He stopped. "On the morrow...I will be executed."

"No!" Quenton cried out.

Ian scanned the corners of the palace to see if anyone was alerted to their presence. No one came.

"Glynn, I'll not allow it! I'll kill Lazare, myself!"

In the softest of voices, Glynn comforted his older brother. "No, my brother. I am ready. There is much

they have done to me. I am...less than a man now."
A single tear filled his eye and spilled onto his cheek, as he hinted of his emasculation.

"Fucking bastards!" Quenton raged.

Then, against all predictability, Glynn's face illuminated.

"Brother, you can do nothing for me, but there is some good that comes of all this misery." His chest swelled. "My sweet Monique, the chambermaid you warned me about, is with child...my child. If you return with our brethren, return for my son. Take him and my precious Monique back to Scotland, where they belong."

Quenton was an emotional man and bore great love for his brother. Smashing his hand into the rock of the palace wall, he drew back a bloody fist.

"I'll not surrender you to this evil son-of-a-bitch," Quenton promised.

"Shh," Glynn consoled. "My child, and the love of my heart. They are the ones that matter now. They are the ones who need you now."

Crouched there in the shadows, Ian, the sorcerer brought a finger to his lips. A sentinel walked past the corner of the palace wall and peered suspiciously into the darkness. Finally, after studying the shadows, he turned and walked back in the direction whence he came.

"Come now Quenton, we must leave," the sorcerer instructed.

"I will not forsake thee, my brother," Quenton whispered, as he and the magician retreated into the concealment of fog and shadow.

Glynn MacTavish shook his head imploring the elder brother to release him to death, but Quenton and Ian were gone.

Sunrise compromised the thick fog and was, therefore, late in its arrival. A platform had been erected in the courtyard. Upon it stood a cross section of a magnificent oak, taken from the nearby forest. It was to be the chopping block on which Glynn MacTavish would lay his head.

Peasants began to arrive at the palace, as ordered. Lazare's executions required attendance from his subjects and were a reminder of the consequence for disobedience. An hour after sunrise, the courtyard was filled with people from the French countryside along with those enlisted in Lazare's service.

Monique stood against the wall of the castle alcove, her face filled with anguish. She desperately needed to see him, but not this way. Misery gripped her, as Glynn MacTavish was marched out of a tunnel that led from the dungeon.

Penetrating cold found nearly every peasant in a hooded cloak, and from a distance, they appeared as monks attending an outdoor mass. Two of Emilien's elite escorted the longhaired Scot to the platform. Immediately behind him marched a hooded gargantuan carrying a semi-circular axe, its blade as wide as a wine barrel. MacTavish scanned the endless crowd, and somehow, found the face of his love. The murmuring of the throng, and the distance between them silenced his words, but she could read his lips. His message was simple.

"I love you," he mimed.

Monique patted her swollen belly.

"Your child," she returned managing a grieved smile.

Lazare ascended the platform and held his hand to the sky. The drone of the crowd silenced and he began to speak. "Those who are not with me are against me. Those who seek to take what is mine shall find themselves here on the block, as does this arrogant Scot. He chose to pluck the fruit of my orchard, and now he shall compensate me for his crime."

A single, hooded, obscure figure moved erratically through the throng, approaching the platform. Monique's eyes cast to the ground, as the executioner's assistant forced MacTavish's head to the block, his hands bound behind him. Glynn MacTavish's face remained stark, and he awaited the blow. Yet, before the beastly assassin could raise his blade, another mountain of a man leapt to the scaffold.

Peeling off his cloak and drawing his long sword in a single motion, Quenton MacTavish pirouetted with the ballet-like grace. Singing as it sliced the air, the melody of his blade ended abruptly, as it sunk into the jaw of the muscle-bound executioner. The disciple of death crumpled to the wooden stage, as a sack of flour. Quenton spun and was facing Monique when the archer's arrow found its mark. The elder MacTavish grasped the short remainder of arrow that protruded from his chest, then he too fell.

Ian, the mage, watched without outward emotion, as the foray ended.

Lazare stepped up to the still kneeling Glynn MacTavish. "I shall do this myself," he decreed. Struggling to lift the cumbrous axe above his head, he paused with the blade directly above him. Quickly it fell, ending the life of Calvin Glynn MacTavish.

Monique wept, as she listened to the sigh of the crowd, signifying her lover's end. Grief-stricken she ran from the courtyard, back to the isolation and sanction of her chamber.

A nondescript figure made his way up the platform. He was unnoticed by Lazare, as the dark overlord held high the head of MacTavish and screamed out his revenge. The cloaked visitor stepped quietly to the Marquis' side and whispered in his ear. Horror and ire filled the wicked one's face. He turned left and then right. Grasping a palace guard by the arm, he ordered him to arrest the dark robed intruder. Yet, when he turned around to show the guard whom to apprehend, the mage was gone.

The tenacious fog had lifted the next morning, as Monique rose from her modest bed. A stitch in her back caused her to twinge, when she stepped onto the burlap rug on the floor at her bedside. Brilliant light shone through the window, and she made her way to a porcelain bowl of water on a stone pedestal. She had not slept. Images of the crowd, and their damning sigh replayed in her mind. Emptiness filled her, and even the joy of a coming child was ineffectual in raising her spirits.

Lazare left her alone since she had begun to show. A woman with a belly disgusted him and he fed upon the others of his flock. There was some solace in that. Emilien thought the child to be his, but Monique knew differently. She knew it the instant that Glynn had come, and was at least encouraged to be carrying the offspring of her lover, and not that of the baneful one. A month earlier, she told her wonderful secret to Lucienne Treaudeaux, another of the vampire's fold.

Signs of pregnancy had not yet presented themselves, and Lazare was ignorant to that which grew within her. Monique had been ordered to the kitchen to help Lucienne with preparations for dinner guests. Normally, Lucienne's partner was Alicia Pontiff, but Alicia had fallen ill from blood loss. As they toiled in the kitchen, the chambermaid radiated joy, nearly bursting to tell someone. Lucienne and she had become friends over the months and years.

"What joy is it that you keep to yourself?" Lucienne asked.

Erupting in a gleeful whisper, Monique replied, "I carry my lover's child."

Her face then dropped, as she considered Glynn's imprisonment. Vile as Lazare was, she still hoped for MacTavish's release. That was before his execution had been announced. Even in the cruelty of life, she had found joy, and yet somehow, the *beast* had found a way to take it from her.

Splashing cold water in her face, she met the day with melancholy. Monique reached for a towel and noticed a chipping sparrow on the ledge outside her window. It paced hither and to, never taking its eyes from her. It were as though it would speak to her if it could.

"Poor thing, I think you are hungry, oui?"

Dubois scanned the room and then spied a small dish with crumbs from last night's meal, a half loaf of hard bread. She pulled a stool to the window, climbed upon it and gently eased the window open. Carefully, slowly, Monique slid the plate onto the ledge. The sparrow hopped but once, undeterred by her presence. Reaching for the window hasp, she prepared to pull the glass back into its place. The drab little bird flitted inside before she could again seal her tomb. It lit on the washstand.

"Precious…you are cold too, oui?" she asked, as if expecting a reply.

Then, from the time it took her eyelids to drop and rise again, the sparrow had miraculously transformed. Before her was an aged gentleman, well creased of face. He wore a seamless black robe, its hem trimmed with a gold band. On his head was a simple cloth skullcap, also black.

A rare smile grew on the ancient face, and Monique stood speechless.

"My name is Ian," he began. "I am…was…the consort of the MacTavish clan. Glynn was the last of the family lineage. 'Twas up to Quenton and him to bring offspring that would further the family name, but sadly that will not be. But you my child, do carry the MacTavish blood within you, so truly the clan still lives."

"You are a sorcerer?" she finally asked.

"Indeed."

"Sorcerer…," she began.

"Ian," he corrected.

"Sir Ian, the child of my lover is in grave danger. The one who imprisons me is a wicked servant of darkness. He is most vile, most despicable, and most dreaded of all creatures in France—nay of the entire earth. He thinks the child to be his, but it matters not whom he believes the father to be. The child will be damned if taken into his care. Will you help me?"

The bow-backed magician smiled warmly. "My dear child, that is precisely why I am here. I have a power." He paused. "Not understood by mortal men. I advised the boys, Quenton and Glynn of mixing with the likes of Lazare. I know of him through the channels of magic and mysticism, but the young MacTavishes were desperate for alliance against invasion. Against my urging, they came here, and so came to their end. But, perhaps it had to happen. Perhaps this is providence, and perhaps this is the only way that your child, the future of Scotland could come to be.

"To answer your question, yes I will help you. I am honor-bound to do so. When the child is born in late autumn, I shall return. I shall take him to safety, and you shall fear not for his well being. It is foretold that a child who is born of Scotland and of darkness shall lead our country against its enemies through this century. The good of his mother, in consonance with her dark powers and the strength of his father shall make him a warrior of which legends speak. And in seven years times seventy, a descendant of this child shall avenge his ancestral father's death. This child shall forevermore end the evil reign of Emilien the Wicked. So it shall be."

"And kind mage, might I ask your surname?" she inquired.

"Of course my dear, it is MacLeish. My proper name is Ian MacLeish."

Chapter 27

The ancient vampire continued pampering his scar of centuries passed. It burned him, haunted him, and reminded him of words whispered in his ear by a stranger on an executioner's platform, in the year 1508 A.D.

"What is this that 'Emilien the Terrible' displays?" Monique taunted. "What is it that I see? Ah, yes. Now it becomes clear. I not only see it, but yes, I smell it too. It is fear! After five centuries of your wicked intimidation, it is you who is hunted, you whose bladder releases from the dread of one who will harm you. Please do tell Emilien. How does it feel?"

"Silence, bitch! You go too far! Think on this ... vessel of my semen. What if you are wrong? What if the one you think that comes to save you, forsakes you? How will you beg, when I return night after night to drive my spike into you, and suck you until you are dry? Trust in this and nothing else. If he is not mightier than any of the warriors that I have faced in six hundred years, then your agony will grow tenfold. That, which I have subjected you to, will seem as a tea in the courtyard of my palace. Boast as you will, but I think this a rouse, a clever deception to lure me from you. If your trickery, your threats are empty, pray for death. Death would be a pleasant option, given what you will face."

"Hah," she scoffed. "It is not deception. The great one that traverses time will strangle you with his mighty hand. Be gone!"

As a thousand times before, he that commanded the undead snapped his garment and was gone. Her eyebrows hung, as she peered from under them. Then a sly grin emerged. It could be that she would pay dearly for her scorn, but this delight was worth the risk. Somehow, someway, he knew of Timetravellar and his fear was genuine. She hoped that her knight would contact her soon. Saving face was important, but if he did not come of his own accord, she would have no choice but to ask his help. Thunder rolled in the distance, and feeble lightning flickered intermittently. She closed her eyes and imagined that the thunder was the pounding hooves of his steed and that the lightning was the clash of his sword.

"Goodnight, Mon Couer, wherever it is that you lay your head."

A week and a half passed and still no word from Travellar. Monique became restless, uneasy, as anxiety over cyber-silence and hunger pangs grew into one twisted mass of frustration. That night, she would message him. She would beg for his intervention and hope above all hope that there was substance in his words. The time for romantic banter was gone. She needed him sorely. Her savage tormentor of the night had not returned since she insulted him, but pride would bring him back soon.

Hunger took precedence for the moment, however, and she prepared for the hunt. Intuition spoke, warning her to remain cautious of the constable that stalked her. She had frightened him well, but she knew that he would remain tenacious. His kind always was. She would change her habit to throw him from her trail, but deep down she knew what his pursuit meant. It meant that for the twelve hundredth time, she must move. The little stone house in the forest was perhaps her favorite residence of all her years. Still, once the vampire hunters began, she would be forced to a new place. They were ruthless in their pursuit, and she would be driven to a home where vamps had not been, at least in many years.

That particular night, she began her hunt shortly after dark on the outskirts of the downtown area, rather than in the center of town. Hollander would be following a cold trail near the clubs at "half-past-as-cold-as-a-witch's-titty." She hugged the walls of the buildings lining the street and felt awkward in that new part of the city. Over time, she had become familiar with the nightclub area and the moving patterns of her quarry.

Automobiles whizzed past creating frigid gusts that blew under her Gothic attire. The occasional pedestrian that passed would gawk. Even in the faint light of the poorer area, passersby could see the paleness of her complexion. She hated every step of her vigil. It marked the beginning of the end of her time in Ottawa.

A weathered two-story brick building lay before her and she spied a single lit office on the second floor. As an osprey might eye a fish from high above, she watched the illuminated window. A single figure moved about, and appeared to be alone. Monique ducked into the doorway and became part of the darkness under the stairwell, patiently waiting to feed. Unaccompanied, a lone figure moved down the dimly lit stairs. The thief of blood listened, as the footsteps approached. She prepared for the assault.

Nose raised into the air, she sniffed. "Sacré bleu! What is this? Do my senses decieve me? How can this be? Soft curls on the back of her neck bristled, as she sniffed again. It was the unmistakable scent of the pursuing constable. Biting her lip, she nearly swore aloud. Anger raged within her. Hollander had been warned. However he had managed to find her was of no consequence. The dark huntress did not wish to kill him, but he had not taken heed.

With the speed and agility that a mongoose strikes a cobra, Vampyra pounced upon her unsuspecting victim. Glossy nailed fingers, like a steel trap, clutched the throat of a petite woman. Predator and prey beheld each other in complete astonishment. Vampyra gaped at whom she beheld, and her target blinked in shock from the unexpected attack. Sleek black fingernails dug into her prize's throat. Vampyra pulled the woman to her and sniffed. Puzzlement filled her face, as she tried to cipher the contradiction before her. Unmistakable was the scent of the one whom hunted her, yet this was no policeman. Very simply, she was a delicate, beautiful woman.

A smile as wide as the horizon appeared on Monique's lips. "You are his woman, oui?" she asked politely.

The African-Canadian female looked upon the vampiress's face in horrified disbelief. She did not, could not, answer. The enchantress moved her head forward only slightly, and then exposed a tongue that protruded seven inches beyond her lips. It flicked, sensing and tasting the mixture of fragrances in the air. There was perfume and there was fear, but there also was the unmistakable scent of Isaac Hollander, the vampire hunter.

"This is providence, I think." The Dark Princess laughed. Still clutching Michelle Hollander by the throat, she eased her grip and moved her lips to the cinnamon neck of her prey. Sliding her hands to the small of the fair Hollander's back, she pulled her close. To the brown woman's surprise, Vampyra gently moved forward and kissed her full red lips.

"Oh my!" Michelle sighed, opening her pale green eyes after the tender caress. "That was very nice, very pleasant, indeed!"

Monique smiled sweetly, brushing Michelle's shoulder length, honey-brown, hair to the side.

"Mostly, I never do this except out of hunger, or out of hate. But tonight, my bite is my gift to you," she said.

Vampy's lips instinctively curled, and her mouth opened exposing her elongate, ivory, fangs. Michelle's knees almost left her, as the punctures opened deeper and deeper into her satin flesh. Dubois' warm, moist lips sucking around the two wounds and the sensation of her tongue swirling and lapping the fountain of crimson, was strangely sexual—undeniably stimulating. The bite was protracted and lasted far longer than a feeding or attack strike. It was sensual and unique.

The dark Canadian stretched her neck farther to the side to allow the mistress of night every possible comfort, as she fed. Her breasts tensed and her nipples firmed. Chill bumps burst forth on every part of her smooth skin. Michelle sighed and shuddered simultaneously, as her courtesan pulled away from the erotic prick. Eyes that had been rolled upward, showing only their whites, now returned with elliptical pupils. Her chest heaved and she struggled for breath.

"Ma chéri," Michelle cooed. "That was beautiful! Would you like some more?"

Monique caressed her lover's wavy tresses.

"Mmmm...oui. Yes, more would be nice. More would fill me completely, but it would be more than your body could withstand. To continue would take your life."

"But, will you come to me again, or may I come to you? There is so much love that we could share, in the seclusion of a bedroom," Michelle pleaded.

"Perhaps oui, perhaps non, my sweet brown childe. What matter is that you take the new creature that you are home to your mate. Make love to him, drive him mad, and when he near his climax, plunge your new toys into his throat. Never have he felt such ecstasy, never will he look upon desire in the same way, and never will he hunt vamp like us again.

"For he and you will be vamp together, and you will roam the nights of eternity, arm in arm, in bliss. Such a union of the undead is rare, but it *can* be beautiful when there are two who share it. You shall feed upon him and he upon you. Undeath for many, is misérables, but for you and your valiant stalker, it will be wonderful." Monique became more serious, more adamant, as she began to lecture the novice vampire.

"Then there is the matter of your appreciation of the fair form, the femme. Centuries may pass before it come to you, and while you love for him will not die, a change may come over you. Some night when you go out to hunt, when your prey is in your hand and you are about to extinguish her, you will be taken by her beauty. You will look upon her, as I have looked upon you this night, and your breasts will peak. Gentle waves of desire will ripple in that part of you that is woman. You may take her to lie with you. Between satin sheets you will caress her and passionately clench her throat.

"An ethereal sense will intoxicate you, as her lustful, hot, scarlet flow down your insatiable throat. When you pull back from her and look into her eyes, they will be the eyes of vamp. Her desire for you will never leave her, just as your desire for me will never leave you. A bite of passion will burn that searing desire into her heart and soul, forever. I only tell you this so that you will be prepared. When the vampire in you stirs the lust in another female, it is intense powerful and it is forever. So, choose carefully your female consort. Consider if she would be acceptable to your male mate. A time may come when the three of you, for a period, roam the nights together, and share a bed together.

"Be careful when you choose. If you use this power unwisely, there will be many femme that will clamor for your affection and those who may even choose to challenge your mate. Once in a great while, you will desire a soft curvaceous bed partner, but consider all things when you choose, and do not choose too often."

"Oui, my queen," Michelle replied.

A gentle kiss of her siress's lips, a snapping salute of her arms upward, and she was airborne. The Ottawa detective's wife shape-shifted to vampire bat as would a veteran of the night. The gentle buffeting of her wings quickly silenced, and Vampyra watched her disappear into the dark sky.

"I think chéri, that you were born to be vamp." She smiled. "Sadly, I was not, and while this existence may be quite satisfying for you, it remains my personal hell."

Her belly was not full and she was not satisfied, but weariness and despondency subdued her. Trotting down the unlit section of sidewalk, she changed again from biped to quadruped, and proceeded back toward her quarters.

Another abbreviated night in the cave and a hurried trek home before daylight found her again entering the safety of stone walls. This time she was cautious, wary, and suspicious that Lazare might be there, but he was not. Her computer was on and tied to the line, but she was too tired to get involved. Almost certainly someone would detect her presence and want to talk Goth, or ask her advice on some mundane, mortal issue. The sparkle of cyber-fame was wearing off, and served as no more than a vehicle by which she communicated. The next day, after rest, she would travel the channel and find Travellar. If there was anything still in his heart, perhaps he would help her. He must.

Morning ended with the sun high above her secluded nest. Normally, she would take her rest until late in the afternoon and then rise for night's journey. Up until she awoke, bizarre hallucinations of the chestnut beauty she had just met and the loathsome tormentor of ancient France haunted her dream-state. Monique sat up quietly in her bed just after noon. Swollen eyes and a troubled face spoke of her restlessness. The time had come. No longer could she wait for salvation. Female pride must be set aside, and she must pursue with rigid tenacity, the Timetravellar.

Lazare's weakened and vulnerable state was a fleeting glimpse of hope; she knew that. He was too shrewd, too cunning, and too ruthless to long be held at bay. The previous night's interlude with Michelle was something for which she had yearned. Tenderness and desire were emotions she desperately needed to share. In all her time in this world, those rare moments of gentle affection had been infrequent. When she did indulge herself in them, it was always with a woman. Hatred of her continuous molestation, that contemptible violence she equated with males, had kept her heart from warming to another man. Thus, when her heart became so torn and empty from the barrenness of being alone, she would turn to the prettier of the sexes.

Then, there was her undying devotion to the memory of one she barely came to know, Glynn MacTavish. Even before he had romantically taken her in the mystical forest that surrounded the palace, her heart had bonded with his. The night he defended her against the abusive guard was the moment he entered her heart. She could still see the majesty in his eyes, though she could not remember his face. Five hundred years had a way of erasing the memory of images, but they had done little to extinguish the fire of her heart.

Perhaps the time had come, though, to put the things of days gone by behind her. She had been faithful to the immensity of what he represented, but eternity was forever and somehow, she must find a way to move forward. Once in a lifetime such a great love may come. Sometimes, it never does. By clinging so tightly to her remembrance of MacTavish and to her hatred of Lazare, she may have let another, just as worthy, slip from her grasp.

Normally, Monique did not consume wine until sunset, but her awareness grew raw from lack of sleep. Removing a bottle of ninety-year-old burgundy from the concealed pit in the wall, she fumbled through a drawer looking for a corkscrew. Finally she located one of many scattered about the house and pulled the stopper from its womb. A quickly drunk glass calmed her, and she poured another. Resting her bottom on the computer chair, she logged in and proceeded to her mailbox. This would be her one plea for help. If his heart were full and righteous, he would come to her aid. If not, begging would be of no consequence and Lazare would retaliate.

Monique Dubois decided, as she typed, that if her effort failed, she would fall back on her last resort. Emilien would never again touch her. She would make sure of that. If Timetravellar did not come, then she would present herself to the one who had extinguished Estefan, the one in Fountain known as "The Stalker." No more would she endure eternity in this manner. There would be peace, or there would be death, an end to suffering. For even in a state of undeath, contentment could be found. Michelle and Isaac Hollander were proof of that notion. Thus, if Monique, "Vampyra" Dubois, could not at least find that peace, then she would chose doom. In death there would be peace, and perhaps that way she could be with Glynn.

Vampyra: My dearest Travellar...hmmm...how do I begin?...there is so much I could tell you...but so little of it would make sense...

Sweet warrior...we are much alike you and I...very proud...very stubborn...but the time has come for me to humble myself to you...This game that we play...this prideful chess match between the two of us ends...What

I am about to tell you...it seem unbelievable, I think...but it's true...

Many year ago...almost five hundred...I live in a small town...Strasbourg...in eastern France...I was peasant girl...and taken into the service of an evil monarch...his name Edouard Emilien Lazare...how do I explain?...There is no way but to say it as it is...he is vampire...and so too...am I...he make me what I am...but he is cruel...horrible...He violate me throughout these ages...And now in twentieth century...I draw a line...and dare him to not cross over...The line I draw in the sand is the name of... *Timetravellar*... Somehow... someway...he think my lover from the past come back to hunt him down...Somehow...someway...he think that you and my sweet love of days passed...are one in the same...But please do understand this...my threats and the intimidation of a defender that come to my aid...will not keep him away forever...Soon he will regain his courage...and will come back to punish me...

I do know that what I tell you may sound beyond belief...but it is true...every word...I also know that almost all in the cyber are masqueraders...If you are too (which is my greatest fear)...then do not grieve...it is all right...but I hope above all hopes that somehow...you are that magical warrior that you pretend to be...
Only that brave gladiator might rescue me from the pain of the future...and if I must face that pain...then I think perhaps...death's sting is more desirable...For in death there is an end...in undeath...there is infinity... an infinity of torture...I can bear no longer...

If you are out there valiant one...if you have compassion...if you possess the power of your words...please... I beg you...save me...

Whether you come or no...I will always have great feelings for you...be well brave knight...*soft kiss on your cheek*...

Chapter 28

Divorce papers, that had lain on the coffee table for three weeks, stared at Calvin. A heap of unopened bills, too, constantly reminded him of the spiraling vortex of distress into which he had fallen. Being ostracized from Gothica had been like a sharp slap in the face. From time to time, he would think on his long lost alter ego and consider that he may well have been part of something special, something fantastic. His mind's creation, though, had been gone for weeks and it was he, Calvin, who had driven him away. Re-entering reality and taking responsibility for his laxness was more than he could endure sober.

Popping like green wood in a hot fire, the cubes of ice in his cocktail glass protested loudly, as the whiskey poured onto them. Self-pity and regret hung over him like an intense thundercloud. Maggie, it seemed, was right. He was irresponsible and destined to fail, no matter the endeavor. Even as a role-playing character, he had earned the disdain of others in virtual reality.

All of his savings were depleted, and his wife's lawyers were hounding him to either agree to her conditions for divorce, or contest them in court. Between addiction to the Internet and his most recent obsession, Cathryn "Panthera" Meeks, he had let his world crumble before his eyes. The electricity had been cut off twice in the last three months, but most recently, it was the gas. Credit cards, utilities, everything, had been sacrificed so that the little money he had left, kept him with food, drink, and Internet access.

A .380 caliber pistol lay next to him on the end table. He was despondent and suicide became a real option. Calvin did not really think he could do it, but if the alcohol so convinced him, then so it would be. The telephone chirped annoyingly.

"Now there's something that wouldn't break my heart if they disconnected it," he said to no one.

"Yeah," he answered impolitely. "Oh...hi Cat how are you? What? Well no, actually I haven't been on in a day and a half. Trying to quit, you know. Oh, hell I had forgotten all about it, my birthday I mean. Sure darlin', I'll check it out. Thanks, you're a sweetheart. Bye."

Just when things seemed at an all time low, Panthera called with her unique wit and brightness. He almost resented the fact that she had cheered him up. Beating himself up was the only thing that he seemed to do well. He logged onto the computer for the first time in thirty-six hours, and proceeded to his mailbox. Panthera's message was there, highlighted as an unread message, but there was another flashing with an "Urgent" tag attached. It was Vampyra.

Part of him did not want to even look at it. The other part felt obligated to do just that. Timey was history. Anything he could say to Vampyra would hurt her feelings. He simply was not the romantic that Timetravellar was. Still, he owed her an explanation. The relationship needed closure, and she at least deserved a Dear John letter.

Yet, when he opened the electronic distress call, it was as if something instinctive, something chromosomal rose from the most primitive part of his being. A dominant trait of his heritage raged from its dormancy and stood in defiance of all of his frailties. Courage abounded within the child of Scotland, yet there was also confusion in his soul.

Vampyra's cry of anguish lit a fire under Calvin Ian McLeish, but what to do? In his heart of hearts, he knew that all she said was true and desperate. In the face of such a fantastic tale, he stood a believer. The MacTavish blood that flowed through his veins howled for retribution, but he was powerless to charge to her rescue. How would he battle such evil? What would his weapon be? He felt for that one indescribable, decisive moment, that finally the purpose of his miserable existence had been revealed to him. Still, he drowned in his own mediocrity and helplessness.

Calvin stared at the monitor for a full hour, unsure how to answer. He, as Calvin McLeish, had snubbed her and even cursed her. Now she came to him begging for his intervention. Her total existence depended on his heroism, and there he sat, not knowing how to be a hero. Finally, the truth rested itself upon his shoulders and its weight overwhelmed him. Her salvation, it seemed, lay not with him, the mundane cyber-surfer, but with the one he had created, the one he had let slip into a quagmire of despair.

After all the time and after all the guilt and misguided emotion, his mission became clear. Calvin, the man, could not rescue the enigmatic gypsy of the centuries, but perhaps he could resurrect one that could.

Finally, he hammered out a response to the sensual siren.

Timetravellar: Where do I...how do I begin?...As fantastic as you may think that your story is...I have one equally unbelievable...Somehow our destinies seem intertwined...Some way, it is I that stands between you and your champion...You see...in the beginning... Timetravellar was just an idea...his words were to be my words...but very quickly...I lost all sense of control of him...he became his own entity...and he has come to me on more than one occasion...

There is one thing that you must believe...any words that touched your heart...any sentiment that warmed you...those were his words...my hands were the pen that he used to scribe to you his great passion... Beyond that...I was an obstacle that he constantly struggled with (with the greatest gentility, I might add)...

He continuously exhorted me to treat you as a queen... a princess...When you read words that were crude or unkind...they were mine, not his...That day when we bickered...when you were ill...it was he that spoke of *"moon's amber oil"*...It was I...*hang my head*...that was disrespectful...The duality of our being drove me to near insanity...and I prayed that he would vanish...and now...it is with the greatest sorrow and regret that I must tell you...he truly seems to have dissipated into that world where broken hearted lovers go...that abyss of despair where unrequited sweethearts spend their eternity...

Truly...his words were that of the greatest romantic that I have ever had the pleasure of reading...Yet it was my carnal lust, and promiscuity that kept him from you...my selfishness that drove him from cyber-consciousness...

Timetravellar was...*REAL*...I have seen him...and been touched by him...the last remembrance that I have of him is a photograph taken of my bedroom...In that photograph he lies on my bed (although never visible to the one who took the picture)...and appears at death's door...my own guilt and self-centeredness has kept me from emancipating him from his misery...but now...I fear that it is too late...

Long has it been since he made himself known to me...and just as I created him...so it seems I have put an end to him...Perhaps it is my own great disregard for myself...my own self-hatred that led me to treat the child of my mind in such a way...a child that grew to become greater than the parent...And just as with a child...he had my looks...my walk...yet he was taller, stronger...and more true than Calvin McLeish could ever hope to be...he was the living illustration of what I had always strived to be, yet failed so miserably...

Now, out of reckless abandon...out of jealousy...I have driven him to who knows where...if I have not indeed destroyed him completely...He was a handsome and likable fellow...but he would not stay here...in my mind...where I made him so unwelcome...Now, I do believe with all my heart and soul that he is real...and that it is him that you seek...but I know not how to bring him back...or send him to your aid...For my foolishness and for your pain...I am sorry beyond the pitiful expression of words that I convey to you...

I may only say that I am regretful...and shall carry this remorse with me...for whatever time I have left in this pitiful existence...*kiss on your cheek*...

Please forgive me Lady Vampyra...for my weakness ...my thoughtlessness...and my unworthiness... Were it within my power...I would stop your suffering...but as you can see...I am less than nothing...and I have foiled any chance of your salvation...I hang my head with the shame that is my curse...my burden...and my dishonor...

Sincerely,

Calvin McLeish

Calvin deployed the message and turned his computer off for the very last time. He walked back into the living area and picked up the empty cocktail glass. The ice had melted, and he calmly hurled it through the window. It fell into the shrubs in front of the house, and his eyes turned to the pistol that seemed to call him saying, "Take me, use me...I am your only way out."

Inverting the whiskey bottle above his head, he gulped and waited for some sense of numbing. Drunkenness would come, but relief from his agony would not.

Foggy awareness drifted back into perspective, as he returned from a nap and from the bottom of the bottle. The radio was on louder than Calvin ever listened to it and he was puzzled.

"Good tune," he thought. "But I don't remember turning that on."

He gingerly rose from the sofa and walked to the entertainment center, turning the volume down. Sitting on an ottoman between the couch and stereo, he listened.

"Come to my window, ah ha...
Crawl inside, wait by the light of the moon,
Come to my window, I'll be home soon,
I'll be home, I'll be home...I'm comin' home..."

He closed his eyes and floated on the raspy voice of Melissa Etheridge.

Opening his eyes, he pondered the gloom of his reality. Something, an irritation, just out of his field of vision kept vying for his attention. It was there when he had awakened from his stupor and it remained. Turning to the window, he could see the outline of the largest honeyed moon he had ever beheld. But, what was it that obscured its form? He moved his head from side to side and squinted. Reflection from the greatroom lights interfered with his line of sight. He stood and walked toward the window. When he was but two steps from it, the cryptic form took shape.

Collapsed, it seemed, his lungs would not take breath. The offending silhouette was that of a woman in a flowing dress, and she hovered just above the shrubbery in front of his window. Awestruck, he stood motionless for a time. He could not see her features, only her dark shape. Part of him wanted to bolt, but the part of him that was curiosity won out. He tentatively pulled on the latch that secured the window and positioned himself in the opening. Contours of her face were indistinct, but he saw enough to know that she was beautiful. Her flowing hair drifted behind her, as did the sheer dress. Finally, flabbergasted, he spoke.

"Ma'am, can I be of some service? I'd offer you a broom, but you seem to levitate quite well without one," his voice cracked.

"Monsieur Calvin," she began. "Much of what you have learned of vamp are nonsense, but that we must be invited inside a mortals home is indeed, true."

"Oh, well. Hell yes, do come in. How completely rude of me to have forgotten my vampire etiquette," he jibed.

Calvin turned to re-enter the main part of the room. "Well, I knew I was screwed up, but I sure didn't think alcohol could have this kind of affect on dreams," he thought.

"This is no dream Monsieur," the vampiress replied.

"Huh?" he responded. "I didn't say anything, how did you...?"

"It matter not, sir," she replied calmly, stepping from thin air into the house. "I come to speak to you of the knight."

Calvin's mouth dropped like the bucket of a front end loader.

"Timetravellar?" he whispered. "You're...?"

"Oui, Monsieur McLeish. Forgive my uninvited intrusion, but I have traveled very, very far. Shape-shift require much effort. I fly from Ottawa, as soon as you log out of Fountain. I must speak to you about the one that was born of your mind, the one you named Timetravellar."

Calvin stood in front of the couch. His eyes rolled back in his head and his knees unhinged, as he crumpled unconscious, onto the sofa. When he awoke, an exquisite, most fair-of-skin-woman dabbed his head with a wet towel.

"Monsieur Calvin?"

Her eyes were soft and kind, but their tenderness and the simultaneous presence of her protracted eyeteeth confused him. Vampyra sensed his anxiety and spoke.

"Non, Monsieur. Do not be afraid. I have not come to harm you."

McLeish blinked hard. "Why *have* you come, Vampyra? I explained that as sorry as I am, I do not know how to put you in touch with the one that you seek. He is gone. I did not ever summon him. Always he came here to me. My God, you're beautiful."

Her alabaster complexion flushed from his compliment, and she scooted close, so that she might touch him.

"Something about you look like him," she whispered, as she stroked his long hair.

"Timetravellar?" Calvin asked.

"Non, one from long ago. It is just now, after so long that I have been able to remember his face. Yours has brought his image back to my mind...so strange. Tell me about him, describe him," she implored.

"Well, he *does* favor me. He's taller, looks like Schwarzenegger. Wears a dress." Calvin chuckled.

Eyes popping, a whimsical smile bloomed on her face. "A dress?!" she inquired.

"Nah, a kilt."

Vampyra's mirthful expression turned to bewilderment. "A kilt? Like a Scot wear?"

"Well of course. You've read my homepage. He is a *Scot of ancient lineage*, remember?"

"Yes...of course," she said, confused. "Tell me more. Where is it that he has appeared to you, Monsieur Calvin?"

"Come. I'll show you." Calvin took her by the hand and led her to the bedroom. "Sorry for the mess," he said. "Both times that I have spoken to him—in person that is—has been right here in this room."

Stopping between the doorway and the computer,

she closed her eyes, held back her head, and inhaled deeply. A wave of shudders rolled through her body.

"Ah yes. Oh, that wonderful smell," she celebrated.

Calvin hung his head, "That'd probably be the tuna I ate earlier."

"Non, it is the smell of my lover! The one that come to me in France. Monsieur Calvin, there is magic here, great magic. Is there no way to summon the child of your mind?" she begged.

Calvin frowned at his ineptness. "Vampyra..."

"Please, call me Monique," she interrupted.

"Monique, if your presence has not brought him, I don't think anything possibly can."

A shrill howl burst from the night outside the opened great room window.

"Listen," she said, placing a finger to her lips as a request for silence. "It is my brother the wolf. He try to speak to me, as he often do."

Calvin paused reverently to allow her to listen, and then spoke. "It's not a wolf, probably a coyote. If wolves have ever lived in South Georgia, it was way before my time," Calvin assured her.

Stubbornly she insisted. "Non, it *is* the wolf. I know his voice."

"Well, whatever it is, it sounds like it's standing in the front yard," he submitted.

Still holding hands, the couple moved back into the great room to have a better listen. As they stood together waiting for the next howl, a tremendous figure bolted through the open window. It was that of a gigantic silver wolf. The creature stopped in the center of the room gazing hypnotically at the mortal and the vampire. Its eyes demanded the couple's complete attention, and locked their gaze with his. A voice emanated from the beast.

"Greetings, Monique and Son of Scotland."

Calvin stared for a moment, completely unaddled by the animal's arrival.

"Well let's see, I started off the night by getting drunk and contemplating suicide. Then, a lady vampire stops by for tea, and asks me to invite her in. Then, her brother, who just happens to be a wolf, stops by. He hops through the front window and begins talking to us without moving his lips. No, nothing unusual here, just another night in the sleepy little town of Candler."

"If I may continue," the wolf implored.

"Oh sure," Calvin conceded, waving his hands in mock reverence. "I just don't know where my manners have been this evening. Please allow me to make things right. Monique, could I get you something? A pint of blood? Brother Wolf? A Milkbone perhaps? I think I've got some choice raw steak in the fridge. Won't take a second."

"Silence!" the wolf commanded.

"Yessir," Calvin replied with wide eyes.

"This journey, for both of you has been difficult. Monique Dubois, for you it has been one of endless misery and suffering. Calvin Ian McLeish, for you, it has been one of total ignorance. You have not even been aware that it has taken five centuries to get you here. You are..."

Calvin interrupted, "Yeah I get the idea, I'm an idiot."

The wolf cocked its head and then continued with a stern voice, "That is not what I implied, but as time goes on, you do convince me that you are correct. Do not interrupt me again, lest I be forced to discipline you."

Calvin nodded.

"Before I was so discourteously detoured, I was about to make some sense of both of your existences."

"Uh, I hope you won't eat me or anything, but before you go on, I have to ask a question," Cal asked like an impatient schoolboy needing to go to the restroom.

"What *is* it?" the wolf asked in the most irritated of tones.

"Who the hell *are* you?" Calvin continued.

"Ah. I am *the Sorcerer,*" the wolf answered.

"Okay, that answers that." Calvin smirked, not remembering that they had spoken before.

"Oui!" Monique squealed. "From the room."

Curling his lips, the wolf smiled, as best he could.

"Wait, you mean *the Sorcerer* from Gothica? Now I'm really confused," Calvin interrupted.

"Boy...if you will silence your tongue long enough, I will get on with this. The one called Timetravellar is, as you know...real. In the future, rather...in the past, I shall reveal more to you, but for now I will tell you only what you need to know. I have been with you and tried desperately to mentor you, Calvin. If you will recall, I attempted to guide you when first you entered Gothica. Your stubbornness and lack of discipline, however, have required me to adjust continuously since you entered the cyber.

"Listen to me carefully, Calvin McLeish. It is vital that you comprehend and comply with my command. Will you?"

Calvin sensed the urgency in the wolf's request and simply replied, "Yes."

"Monique, you must unleash the power of your offspring of centuries gone by. That offspring was part human and part vampire. To liberate that strength, you must call to the ages by that which is your nature. You must awaken Timetravellar, through Calvin, as... Vampire!"

"What must I do great shaman?" Monique asked in earnest.

"You must bite, and suckle the blood of...Calvin McLeish."

Calvin's mouth dropped and his eyes bulged.

"Huh?" was all he could mutter.

"You agreed to this Calvin, just moments ago. Yet, there is more to it than just allowing yourself to be bitten, my son. You must understand what it is that you sacrifice by such an act of selflessness. Once bitten, you will fade into non-existence, just as Timetravellar has. Your demise will give him immortality, memory, and the strength to do what it is that he must do. You will not die, however. For just as the Timetravellar has been in your mind, so shall you be in his. But beyond being a part of his mind, there will be no Calvin McLeish. You must understand that. You and Timetravellar trade places, forever.

"I do know that what is asked of you requires absolute blind faith on your part, Calvin. Still, it is vital that you sacrifice yourself for the good of many. What say you, Son of Scotland."

Calvin stared past the wolf at the open window. Somehow, it seemed a doorway to another reality, a place where he could be that knight of his dreams. A place where he could finally make restitution for the miserable failure that had become his life. He had no purpose, as he existed at that moment. So, why not walk on the wild side? Why not submit selflessly to the Sorcerer's request? Perhaps it was escape, salvation from certain, continued misery. And, just that quickly, he turned to the wolf and nodded.

"Yes, for the good of many, and for the good of myself, I will do as you request."

Vampyra looked into the wolf's eyes and asked, "Sorcerer, how must I bite?"

"Bite as you would to transform him to vampire," the sorcerer answered.

"But, great master..."

"You must. It is the only way."

The vampiress stepped as awkwardly as a schoolgirl at her first dance. She had taken many over the centuries with great ease, but never had she taken one to which she had become so bound. The act seemed obscene when purveyed upon the mortal. It seemed wrong, yet she knew that it must be done. Looking into Calvin's eyes, her countenance was one of apology. McLeish held his head to the side without hesitation, and quickly felt her plunge into his flesh. The wounds were deep and his eyes teared, as she extracted his blood. A wooziness came upon him when she finally pulled away.

"Forgive me, Monsieur," she implored.

A trickle of his blood oozed from the corner of her mouth. Calvin smiled, as his flesh became chilled and he felt life seeping into another horizon.

"It's all right," he assured. "It's almost pleasant, almost..." He stopped and looked at the transparency of his hands. "Happiness to the both of you," Calvin uttered.

Those would be the last words that Monique Dubois would ever hear from the lips of Calvin McLeish. He became more ghost-like by the moment, and Monique was racked with guilt, until the wolf finally spoke.

"Go to the bedchamber Lady Vampyra," he instructed.

Monique obeyed, and when she crossed the threshold of the doorway, her heart leapt with jubilance. Sitting up on Calvin's bed was the monolith that she had not seen in five hundred years. As Calvin faded, Timetravellar grew into the third dimension.

"Mon Coeur!" she shouted, as she bolted to his arms.

His flesh was complete and the momentum of his lover's embrace knocked him backward onto the mattress. Timetravellar looked up at his ladylove in astonishment and began to speak. "Sweet Monique," he cried. His voice, now, was the thick Scottish brogue that it had been when he lived in the time before. The intensity of the embrace was emotional and gratifying. Her kisses covered his face, as he reveled in the wonder of her touch. Passionately, the couple progressed. It seemed nothing could steer them from consummating their passion, when unexpectedly, Monique jumped up.

"Glynn, wait! Hurry, come with me!"

She dragged him by the wrist into the great room. There, almost a memory, were the faint remains of Calvin Ian McLeish. Monique sheltered her eyes with a hand to block the glare from the room's light. For that one twinkling moment, she was able to see the last of Calvin. His smile was as broad as the night sky. He mimed a kiss, winked, and was gone.

"Bonsoir, valiant knight," she whispered.

The reunited couple, arm-in-arm, turned back to the bedroom, back to the love that had escaped them for so long.

Chapter 29

IV

Love, it seems, transcends all barriers—be they physical walls, or barricades of the heart. Yea, even creatures of unlike kind may find an immaculate passion that sends them soaring, hand in hand, up into the magnificent deep blue of night's remarkable canvas.

Timetravellar's eyes were torn between the loveliness of the blazing orange sphere sinking into Canada's western sky and the visage of his woman, as she splashed playfully in the lake. Spring's first warm wind caressed his immortal flesh, and Monique's sensual form softly caressed his eyes. "Truly, this must be heaven," he thought.

The image of his eternal love bathing in the chilled water, and the majesty of sunset were both miracles that nurtured his starved soul.

Hidden from her view in the columnar shadows of the spruce trees, he marveled at their bliss. Only two days had passed since he had come back from the dark reaches of Calvin's mind, and his heart brimmed with happiness. She was undead and he was immortal. The very idea confounded him, not so much that she was vamp, but more the notion that he was now deathless. He had been killed in 1508 A.D. He remembered it, and yet, there he sat at a lake's edge, watching the most rapturous of creatures, his mate. Timetravellar popped his face with the palm of his hand just to make sure that it was really happening, but happening it was.

Chilled as the water was, the fire in her heart kept her warm. The cool moss at the lake edge greeted her feet, as she stepped out from her bath. Monique reached for a towel, when she heard the crunch of approaching footsteps.

Smiling she said, "Mmmm...come hold me, my handsome knight. Let me feel the warmth of your skin upon my own. Ooh, my! What is this? Your kilt has a new prominence," she said giggling. "You have been watching me from the shadows, oui?"

"Oui, mon amour. But, it is not just your body that affects me this way. Just thinking on you gives rise to that within me which is male. Truly, a glimpse of you, your residence in my mind, or the fragrance of your scent are powerful forces. Any one of them drives me, and creates a yearning to be nestled in the ecstasy of your depths. It is there that my happiness lies, at your center. When I am there and we are one, there is no greater exhilaration in the universe. For that, I would march into the depths of hell and fight Satan's army. I have lost paradise once and I shall never lose it again."

In his eyes was the truth of his words, and there she curled in quiet peace. Exuding strength and gentleness, he moved to her and pulled her wet body to his. He drew his cloak around them both, and it became their cocoon.

When he watched from the distance, her graceful comeliness inspired him. While she excited him physically, his thoughts remained in his mind, and he was awed by his contentment. Now, with her petite frame against him, the softness of her breasts upon his chest, his thoughts turned to exploring the treasure of her body.

She, in turn, became pensive, as she frolicked in her own happiness. Her knight's chest was thick and taut. Pressing herself against it, sensations only known to Woman illuminated her long-starved heart. Raising her head, she found the home-fire of his eyes, as she knew she would. Their embrace began with a gaze, and it was there that lovemaking began. Without so much as a word, he told her of his worship. Without even a whisper, he proclaimed his eternal affection. Above his physical grandeur, were his eyes and it was his eyes that brought her surrender. He was the matepiece to her incompleteness. Only together were the two whole.

Lowering her onto his disrobed cloak, the sun traded places with the moon. Rising to reflect off the crystal lake, moonlight captured the magnificence of his eyes, just as the stars had in the French forest. Eyes drifting shut, she became the sweet music he composed. Plucking and caressing the strings of her passion, he brought to her lips the song of love. Tender touches of her waiting flesh, she now flushed with the heat of desire. So long had her skin been cold and without radiance. So empty had her aching arms been.

That night, as with their first night in Calvin's bed, her body burned with passion. Gentle strokes of her hair, her breasts, and her thighs, evoked soft coos and maddening desire. Lips of one lover pressed against the lips of the other; there was no timidity in their play. It were as if they had been together all that long, lost time. And, as she unfolded and as he entered, the indescribable heaven that magically comes from lovers meshing was created. Her passion flowed, and he dipped deep inside to taste of her sweet nectar.

He felt enormous at first, as she accommodated him. Still, she would have had it no other way. Timetravellar was the essence of manhood, and her thirst for him seemed unquenchable.

When the lovers' parlay eased from frantic pitch to gentle sway, he breathed into her those words for which her craving heart had longed.

"I love you, my sweet Dark Princess, my flower of the night. My heart is seared with a desire for you that is inimitable. Never shall I forsake thee for another, and should my immortality fail, it is your name that will be the last word I speak in this life."

His dark mistress smiled warmly, and then asked, "What is that delicious aroma?"

"Arghh! The wild pig," he cried.

Travellar leapt from Monique in all his naked glory and sprinted, flopping from side to side, up the hill. His lover lay on the lake bank moss and laughed wildly at his display.

"Oh, this is wonderful!" she bragged. I do not require mortal sustenance, but I had forgotten the absolute pleasure in its taste. I do not remember the last time that I partook of something other than blood."

"Hmmm, it seems that I, neither require it, but anyone, even immortals, would have to admit that a roasted pig is...marvelous."

"From whence did this magnificent meal come," she asked smiling.

"Just after you left the house to go to the lake, the poor beast chose poorly his path. He strode past my line of sight, and my arrow found its mark."

Travellar poured her glass full of blood-red wine and looked past her physical eyes into her soul. "So...this is heaven? He smiled.

She returned his smile. "Mmm, it would seem so, Mon Trésor. Heaven, save for one blight that mars the perfection of our togetherness."

Shaking his head and licking the pigs grease from his ring finger, MacTavish contradicted, "There is no blight, nothing that I cannot quell."

"Yes, of course you are right, my lover," she assured. Yet, she, herself was not convinced. The merciless curse of Emilien Lazare still plagued her consciousness.

Immortal or not, MacTavish was still a man, and still lacked insight. Had he looked at that moment into her, as he had when they made love, he might have seen the fear and the worry. Still, as any mortal male might have done, he missed the telltale signs of the storm that brewed within his passionflower.

The witching hour found the two deathless lovers naked and basking in front of a blazing fire on the hide of a great bear. Neither seemed satiated by repeated lovemaking. So much time had passed, and they drank of each other, as though tomorrow might never come.

"Does it bother you?" she asked, the fire's light dancing off her pallid flesh.

Smiling, almost as if he knew, he asked, "Does what bother me, my desire?"

"That, I cannot go with you into the warmth of sun's light. That, the earliest I may step into the world is at dusk. Does it bother you that these lengthy daggers of my mouth represent violence? And when we explode in passion's bliss, that I cannot curb my desire, and that I sink them into your sweet, precious flesh?" Monique looked up at the masterpiece that was her lover and gazed upon the two punctures that she had just inflicted in his throat. Two crimson streams progressed from the wounds of passion down to his thick pectoral muscles. Light from the fire and fire from his soul projected from his omnipotent eyes.

"Does it bother me that night's goddess gives herself to me, and brands me as hers with her own special mark? Does it bother me that I drive her to such passion that she inflicts her satin sting and tastes of me? My eternal love, you might as well ask me if I am bothered by being thrust into paradise."

She raised her head from his lap and kissed him. Extending from between her succulent lips, the apex of her tongue flicked the two bleeding perforations just below his jaw-line. In the time that it took for him to inhale and exhale, the punctures sealed and vanished. Tenderly, she licked the cerise trail that painted his neck and chest and all signs of the bite were gone.

Reunited, the two wanderers of night retired to the sanctity of Monique's crypt. Sunrise would come soon, and the clock that lived inside beckoned her to seek the refuge of sleep. Her great sinewed lover lay so close, that it seemed that they were one, save for the distinction of their minds. It was Monique's mind that thrashed in the turmoil of what might lie ahead.

MacTavish was a magnificent, fearless warrior, but as formidable as he was, so was Emilien. Desperately wanting to believe what he said, that no blight existed which he could not quell, she was still apprehensive. Lazare was the epitome of wickedness, and while Timetravellar was immortal, so was her dark master. Had she been brought together with her lost love only to put him in harm's way? She would rather suffer endless humiliation than to allow a single strand of her lover's mane to be molested. Should she speak to her knight of the nemesis? Would he be angered that she doubted his mettle? Glynn MacTavish had once been slain by a blow struck by the Marquis himself. He had surrendered himself to the evil one so that no harm would come to her. Was it now her turn to sacrifice herself for his welfare? Sunrise passed, as did noon, as did dusk, yet rest evaded her.

For the time, she carried her burden alone and endeavored to float in the symphony that was Glynn "Timetravellar" MacTavish. Monique's love for the Scot was of a magnitude beyond her own comprehension, and she would protect him at all costs. Still, deep within her own ageless being, she knew that one day the conflict would come. Should that happen, and should Lazare find a way to vanquish her deathless love, she would throw herself upon the point of a stake, and forever end the desecration of her body and her soul.

Minutes before she normally rose, Monique drifted into dreamless infinity. Hours passed and she slept, as would a mortal, with a blanket of stars above her. Then, from the far reaches of slumber she was ripped back to consciousness by a shrieking moan that scared her so badly, that a small trickle of urine streamed down her inner thigh. Surely it was a demon from hell.

"Ahhh!" she cried out. "Glynn! Help...help!"

The noise ceased and Glynn MacTavish burst from around the corner prepared to fight whatever had accosted his love. She trembled and held a post at the footboard of the bed. Rushing valiantly to her, he lifted her up in his arms, scanning the room for a sign of the intruder.

"But, what is it my love? What has frightened you so badly, a nightmare? You seemed so tired; I left you to your rest. Tell me, why do you scream in such horror?"

"Did you not hear it? Surely, it was a howl from a hellhound," she bleated.

"Ah ha...Ah, hahahaha!" he delighted. "'Twas not a beast of Hades, nor any other place. 'Twas just my pipes," he replied, eyes dancing.

"Pipes?" she puzzled.

"Yes, my love, my bagpipes."

"And where did these pipes come from, in that short time that I slept?" she queried.

"I dreamed until that time I awoke. My dreams were of that distant life when I was a warrior nobleman. I dreamed of my father, my mother, and my brother Quenton. Just before waking, the dream took me to the highlands, where I sat on a pile of stones overlooking a field of heather. There I sat happily, playing my pipes. When I awoke, a short time ago, my pipes stood in the corner, over there. I could not resist, but to play a soothing tune."

"Soothing?" Monique growled. "I do love thee Scot, but you must promise me."

"I would promise you the moon, if you asked it of me," he replied.

"What I ask, is not so much as the moon, my knight," she countered.

"Then what? Ask of me. I exist only to make thee happy."

"Promise me you will not play the hell pipes...not while I sleep anyway, mon chéri."

A mischievous grin stretched across her lovely face, and Timetravellar burst into laughter. For the first time, as the immortal Timetravellar, Glynn MacTavish had unwittingly been transported back in time, and equally unwittingly brought back a souvenir.

Calvin had made similar voyages in dream-state, and similarly was unaware that his journey had actually happened. To Glynn, it was but a dream directed by the bizarre gremlins of a sleeping mind. Soon though, he learned to command the ability to take such a journey at will, and become a veteran wanderer of the fourth dimension.

Chapter 30

Days of contentment became the routine in the stone tenement and Monique nearly forgot about the threat that Emilien represented. Soon, though, the time did come when hunger forced her from the protection of its walls. MacTavish understood her need to hunt. He wanted her to be nourished, and yet, the idea of her in the city at night without protection frightened him. "Monki," as he nicknamed her, had told him of the debilitating injury that she had suffered not so long before.

As frightened as he was for her, so too did she fear for his safety. Lazare had been petrified when last he came. Still, the Marquis was ruthless and cunning. He sensed the time knight's presence and likely would not submit so easily.

A glossy, black, spider the size of a woman's palm scrunched in a ceiling corner cranny. With naught but firelight, the ominous creature kept a vigil watch, as Timetravellar bid his Monique adieu. Stepping onto the patio, she breathed in the clean, crisp air.

"It is a good night to fly, my love," she said, as she kissed him. "I shall return before you rise."

"Be watchful Dark Princess…that no harm may come to you."

"I always watch my back. You too, be aware of the dangers of night. Should you go from me, I would no longer possess the strength to carry on. If I could take you with me, I would, but I am lone hunter. It is safer and quicker if I do this way."

MacTavish kissed her deep burgundy lips and stood back, as the ritual began. Head falling backward, she closed her eyes and moaned softly. Shape shifting required great exertion, but was the most practical means of travel. Living closer to Ottawa would have made hunting easier, but also, it would have made tracking easier for people like Isaac Hollander. With awe-inspiring quickness, she burst from human to nighthawk, and fluttered eastward toward the rising moon.

Worried eyes and a knitted brow clung to Travellar's face like a moss-covered rock outcropping. Not separated since the time knight's liberation from Calvin's mind, the couple behaved as a young married couple. Separation from each other was unpleasant and worrisome. Still, Monique needed blood, and when hunger came, it came.

MacTavish sauntered to the hearth and stared at the fire's dying embers, then stoked the pit with several logs. Perhaps they would still be burning when the black orchid returned. She would be cold, and he knew how the dancing flames enticed and hypnotized her. It seemed a little thing, but was one of those small gestures that she found so romantic about him. The huge spider was no longer in the ceiling corner.

Without looking, Glynn grasped a split stick of oak and then, another. The octi-ped scaled the angular surfaces of the stacked logs. Igniting quickly, the flames lurched high into the chimney's stack. They warmed his noble features, as he almost thoughtlessly added another log, and then another. When the fire pit reached its capacity, the warrior stood back and smiled. Vampyra would love it, and she would love him for it.

Something tickled his forearm, and he looked down just before swatting. His eyes swelled in their sockets, as he stared into the compound eyes of a tremendous Australian Funnel Web Spider. The assassin lunged from his arm to his throat, sinking its long, hollow fangs perpendicularly into the side of MacTavish's neck. Raking the attacker from his flesh, the giant flung his eight-legged foe across the room.

Paralyzing pain gripped Glynn's throat and chest. His abdomen convulsed and his legs almost immediately began to quiver. Objects within his line of site doubled and a voice came from his painful dream. A sinister laugh emitted from across the room.

"She is my slut, immortal, and you may not be as deathless as you think. Wherever you go, wherever she goes, I will be there. When you leave her, I will ravage her and when she leaves you, I will strike you, as I have this eve.

"I have felt you in the channel of the undead for some time now. You do, indeed, seem to be the one whom I decapitated so long ago. Nevertheless, understand this, vile Scot. Edouard Emilien Lazare fears no mortal, no immortal, and no vampire. It is my cleverness that is the difference between us, and it is my wicked deception that shall be your undoing."

Glynn MacTavish lay on the cold stone floor, eyes spinning uncontrollably. The figure that stood above him was indistinct, but the voice was without doubt, his demon of the past. Helpless, MacTavish's body seized, and a white froth poured from his mouth. Immortal though he was, the bite was deeply venomous and wickedly violent.

Nosing the door, as she always did, Monique breached one of the fortress doors. It was just after five a.m., and the journey had been tiring. The difference between this homecoming and all others of the past was that someone waited for her, someone that loved her. Trotting through the kitchen and around the corner, the faintest of light outlined her fallen hero. Sweat beaded on her lupine flesh and the horror of what she beheld caused her to immediately transform back to human-like form. Her heart turned cold, refusing to beat, and for a moment, she thought the invincible one had been slain.

Rushing to him, she lifted his head into her lap. Dried white residue around his blue lips created a corpse-like image.

"Glynn! Timetravellar! Please rise, what evil could fell my great knight?"

Monique swept a candle from the mantle and lit it on a beaming coal. As his face illuminated, she could see the two punctures resting in the center of his deeply bruised and damaged flesh. Thumbs width apart, they were too small to be vampire. The necrosis implied that it was an animal's bite. Still, she knew of no creature in that region that could deliver such a wound. As panic apprehended the vampiress, he stirred.

Her lover's eyelids opened, but only the whites showed, rolling aimlessly in his skull. Finally, propped in her lap underneath her adoring, but worried face, the glacier blue disks that were his eyes returned. Searching for focus, they ultimately fixed on Vampyra's worried stare.

"What in *the* hell, happened?" he asked. Reviving partially, he recalled nothing of what had happened a few short hours before.

"Are you hurt?" he inquired.

"Non, my love. I am not hurt. It is you who has been stricken," she doted. "It appears to have been spider."

"I should be thankful for immortality," he smiled. "If I weren't, I have to believe that this creature would have killed me."

"Oui, Scot. I believe what you say is true. Fang marks are thumb's width apart. A nasty creature," she replied with suspicion in her delicate voice.

MacTavish sat up and wiped the dried fluid from his face.

"Timetravellar, I believe this is mark of the one that hunt me, the one that punish me. Now he punish you."

Still without his full memory, he assured his lover, "Do not fret, my dark love. You worry too much. 'Twas but a spider."

"Did you see the creature?" she asked.

Timetravellar closed his eyes and concentrated. Delirium from the poison still clouded his thoughts.

"I do remember something. Whether it was real or a dream, I am not sure. I remember a creature, yes, a spider perhaps, on my arm. Mmmm, I am not sure. What I recall was something the diameter of a pear, black and shiny, I am not sure. You should have warned me of the nasty creatures in this land. I would have been on my guard," he said, trying to make light of the incident.

"I wish that I could tell you that what happened was one of Canada hazards, but alas, it was not."

Timetravellar's head throbbed, as he tried to be attentive. Eyelids closed, he rubbed his aching eyes with a large thumb and forefinger.

"Please say what you mean, Dark Princess. I am still in a mist."

"The one that attack you tonight, was your murderer...and my tormenter."

Chapter 31

Two uniformed police officers stretched the yellow and black "Crime Scene—Do Not Cross" tape around the perimeter of the house. A navy blue and white patrol car slowly rolled to the curb in front of the house, and Maggie stepped out of the front seat. An hour before, the station had called and told her of their concern about Calvin and that a missing persons report had been filed. Maggie asked if they would escort her to the scene and they complied. In actuality, they were calling to ask if she would come to her former residence, anyway, for questioning. The fact that she requested Candler's city police to give her a ride simply made their job a bit easier.

Maggie and Officer Elijah Clarke walked through the unlocked garage door to find Chief of Police Ernie Evans and Aaron McCall standing in the great room. Three feet from where they stood, an officer took pictures of what appeared to be bloodstains on the beige carpet.

"It's really not that much blood, Mr. McCall," Evans said. "The thing that is probably most disturbing is that you haven't seen or heard from McLeish in a week. This is probably nothing. When you called three days ago, I thought perhaps he had just gone on a road trip or something. A week, though. Well, I'm a little concerned. I've checked around town, and you've probably seen him more recently than anyone. We're gonna treat this with kid gloves. More than likely he'll show up hung over or with some other plausible explanation. Still, you've done the right thing. We'll start digging. Oh, Hi Missus McLeish."

"So what's going on?" she asked with worried eyes.

"Now, don't get too excited by all the hoopla, Maggie. Aaron's been concerned about Cal. He's been gone for a few days. There's a little blood on the floor, but not enough to…Well, we don't think he's dead or anything. Aaron, do you know of anyone that would want to do Cal any harm?"

Aaron stroked his chin and then said, "You mean like people he's owed money to for the past few months, or like a wife that just left him and hates his guts, or like that Muscle Beach guy that's been seen over here? Actually, I think all of those people want him very much alive.

He can't pay his bills if he's dead. Can't pay alimony if he's dead. Can't…," Aaron paused. "Well, he can't do for that muscled up live-in, whatever it was he was doing for him…if he was dead. No sir, I don't think that any of those people would want Cal gone at all."

Evans chimed in, "I agree Aaron, no one would want him dead."

"I didn't say that," Aaron refuted.

"No?" Evans puzzled.

"There is *one* person that I know of, without a doubt, that would like to see Calvin come to some harm. I have proof. Wait here," Aaron instructed.

Moments later, Aaron returned with Bitsy's diary. He flipped to the pages where his disloyal wife had written that she would like to see Calvin McLeish dead.

"Whatya think?" Aaron asked, trying to keep a smirk off his face.

Ernie Evans's eyes intensified as he read, "Where'd your missus be, Aaron?"

"My guess is, if she's gotten wind of any of this, probably right outside, spying from behind a bush."

Maggie's eyes darted from Aaron to Ernie and back again.

"What is it that you're saying, Aaron?" she asked.

"Just that in her sick, twisted, *Days of Our Lives* little mind, she had reason for revenge. Didn't know she had a thing for your husband, did you? She was always a little jealous of you, Mags. You were prettier, had a flat-bellied, longhaired husband that aspired to be an author... couple of good kids. You, and what you had, always stuck in her craw. Me, I'm bald, big bellied, very technical, but void of creative talent. I was everything she despises in a man. She just didn't figure that out until she'd been married for a while." He smiled and then continued. "It's o.k. though. I've never been *that* big on her either."

Chapter 32

Perched in the top of a great birch tree, Glynn MacTavish stared at the lake's glassy surface below. He had risen from their nest after only a few hours sleep. He tenderly touched the spider bite on his neck and reflected on the previous evening. Lazare's words had come back to him that morning, almost as soon as he arose, and he knew that what Monique told him had been the truth. Baffled by the scenario that presented itself, he must find a way to eradicate his hated enemy. His own vengeance was at stake, but more importantly, the fate of his twin fanged mistress.

If Lazare could inflict such devastation upon MacTavish, the immortal, what would he do to Monique? What had he been doing to her all this time? Rage peculiar to Scottish blood simmered, then boiled. Glynn MacTavish represented many things, but nothing radiated from him, as did honor. Even as a mortal child in Scotland of old, he had rushed to defend the weak and the bullied. Now, five hundred years later, one who had chosen the evil of darkness was still persecuting his mistress. Head afire, he came to a conclusion and then lunged from the thick branch he sat upon, out into wind-kissed space. Frigid water shocked his magnificent body, but did little to cool the fires of revenge burning in his heart. He stepped out of the water, and scaled the steep hill that led to the hidden stone lodge.

Dried off and kilt changed, he sat on the corner of the mattress. Glynn gazed upon his sensuous goddess and filled with all of love's emotions. She was his answer to existence, his purpose, his fulfillment.

The tiniest of smiles grew, as she dreamed, followed by soft giggles. Timetravellar leaned forward and kissed her lips. She moaned and batted her long lashes, fighting to awaken.

"Hmmm, that was so pleasant, my handsome mate," she surrendered. "Will I be so lucky to awake to such perfect amour each day of eternity?"

Travellar crawled onto the center of the bed where she lay and straddled her with his banded thighs.

"Ah! Well it seem that at least *this* day, I shall benefit from your passion. What a lovely salute you bring me," she said admiring his heightened maleness.

Again, the Timetravellar kissed her willing lips. He separated the neckline of her gown such that her delicate, perfectly proportioned breasts revealed their own salute. He kissed the apex of each. Desire soared at the feel of her softness, the elegance of her form, and the erotica of her scent.

"Mmmm, mon chéri, do ask your beautiful pet to come inside, where it is soft and warm."

Vampyra's gentle moan caressed his ear, as he lowered himself and then penetrated her sanctuary of love. Shuddering in ecstasy, her melting hollow gripped his advancing intrusion. Her lover almost always began slowly.

It was the gentleness, and sweet caress of his smooth impetus that caused her to quake with an unbridled craving. MacTavish would coax her to a pinnacle of floating desire and she would burst as a dam, her flooding ardor bathing him in reward.

Still there were other times when he, as well as she, would tangle in the roughness of animal lust. There were those encounters when he would see her across the room or walk in from the outdoors and look upon the shape of her body. The beast that is masculinity would seize him and he would take her. On those occasions, he might force her onto the bearskin or mount her, as she stood at the sink. Their love and passion was perfection and treasured by each, above all things. When love was meant to be tender it was, and when it was meant to be rough, it was. Their bond was mighty and each instinctively knew when love should be soft and when it should be untempered.

Lying in the dreamy satisfaction of each other's arms, the inseparable lovers listened to the quiet. Nothing but their beating hearts stirred the silence, and nothing but the threat of Lazare intruded their euphoria. After an hour of speechless tranquility, Timetravellar finally broke the stillness of Monique's bedchamber.

"What you said was true. I do remember the events after the spider's bite. Twas Lazare that did come and Lazare that took the form of the iniquitous beast that smote me. He *shall* return. He means harm to me and to you, as well. I vow this to you, sweet Monique. I shall hunt him down and destroy him. He may be vampire, but I too, am immune from death's sting. I shall find a way, and vanquish him. I promise."

Monique's fingertip traced the outline of his lips just before she solemnly warned her eternal companion.

"None of us are indestructible, my sweet prince. Not one of us can truly stave off doom if someone is bound to send us to the beyond. Neither vampire, nor immortal is invincible. We all have our weakness. You must learn that. Words like "immortal" and "deathless" are words that mortals use to describe us, but it is a fool who thinks that no power is greater than he. I fear that there must be an end, a final conflict between you and

Emilien and perhaps even between Emilien and me. Things cannot continue, now that you walk the same path that we do.

"Promise me that you will take heed of my words. Last night, you were hurt. That was a warning. The Master of Darkness, the Prince of Night would not show you his greatest blow the first time the two of you met. He is afraid of you, and he will try you to determine your strength...and your weakness. Yesterday eve was simply testing the waters.

"You are correct. He *will* return. Edouard Emilien Lazare is ruthless and sadistic. I know. He has castigated me since I was a young girl. Now, when he comes for me, when you are not by my side, his evil will be multiplied, but as much as I fear that, I am more afraid for you, my precious love. For I am nothing, if you are gone. If you are hurt, so am I hurt."

Her soliloquy ended with a gentle stroking of his long, soft, hair.

"I shall learn from the wisdom of your words, my beloved Monique. I suppose that deep within, I have known all along that what you say is true. Perhaps I have been bolstered by my newfound immortality, but in my heart, I know that no one is endless."

Smiling, she teased, "It is well that you understand this. For the passion of my loins has taken great strength from you. I render you quite helpless, no?" A long blink and an affirming smile acknowledged her amusement. "You sleep my warrior. You do look quite weary. I will wake you when night falls. Je t'aime, I love you."

* * * * *

Again, by way of sleep, Glynn MacTavish found himself back in his native Scotland of years long passed. He sat in a great chair in the MacTavish castle and was laughing with his brother Quenton and his father Lachlan. Sun was setting on the Scottish moor, and the scent of the dark ale they shared filled the room. He would not remember the joke that Lachlan told, and it was not important. As the three Scottish knights sat at the great oaken table and reveled in their fellowship, a majestic ram walked into the great hall.

The absurdities of dreams require no logic, and in the dream, the ram's presence seemed quite acceptable. Vertically pupiled eyes captured the attention of the noblemen, as a voice came forth.

"It is the power of your sword, Glynn MacTavish, that gives you strength to defeat thy foes. Yet, its power lies not in its length, nor in the forging of its steel, nor in the keenness of its edge. Its greatest magic, your greatest power, lies in the ruby of the eagle's claw. Hold it high and find its enchantment."

* * * * *

"Glynn, wake up!" Monique begged.
"What is it?" MacTavish asked sleepily.
"Come look!" she continued.

Rising from the bed, she dragged him to the large room where the fireplace lay. She pulled him by the wrist, and the two stepped out onto the slate patio. Dusk's light was poor, yet sufficient to see the thing that so excited the mistress of the house. It was a great white ram standing atop one of many surrounding boulders.

He smiled and gazed upon the beast, his arm around the waist of his female half. It delighted her and he saw no point in relating the dream from which she had pulled him. Just as with the funnel web spider, that species of ram did not belong in southern Canada. They never discussed it, but MacTavish understood its significance. When he returned to their small love nest, he found in the corner, next to the bagpipes, the sword, which he had not seen since he fought the Marquis' brigade, so many years before.

Sadness filled him, as he beheld his weapon. Signs of what was to come continued to appear. Although Glynn tried not to determine precisely what it all meant, something instinctive told him there would be a time when soon he would have to leave his lover.

Monique entered just behind him and saw that he looked at the sword. The very fact that it was there hinted of his mounting quest. Objects appearing from another dimension could not be a good sign. She too felt that a disruption awaited their union, but would not speak of it. The anxiety on his face confirmed her uneasiness, and she made an unspoken promise to make the most of however much time they had.

Monique and Glynn turned their attention from the blade to each other's eyes. There was an understanding that what would happen, would happen. There was also a silent commitment exchanged to conquer the forces of darkness, and to find each other no matter the circumstances. Eternity lay ahead and it was the future where their final peace and happiness waited.

He placed his arm around the pleasant curvature of her waist. Propped against the bagpipes, the sword, its scabbard, and the belt waited patiently to be donned. A dim glow grew in the ruby sphere of the handle, but no one was there to see.

Cuddling again by the fire, the two timeless agents of passion stared into the hypnotic flame. Communication occurred only through their eyes and through the clairvoyance of their hearts. Neither was willing to accept defeat. For, within two hearts grafted together and bound by that strength, came never-ending hope. Unfortunately, hope for the future meant confronting the past.

Chapter 33

Forty-eight hours passed before the next and final omen revealed itself. On that particular evening, sleep again eluded Monique. She rose from the red satin and slipped on gossamer. Walking down to the edge of the water, she basked in the death throes of the sun. She did miss its warmth and its smile. The creature that she was could not endure the intensity of earth's celestial father, but she did remember its gift. She did recount the elegance of its touch on her skin and frolicking in its light. Save for her regained union with the warrior, she was without the beauty of light.

The noble knight had filled the void of her past, and although deprived of simple things like walking in the sun, she had found her own warmth. In the failing light, she watched tiny fish kissing the lake surface. Monique laughed softly at their antics, filled by one of life's simple pleasures.

Only an arc of brilliance remained on the horizon, but it was sufficient for her to perceive the shadow that appeared at her side. Turning quickly, she bared her hands as claws, preparing to defend herself.

"Oh God...," she whispered.

Standing there, cloaked in darkness, shrouded in evil, was the one she feared most, the Marquis.

"The one that has trespassed inside my property, the one that now separates the lips of your loins, sleeps, oui?"

Tears surged into eyes filled with horror and hatred. The vampiress looked to the rock estate, imploring Timetravellar to rise and come to her aid. Lazare hushed her, just as she opened her mouth to scream.

"Are you sure that is what you want to do, my delectable chambermaid? The one you fill your lungs to shout for, is the one whom you condemn to agony if you shriek out his name. For if you do warn him of my presence, the next time I come here for him, I shall take a more dreadful form than the spider. Next time, he will suffer more, perhaps meeting his own end."

Emilien's depraved laughter chilled her and frightened her to silence.

"What is it that you want then?". What must I give you for you to leave us forever in peace?"

Moving very close, he leaned forward and licked her willowy neck. "Hmmm, you know what I want, strumpet. I am hungry...hungry for blood and the delectable taste of your flower's flesh. Give these to me, and your warrior shall be spared, at least, this night. As far as forever? I am afraid that you have no gift so great, as to keep me from you forever."

Perhaps more devastated than she had ever been, she surrendered herself to his debauchery. There was no other choice. To bow up against him would be to put her lover in harm's way. Looking back to the water, she watched the small fish again. "All right," she submitted.

Vampyra untied the laces of her lapel, allowing the garment to gape open. Lazare saw nearly half of her breasts, but her nipples remained hidden.

"Pull it open," he ordered.

Shame and defeat crushed her, as she exposed her femininity to her abuser. The sun fled, but the curvature of earth in the distance still hinted of light. Farther up, night's concave canopy faded from dying light to brilliant and then darker blue. Anxious stars exposed their pinpoint light. An impressive spring night was about to witness the latest in an endless string of the Marquis' molestations.

"Lie bitch," he ordered.

His humiliated concubine descended to the soft grass and moss of the lakeshore, her heart bleeding. Lazare unbuttoned his trousers, revealing his contemptuous weapon. Monique turned her head on the chilled mattress and waited for his vile entry. Her eyelids clamped and her heart raced in fear and grief. For what seemed an endless wait, she braced herself.

"Damn it, just get on with it," she thought.

Despite her clenched fists, her gritted teeth, and her bitten tongue, the ravishment did not begin. Instead, she heard a stifled gag, an intense gurgling. Opening her eyes to see what detained her most hated of all creatures, she could makeout the dark image of Lazare, his shoulders shrugged and his body tense. Behind the demon stood the cause of his discomfort. Lazare panicked and thrashed in the grasp of his assailant. As he struggled and moved to the side, Monique saw the source of his anguish. Covered in but a loincloth, sword dangling at his side, MacTavish twisted the vampire's collar from behind.

The viper's member turned flaccid, but was still sufficiently erect to provide a handhold. MacTavish relinquished one hand from the incubus's throat and grasped his male organ with the other. Then, with a strength known only to the deathless, he hurled Lazare across open space. Emilien smashed into a large boulder at the foot of the hill. His head thumped like a dropped melon, and for a moment, he did not move. MacTavish marched toward his archenemy. Craftily, the Marquis feigned defeat, lying very still.

Timetravellar reached down to grab the throat of the faking vampire, when Lazare lunged. Inch-long fingernails, like ten short daggers, thrust into the eyes of the noble Scot. Reeling in pain, MacTavish staggered backwards, blinded by the attack. Blood streamed from beneath his hands, as he defensively covered himself. Vampyra leapt as a protective cat, coming to her mate's defense. Wheeling from left to right, Lazare savagely smote the left side of the fair one's face. She tumbled and landed on a bed of rocks the size of ostrich eggs. Timetravellar heard her cry out, as she landed on the jagged stones. She did not move, nor did she make another utterance, and while he could not see, he knew she was hurt.

Emilien's sadistic snicker joined the sound of tiny waves lapping against the rocky shore. The valiant one dropped his hands from his face and stood in absolute darkness. His enemy was powerful and savage, and he knew the next strike would come quickly. Dropping to one knee, Glynn of Argyle placed his palms at his belt and listened.

Footsteps crunching the rocks beneath them approached at a near sprint. When he was certain that Lazare was upon him, just a moment before the next debilitating blow, the time warrior grasped the golden eagle's claw and slashed at the oncoming devastator. A sweet soft thud stopped the blade, as it knifed through the darkness. Lazare huffed in pain. The broadsword sliced through his ribcage into a lung, and hung in his flesh and bone.

A loud "thwump" echoed across the still lake, speaking to the wilderness of Lazare's fall and of his defeat. MacTavish listened intently for sounds of another attack, but none came. Blood bubbled into Lazare's throat, garbling his threat. "This is not the end Scot, but just the beginning. I shall return again and again. Each time I will know more of you...and your weakness. Inevitably, I will find the heel of the Celtic Achilles, and I will strike the final blow." Sightless, Timetravellar did not see his opponent change to the serpent that slithered into the night. Somehow, though, Glynn sensed he had departed. It would not matter, for the moment. His eyes burned, but would heal. Groping in darkness, he found the stilled body of his vampire love. He took her into his arms and negotiated his way through the darkness, back to their quarters. Hidden from his line of sight, the spherical gem of his sword's butt glowed its warm, red light.

Morning found the warrior-mates without rest—morose in their mood. It was neither Monique's swollen and bruised face, nor the blood-red whites of Travellar's eyes that created the melancholy. Rather, it was the conclusion of a conversation that had lasted for hours. Quiet sullenness dominated the household for a time, when the man-mountain spoke.

"I have not told you of it, but two nights ago, when you showed me the ram, I had been dreaming. My dream was of that very ram. He had come and spoken to me. His mentoring was of the power of my sword, yet he decreed that its power lay not in the physical strength of the weapon. It is the eagle claw where magic lies. It is there that I must find my destiny."

"I do understand what it is that you feel you must do. But, Glynn MacTavish, I do not want you hurt. I have survived the monster this long time. I can endure him more if I know I have you. Please do not place yourself in the dragon's mouth. I beg you," she implored.

"I *am* in the dragon's mouth, my love, as are you. He will haunt us, as long as we allow him to. He will dog us like hunted game. There must come an end. Be it his or mine, there must be finality."

Bloodtears raced over Monique's bottom eyelids and onto her round cheeks, as she surrendered to the truth of his words.

"How will you battle one so treacherous, so cunning?

Where will you go to find such a dark fox? His powers of shape-shift are wizardry. Even if you find him, he will change so that you may not recognize him. He may be a mite on your garment, as we speak. Where would you begin your search? Emilien Lazare will duck you like a prize fighter, exhausting you to weakness. Then he will pounce on you and..." She stopped and began to sob.

What she said was the truth, and the ire of Scotland rose within him. She was his mate, and he would not allow her to be touched or even threatened by one so depraved. Lady Darkness's argument was airtight, and he struggled for a response.

Suspicious eyes of one immortal darted to those of the other, as an alien clatter approached through the back doorway. Majestic in its posture, the ram entered the hallway where they stood. Timetravellar dropped his head, and surveyed the uninvited beast.

"I begin to think you a bit thick," a voice emanated from the fleeced creature. "Have I not spoken to thee? Have I not surely advised you on how you must proceed? I begin to think that your suspension in time has sucked the brain from you."

Timetravellar's eyes all but closed, as he countered, "An impudent goat? Perhaps I shall cook thee over a pit of coals."

"Ahahaha!" the ram scoffed. "Yes indeed, you have lost much sense in five hundred years. You were much brighter as a child, I think."

Vampyra's face illuminated. She intervened. "My love, it is the Sorcerer. He, too, it seems, has great magic."

Unimpressed, MacTavish continued, "Yes, I did see you in my dream. You spoke nonsense. The magic and power of my weapon, you said, are not in its bite, but in its handle. Wonderful advice, I'd say. Perhaps I shall bludgeon my enemies to death with a ruby that is the size of a walnut."

The ram continued. "Listen to me! You allow Calvin McLeish, the one in your head, to cloud your thought! Let your mind and heart be one, and listen to the words of one who has knowledge beyond your understanding. I do not come here for my own benefit. I am here because of a promise I made to Lachlan MacTavish, and I by God intend to keep it. But you, you try my patience, boy.

"Before Lachlan passed, he asked me to always look after his sons, and so I have done. Your father knew not that you would become one that walks through eternity, but it is so written in the Book of Celestia...that out of the Clan of Campbell of Argyle ... out of the house of MacTavish...would come an immortal."

Glynn MacTavish stood dumbfounded, as the beast spoke. Who was this goat and how did he know the name of Lachlan MacTavish? What was the Book of Celestia? Could this be some of Emilien Lazare's trickery?

He thought not. The voice, although stern, was familiar, comfortable, like a favorite pair of sandals. At that moment, his mind and heart did become as one, and he did heed the words of the peculiar animal. Inexplicably, the reprimand felt like the firm love of a mother or father. For a fleeting moment, the beast's identity almost revealed itself, but the skepticism of his mind, the Calvin within him, obscured his understanding. Finally, he submitted to the spirit of the ram. "What is it that I must do, then?".

"When I came to you two nights past, it was not in a dream, as you described. It was as real as the three of us standing together, at this moment. You must gain understanding of your charge--your quest, as an immortal. Until your heart becomes free of suspicion, it will be difficult for you to focus on what it is that you must do. As your mind opens to that power within you, you will gain understanding and wisdom.

"Your crusade will begin with difficulty and your pitfalls will be many. Stubbornness and doubt will make you as an adolescent who ignores the guidance of a parent. Still, you must prevail. Eventually, your tenacity and pig-headedness will become strengths, but I do believe that in the short term, they will aggravate," the mage concluded.

"Are you a god?" MacTavish asked.

"No, there is but one," the ram replied.

"Then what is it that you would have me do?" Glynn asked for the second time.

"I have told you whence your power shall come. I will also tell you this, but no more. The pestilence that you and your lovely lady endure in this time, is but a shadow. You cast light upon it so that you may better see to engage it, and it disappears, just as a shadow. If you fight it a thousand times, nay, even a thousand times a thousand, the result will be the same. You may fend him off, but the evil in that black heart remains. He will return, as many times as there are stars in the universe.

"Answers for the present and for the future lie in the past. It is there that you must return, to confront that which has gone awry. Remember what I told you before. Remember where your magic lies. For, no one is truly immortal, not without magic. Learn yours. It is a great and powerful magic."

The time tripper's eyes filled with dread, as he asked, "But, what of my love? Shall I leave her to the blackguard's defilement? Shall I journey from her such that he may take his way with her?"

"The eternity away from her that you are about to endure will pass, as quickly as a meteorite's journey across a starlit night sky. Fear not for her. It is you whose mettle shall be tested."

The splendid cloven hoof apparition exited the manor, and passed into another world. Timetravellar's face bore the weight of his mage's charge. For Monique, there was no tragedy, no indignity to suffer. For that, the cavalier was grateful. MacTavish's absence from her in the present would be but a moment, but for her champion, the journey back to her would be protracted.

"What is it that you must do, Mon Coeur?" Monique asked.

Silence was her immediate reply, but then he spoke. "I know not the fine points, but I do believe that I must obey his wisdom."

His belt and sword lay slung around the back of a hardwood chair from the previous evening's battle. Slowly he approached it, and extracted the bloodstained length of steel. Timetravellar turned to face Monique and thought back on his first encounter with the goat. Scanning his memory, the mage's words surfaced, as a bubble rises from the ocean depths.

It is the power of your sword Glynn MacTavish, that gives you strength to defeat thy foes. Yet, its power lies not in its length, nor in the forging of its steel, nor in the keenness of its edge. Its greatest magic, your greatest power, lies in the ruby of the eagle's claw. Hold it high and find its enchantment.

Timetravellar held the sword parallel to the floor at waist level. Slowly turning the blade, he inverted it such that its point faced the wooden floor, its hilt oriented toward the ceiling. Inconspicuous at first, the giant polished ruby emitted a dim sanguineous radiance.

Hold it high, and find its enchantment the ram's voice echoed in the chasm of his mind.

As the golden eagle claw and the prize of its talons ascended, the ruby beacon screamed its brilliance. Higher and higher, the broadsword climbed. Streaming rays of crimson darted from the miniature red sun, and as Monique watched in wonder, the time knight too, altered. His physical being sparkled at first, twinkling as a distant star. The continued rise of the sword intensifieda dazzling spectrum that emitted from her lover. Blue-white beams exploded from his gleaming silhouette, until she finally turned her head away from its intensity. Milliseconds before he catapulted to the next world, he dropped the sword and all was as it had been. The novice time traveler gasped and trembled, as the forged steel weapon clanked on the stone.

"Ahh!" he shuddered. "Did you see it?"

"See what my love?" Monique asked, bedazzled by what she had witnessed.

"Reptiles, as tall as trees. Gruesome, impossible giants with tails...maybe three rods in length? Did you see it? What manner of magic could that be?" he shouted.

Monique walked to Glynn, put her arms around his waist, and looked up into his eyes.

"What you have describe, my stallion, are called dinosaurs. They are *indeed* great reptiles, at least they were, far back in time."

Timetravellar's chest labored, as he filled and expelled air from his lungs. "I do hope they are not part of my quest," he murmured. "Immortal or not, I do not think that this sword would convince them of anything."

"I am not sorceress, sweet Timetravellar, but I do not think that your quest lies *that* far back in the past.

The time knight bent over and retrieved his weapon from the floor. "Kiss me my love," he beseeched. "If the sorcerer's words are straight, then I will return in the blinking of your eye. Yet for me, this kiss must last an endless time."

Binding their lips together, the two lovers stood in embrace. Then, stepping back from his eternal passion, he began the ritual anew.

Chapter 34

Thunderous reports from exploding mortars desecrated the pitch of the French countryside. Flares launched by either army illuminated a barren, mud-laden wasteland. Charred, amputated trees stood in the battlefield, as stark prophets of foreboding doom, and the men in that hell hunkered down in their trenches. A flare burst in the night sky, and as it faded, Corporal Silas Yates thought he caught a glimpse of a shadow darting from the sky.

The resounding splat immediately following the darting image caused Yates to jump backwards and thrust his bayonet into the blackness. Another German flare whistled, as it rocketed into the starless sky and the battlefield trench illuminated. Yates strained to see what had fallen so forcefully into his furrow. At first, he saw nothing, and then a massive mound of mud moved and took form. His eyes bulged, as the creature rose, muck sloughing off from its own weight.

"Blimey!" Yates whispered. "Stand fast Nazi, or I'll run you through."

MacTavish used the back edge of each hand as a squeegee and scraped off the thick mud that coated his body.

"My name is not Nazi, Brit. You are a Breton are you not? And, do not threaten me. I am not having a good day."

Another flare burst above, and Yates glanced toward the front line looking for movement from the German infantry. Turning his attention back to the mud-creature before him he replied, "Aye, I am English. Judging from the skirt, and the accent, you'd avta be a Mick or a Scot, I'd guess."

"Scottish," MacTavish growled. "And, it is not a skirt, it is a kilt."

"So you say," Yates taunted, lighting a lantern low in the trench.

"Where's your weapon lad?" he asked. "Are you one of the replacements that we've been promised?"

Timetravellar continued raking the thick ooze from his body. "I think not," he answered in disgust. "And if it is of any concern to you, my weapon is here at my side, buried in this endless layer of mud."

"Blimey," Silas said for the second time. "Well I guess shortages are worse in Scotland than they are back ome. At least they give us rifles to fight with."

"What is a rifle?" MacTavish asked.

"Never mind," Yates snorted. That sword is probably all you'll need anyway. Just about all the fighting here is hand-to-hand."

"Understand me, Brit. I do not run from any battle, certainly not one that is my own. Somehow, I have arrived here quite by mistake. Besides, if I were to engage in this conflict, likely I would choose the other side. The English are not my first choice as allies, as you can certainly understand."

Silas Yates did not understand. The Scots had leaned toward neutrality in the "war to end all wars," but the support that they had provided certainly went to the Allies. He did not understand the icy remark that MacTavish made was based on struggles of centuries past.

"Do you have any water?" the time knight asked.

It had rained for seven days straight. Yates held

the lantern at his knees lighting the bottom of the trench. In the barely substantial light, MacTavish could see that the British soldier stood in mud and water, calf deep.

"Yeah, I'd say we have water."

Travellar unsheathed his sword and dropped the handle into the water above the mud. Rinsing the thick coating of ooze from the ruby, he stood back up. He held the hilt of his sword toward the dismal French sky and the spectacle repeated itself, just as it had in Monique's stone house. Then, within the timeframe of a spark's life span, the filth-covered voyager was gone.

"Hmmm," Yates said wryly. "Didn't really care to share the trench with that ass'ole anyway."

The English soldier pulled a flask from inside his field coat and downed an immense gulp of rye whiskey.

* * * * *

An involuntary groan burst from his lips, as he, again, fell face first onto the ground. Another trench of sorts was his landing place, and he rose from its depths. Standing up in the roadside ditch he looked down at himself to see if he was again covered with mud, and relieved to see that he was not. Stepping from the gutter onto the road, the sun was in his eyes. It was a bright, warm day, and wildflowers abounded.

"This is much nicer," he thought.

Then, from around a hairpin curve, a deafening rumble shook the ground, growing from silence. Startled and defensive, the Scot dived back into the ditch. As his body's tumble slowed, he instinctively grasped the hilt of his sword and blindly whipped its blade in a semi-circular path. Dust boiled from the roadside, as a commotion speeded past. For a moment, MacTavish could not see what caused the ruckus.

"Damn it! It seems that I am bound to ditches

wherever I go!"

The rolling clouds of dust settled back onto the road. Time travellar stared at two chariots in the distance that seemed to be in full race. Inserting his *sword* back into its sheath, he swatted the dust and bits of grass that clung to his garment.

"Immortality is a trying business," he muttered.

Voices that had been masked by the reverberation of the chariot wheels could be heard approaching. MacTavish turned to face five Greek soldiers, as they staggered and swaggered toward him. One stopped and held a goatskin in the air to acquire the last drop of wine, and then cast it to the ground. All of dark hair and golden skin, their laughter encouraged him, at first.

"Hmmm, perhaps these lads are a friendly lot and can tell me to where and when I have stumbled," he thought. "Lads!" he shouted, waving his hand.

The Greek soldiers approached, sobered by the appearance of the hulk. Eyes that had been filled with inebriated laughter, now filled with suspicion. The troop circled MacTavish, eyed the kilt, then began whispering among themselves in the language of the land. Glynn cocked his head and slowly turned, keeping an eye on each of them. They were magnificent specimens of soldiers, except for their drunkenness. His leather chest armor was paltry compared to the brass and copper shielding that adorned their bodies. While their uniforms were similar to Timetravellar's kilt, they found his particularly interesting, pointing and snickering, as they whispered.

Endeavoring to maintain a friendly approach, the Scot spoke again. "I see you boys have an appreciation for the kilt. It appears you beat the Scots to it, although you have no plaid on those handsome garments."

One soldier spoke to another and the entourage burst into cynical laughter. MacTavish had attempted to be a polite guest in the strange land, but even to him it seemed a wasted effort. Narrowed, puzzled eyes told the platoon of his ignorance of their language. One soldier bent over, placing his palms on his knees. A second grasped the waist of the first and humped at his buttocks, clearly suggesting an act of homosexuality.

Quick of temper, the Scot's face reddened. Boiling indignity and animosity surged into the capillaries of his face and neck.

"This will never do, gentlemen," he murmured in controlled hostility.

His sword flicked from its scabbard, as if an extension of his arm, and that quickly, ancient Greece had its first taste of Scotland.

Chapter 35

An evergreen umbrella stole all but scant amounts of light from the forest floor. Dissected rays of the sun's brilliance knifed through the gigantic, ageless, spruce limbs. Bunched like *sheaves* of wheat, they were as a battalion of thin beamed spotlights cutting through the impregnable dark covering. Melodious gurgles from perfect, clear water meandered along a stream's thin, serpentine path. A woodpecker hammered out a coded message on a distant oak. Fat and contented, a gray squirrel stripped the barbed husk of a cone to acquire the delicious seed-treasure hidden within. Completing the picture of solitude was a spotted fawn bowing at the brook edge to drink of nature's marvelous fountain. All was harmonious--in synch.

Abruptly, silence choked the concord of France's timberland. The riveting of the woodpecker ended, as if a quitting time whistle had blown. Pudgy squirrel dropped his fattening snack and whirled to the backside of his tree. There he clung, outstretched, hoping not to be seen.

Young as he was, the fawn flinched, ducking, as if dodging a hunter's arrow. All fell quiet, except for the gossiping brook, and even it seemed to lower its voice to a whisper. The fawn's eyes bugged, as he listened for the danger. A sound, one that he had not heard before, could barely be detected. Slowly rising from his crouch, the fledgling deer stood at attention. His twitching ears turned independently of each other, scanning for the direction and cause of that distant moan.

In but an instant, the far away, almost inaudible cry, accelerated through the heavens and trumpeted its rude creator's arrival. From above, the frightening howl intensified, as did the speed of its approach. Beginning at the treetop, twigs and then increasing larger branches snapped and cracked. The object speeded downward at an incomprehensible rate. Colliding with the forest floor, a thud and blurt simultaneously sent all nearby inhabitants into panicked scattering.

Motionless for a long minute, the gladiator eventually jerked, as if awakened from a deep sleep. Face and clothing adorned with moss, he appeared as a mythical monster of the swamp. Dirt and plant matter spat from his offended mouth. Standing was a monumental task and he wavered circularly, not far from again, finding unconsciousness. His eyes remained crossed for a moment, and then his senses returned. Timetravellar looked down at the perfect depression of his body's outline, where he had landed.

"I really *must* learn to do this more gracefully!" he groaned. "I am not sure how much more of this time travel I can take."

Tiny uniform windows of light filtered through the standing trees and Timetravellar sensed he was near the edge of the forest. Covered with dirt and green lint of the woodland floor, he began hiking. Eerie sensations of déjà vu called to his psyche. This particular place was strange to him, yet he was oddly comfortable here. One silent footstep after another carried him closer and closer to his destiny.

Thus far, he had encountered dinosaurs, a World War I British infantryman, and a troop of ancient Greek soldiers. Timetravellar wondered what his next encounter might be. Then, before actually laying his eyes upon it, he knew he was approaching the lake where he and

Monique had first made love, five centuries earlier. Crisp, cleansed air winged across the lake surface and filled his lungs. Traces of evergreen freshened the breeze and transported him back to that moonlit eve when he had grasped her small, feminine waist. From time to time, moment to moment, he would have sworn he detected her delicate scent. It was the mixture of her hair's fragrance, her perfume, and the unquestionable, indescribable fragrance of Woman.

Merely thinking of her drove him to desire. MacTavish wondered how much time had passed for Monique in the twentieth century. For him it seemed like hours, maybe days. He was not sure. The sorcerer hinted that time for her would pass quickly, and he already yearned to be back with her. How long he would be away from her in this time began to be an issue for him. Going back to deal with Lazare was something he knew he had to do, but he could not help wonder when he would again feel the sensual prick of his lover's fangs.

Nostalgia and yearning were luxuries he could not afford, at least not for the moment. Bumbling and stumbling through the fourth dimension, he had somehow come to France, in that time when he first met her. The path to the palace was just as he remembered, and Timetravellar quickened his pace to find Monique of 1508 A.D. As he approached the countryside fortress, his eyes and movements resembled that of a stealthy cat.

Guards stood their watches at different strategic posts. Encroachment during the daylight was too risky, so he found a laurel thicket just beyond the back lawn. Waiting until dusk, when the setting sun shone on the front side of the palace, he climbed the trellis leading to the third floor. His heart pounded for the young girl that he had lost so long before. Yet, she was not the mature, savagely sexual, female that his vampiress had become, the one that so struck him in 1998.

Ascending the lattice, he achieved the summit. Nimble steps moved him skillfully across the evil chateau transom and he found himself, as he had so long before, perched at the swinging window. This time, Monique was not at her vanity, combing black silk. There was movement in the room, in the corner, where her simple bed lay.

Timetravellar strained to see through the window condensation and through the shadow of the room. His attempts were futile, so he grasped the corner of his deep red cloak and wiped a circle into the steamed glass. Even still, he could not make out the image of who or what moved in the dark recess, so he quietly swung the window gate open. Stepping off the ledge onto an intermediate stone shelf that served as her wishing bench, he entered the room.

The sounds that fell upon his ears crushed him as no opponent ever had or ever could. His vision was still obstructed from the dense darkness, but his ears bore news of terrible heartbreak. Unmistakable cries of passion sounded from the secluded nook. It was his only love, thrashing in her nest with another.

"Monique!" he whispered in pain.

She nor the darkened male figure acknowledged his presence, but rather continued their heightening ritual.

"Monique...it is I, MacTavish."

No reply, but the top mounted lover paused in mid-thrust, as if alarmed. He turned his head and scanned the room, as if looking past or through the trespasser. Finally, anger built in the breast of the brave heart that had come so far back in time.

"Monique!" he shouted. "Did you feel nothing for me? Do you so easily share yourself, and your bed with another?"

Still, there was no response. The angelic, passionate voice of his vampire-princess moaned with rapture, as her current lover passionately lanced her depths. The heavy wooden door flung open and a horde of Lazare's men struggled for first right of entrance. The shadowed lover of his dark queen leapt from her belly to defend himself and his mistress. Bolting into the light for the first time, Travellar beheld the figure that very nearly caused him to faint. The naked image of the man before him was, in fact, himself. Timetravellar had just witnessed himself, as Glynn MacTavish, making love to Monique Dubois on the night that Lazare's Black Elite captured him.

No one in the room paid him heed, and he watched the impossible transpire. Dauntless Glynn MacTavish put himself between Monique and Lazare's dark disciples, ready to die in her defense. Each moment that unfolded was a replay in Travellar's mind and he knew precisely every move, every flick of the wrist before it happened. Vaulting to "Glynn the mortal's" side, he unleashed his hatred from its sheath, the sword singing, as it sliced through the air. The opponent he chose did not respond to his attack and did not move into a defensive posture. Even in that brief moment that the weapon speeded to its target, Timetravellar was perplexed at the lack of response.

The four-foot blade met the caped guard's right bicep and the immortal prepared for his weapon's rapid deceleration, as it buried into flesh. Yet, the steel did not slow, passing right through his adversary. For an instant, Timetravellar believed his sword to be so keen and his blow so mighty that he had lopped the guard in two. That was not the case, though, as the legionnaire of time slashed so furiously that force of his motion took his balance. Spilling onto the floor, he looked up in astonishment. The soldier he had chosen to fight was Glynn's second opponent who stepped in to take the place of the first fallen guard.

There was not a mark on the one that he thought to be severed. What in the world? Clearly, he had made his mark, yet it was as if he were a ghost. No one gave even the slightest recognition of his intervention. He rose to his feet, and all that he could do was stand and watch, as his mortal counterpart ended the life of the third assassin.

The dark lieutenant of the conscript moved to Monique, and the deathless knight leapt to pull his lover from the approaching sword tip. As he flew to her, and saw the apex of the sword racing for the point of her chin, he prayed to win the race. The entity that was Timetravellar would, however, pass through his sixteenth century lover, and sprawl on the floor on the far side of the bed. Nothing he did, it seemed, could alter the course of events. Rising from the stone floor, he looked on as a spectator of history. Confusion and dismay gripped him, as he wrestled with the impossible conflict that evolved.

Glynn MacTavish was bound and abusively pushed out the door.

"Lazare!" Timetravellar thought.

He rushed through the doorway, his unearthly body passing through the detachment of palace soldiers. Racing down the steps, he spied Lazare at the bottom, as he knew he would. He arrived moments before the evil troop did. Tangling and scuffling with the resistance of MacTavish, their progress was slow and hard-fought. The immortal drew his sword again, as he stood in front of the depraved Marquis.

"If there be a God in heaven, let me have this," he prayed.

His knees bent and he thrust forward savagely. As before, he penetrated his target with no reward. Lazare continued to stand and pompously waited for his retrieved captive to be brought. Travellar's heart fell into the cold depths of the earth, as he realized the cruelty of his predicament. His mind turned to Monique, and though he suspected the outcome, he ascended the steps and proceeded down the dim hallway to her chamber.

She lay on her coarse mattress sobbing, and his heart shattered from her despair. Slowly, he approached her bedside, and he spoke, knowing that his words of consolation would fall on unhearing ears.

"Do not weep, my love. I *am* here. It is not so bleak, as it seems. I have come back for you, back to..." he paused.

In his own mind, he was bewildered. He had come back, at least he thought, to right the wrongs of the past, to rescue Monique from a horrible persecution. Yet, the masters of his destiny cursed him with their evil trickery. What manner of heartless magic was this? Who was the sorcerer who had pretended to be an ally, sending him back in time, only to be cursed with impotency?

A breeze of calm anger built to a fierce wind of hatred and vengeance. Withdrawing his mighty servant, he slowly raised it into the air. He would go back to the time from when he came, back to Vampyra where he belonged. The sorcerer would show himself eventually, and an embittered Timetravellar would end his witchery and his existence.

As the eagle talon and its ruby quarry passed his head, he waited for the light, the transformation, but none came. He lowered it back to his waist, eyes never breaking contact. Again, he levitated it above him, and again its power remained silent. Dismally, he returned it to its home. Misery and decrepitude seemed his affliction.

Timetravellar looked back upon the heart of his heart, as she grieved in the shrouded corner of her room. He lowered himself to the bed, and put his arms around her, as best he could.

"I am here with you, my love," he comforted.

Monique's sobbing abruptly seized and she lurched upward from where she lay. She did not hear his words, not in the physical sense, nor did she see him, but she did feel the power of his love...and she was warmed.

"Never shall I forsake thee, Glynn MacTavish. Should I be cursed to endure the vast endlessness of time, my heart shall belong to no other."

A tear meandered down Timetravellar's handsome face, as he listened to her promise. Being there with her and not being able to feel her, not being able to hold her, was more than he could bear. The creature that he was moved his lips slowly, carefully to her cheek. Knowing there would be no physical obstacle to keep him from passing through her, he cautiously moved to the exact surface of her skin. To him it was as if he had kissed the air, but Monique's eyes batted, and the faintest of smiles emerged on her sweet face.

Chapter 36

Deep in the mystical forest that surrounded the palace, a lonesome figure squatted by his small fire. He was an alien, an outsider in a time where he no longer belonged. For the first few weeks of banishment from physical reality, he stayed there in the room with Monique. Lazare's ghastly abuses of his sweetheart, and his helplessness to intercede devastated him. From time to time, he returned to the palatial prison and perched outside on Monique's window ledge. His heart, it seemed, required nourishment, and just looking upon her often eased his pain. Still, he never knew when Lazare would come to her room and ravage her and, on occasion, when he had visited, that is what had happened.

Too, he had visited the mortal MacTavish in the dungeon and had been forced to relive the atrocities imparted against him. Those injustices were easier to endure, though. His own physical pain of the past was miniscule compared to the heartbreak of the present. While he was cursed to be drawn to his vampire love, the visits became less frequent, and the mighty, Scottish immortal embittered over his existence.

He wondered if the fire was real, or for that matter, if he was real. Every evidence suggested he was but an anguished dream with a consciousness. The forest, however, was an enchanted place. It always had been, and things that could happen there, might not be possible, elsewhere. There was nothing magical about it to Timetravellar, though. It was simply a place to be, his *own* prison of sorts.

As vital as strength and honor were to his character, he wished he could be weaker. He wished he could take his own life and end the suffering. Vampyra told him that no one was truly deathless, and if that was so, how could he find an end to his misery? He had fallen prey to the mage's deception, or so he thought, incarcerated in time, powerless to act. After all the years of being dormant in an unexplainable purgatory, he had returned to this? Magic, he thought, was a black enemy. He could neither see it, nor could he fight the one whom had cast it upon him.

Weeks passed. Anger and self-pity rooted deeper by the day. Because he could not bear to go to the palace too often, he would trek off into the wilderness to think and observe. Two months after his arrival, he saw a unicorn drinking at a waterfall deep in the wood. Until that time, he always thought them to be the mythical creatures of children's stories. It was a wondrous sight, and he watched it for hours, as it drank and swam in the pool beneath the gushing fall.

On such excursions, he often found himself so deep in thought that the wondrous magic of the forest passed by him, undetected. Woodland sprites and elfin creatures peered from behind logs and lilies, as he strode by their hiding places. Oblivious to their existence, he did not hear their soft giggles and snickers. The female nymphs were fascinated by his size, but most of all they were captivated by his handsomeness. Soon, the giant became the gossip of Ténèbres. Tiny femme hearts pounded at his attractiveness and squabbling quickly ensued over who would be his forest guardian.

A clock, a calendar of some kind, marked the passage of time within Travellar's being. His memory of every event, from the moment of his capture, until his ultimate demise, was as clear as if it had just happened. One night, as he sat by the dying fire, the villainous dungeon keepers were castrating the mortal MacTavish. That was the final mutilation and humiliation before his execution. Fingers chopped off, chest and back lacerated, earlobe torn off, all had happened early in his bondage. What was the purpose of it all? His mission, it seemed was doomed, as was he.

Four more days passed in the shaded woodland and four more nights found him sitting by the fire. On the fifth morning, he rose and walked to the waterfall and bore the ultimate humiliation. Though he knew his appearance affected nothing, he bathed himself in the chilled water and shaved his face with a keen dagger. His death would be difficult to observe, but he would go. He must.

That day was more difficult and heartbreaking to endure than the day of his father's funeral. Timetravellar grieved, not so much for himself, but more for the fact that he was helpless to change the course of events. He had died courageously, for he was a courageous man. To die a second time was not something he relished, but he could and would face it. Frustration and his sense of vulnerability were the things that enraged him.

Clutching a fistful of juniper, he crushed the leaves to release their commanding fragrance. He dabbed his face and chest, so that the natural cologne clung to his skin. He lashed the sword-belt around his waist, and tightened his sandal straps, and embarked on the two-mile hike to the palace.

Jammed full with summoned witnesses, the courtyard atmosphere was one of dreaded anticipation. Timetravellar arrived moments before Glynn MacTavish was to be beheaded. He watched grimly, as his mortal alter-self mouthed words of promise to a pregnant Monique Dubois. Part of him wanted to leap to the platform in one last attempt to save himself. The other part knew it was pointless.

The paid killer's blade ascended, and Quenton pounced to the stage in his younger bother's defense. Exactly as before, the older fell to the archer's arrow and Lazare assumed the role of surrogate executioner. Timetravellar's stomach cramped violently. He listened to Lazare's hateful oration and watched his own head drop into the large woven basket. Tears flowed down his face, and one droplet after another splashed onto his shirt. He turned to see Monique, but she had already departed. An attractive, demure woman standing next to him in the crowd tugged at his sleeve.

"Did you know the Scot well?" she asked.

Timetravellar did not realize what had transpired at the instant of death and answered.

"Aye, quite well."

One of Lazare's bodyguards on the platform, the one MacTavish brow-beat in Monique's defense, caught sight of him. A moment later Timetravellar's gaze locked with the guard's. The mercenary's eyes narrowed, then closed and he shook his head violently, as though he had seen something impossible. At that moment, Timetravellar realized he could be seen. Before, when the peasant woman spoke, it had not struck him. He was preoccupied with the surrounding events. When he recognized the guard was struggling to place him, he knew he had taken physical form. The shaking guard's head came back to a state of rest. When he opened his eyes and peered back to where the warrior had been, he saw only the woman and the rest of the observing throng.

The immortal hurriedly snaked his way through the crowd. Emilien's elite were everywhere and he feared being identified. Flipping his hood over his lowered head, he briskly exited the gathering and proceeded around the corner of the palace. Head still bowed, his walk quickened. When he reached the open meadow between the fortified mansion and forest edge, he broke into a sprint and disappeared into the refuge of Ténèbres.

Chapter 37

Travellar sat, again, by the fire, saddened and confused by what took place. He searched his mind for answers to questions that had no answers. The peasant woman definitely spoke to him, and he was almost certain the guard saw *and* recognized him. How could that be? For three months, he had existed only as a specter, an aimless soul without direction and or comfort. Why was it that they could now see him? How could the execution of the mortal that he was, give him physical form for a fleeting instant? Logic seemed to have no place in the illogical realm where he existed. His head throbbed, as he searched for answers, and finally, he surrendered. He stretched his large frame out on the ground in the fire's glow, and drifted off to sleep.

The next morning he rose, bleary-eyed and lethargic. Something had awakened him, but he was to groggy to determine its origin. Remains of the fire smoldered, and a continuous trail of smoke snaked skyward. Puffy eyes blinked as he grew more alert. What was it he heard? Thinking back to the moments before sleep, he closed his eyes and concentrated.

"Ah, that's it," he recalled.

Voices, more like giggles, surrounded him in those dreamy minutes before awakening. The voices had been tiny and chirped like a chorus of rain frogs. He leaned over to where the sword laid next to his earthen mattress.

Grasping the hilt, he became a statue and listened intently. Suspicious eyes scanned the multiple green shades of the forest deck-- nothing.

The mirthful laughter of the fairies continued, but struck no chord of danger. The cause of his awakening faded from importance as the new day began. Campfire smoke touched his nostrils, and for the first time since he had come here, he thought of food. Immortal beings did not require mortal nourishment, but the thought of a roasting bird did make him salivate.

Returning in his mind to the previous day, he again pondered the curiosity of what had happened. Eventually he submitted. It was odd, but that was all; it did not matter. Timetravellar did not recognize his appetite a sign that his physical being had emerged. He would not linger on the notion that the woman and the guard had seen him. Before, only the nymphs and unicorns of Ténèbres had been able to see him, but now, even mortal creatures could.

Monique's anguished expression haunted him, just as it had in his dreams. Months had passed since he spent time with her. Beginning that day though, Monique's mortal lover was gone, and Timetravellar felt obligated to at least sit with her in the bedroom. Again, he bathed and again he spiced himself with the scent of evergreen. There was little chance of her smelling it. Wearing the fragrance was more a matter of personal pride. He had done such since puberty, a part of his ritual.

Birds chirped and jabbered, as they performed their aerial acrobatics in and out of the trees lowest limbs. Glorious in its beginning, the morning bolstered Timetravellar's spirits. He dreaded, hated the approach of his former self's death. Finally, it was over. If he was to be sentenced to the solitude of a woodland in the sixteenth century, at least that part of his servitude had passed.

A light breeze licked his skin, as he sauntered down the path to the palace, but a measure of guilt troubled him. The man he had been was murdered but twelve hours earlier, and yet, he was almost blissful. In a way, he felt he had betrayed himself, in another way, he thought that he was past due for a good day.

There was time enough, eternity in fact, to exact his revenge upon Lazare. That day, he would devote himself to Monique, no matter what her chores might be. He would follow her, as she cleaned the guestrooms or scrubbed dishes, all the while whispering sweet words in her ear. Perhaps, if he were persistent enough, she might one day hear. Ignoring his own anxiety, he whistled a melody his mother sang to him as a child. It would be a good day, his best since coming here. That, he promised himself that.

Trouncing the meadow grass with exaggerated stomps, he pranced toward the castle. The main gate stood open, as it often did, with no sentries posted. He strolled confidently through the arched, wrought iron threshold and proceeded to the large wooden entrance doors. Invisibility had its advantages, and on those occasions when he came before, he simply passed through the thick oak. On that particular day, though, the massive wooden gates were propped open to allow the sweet spring air to exchange with that which had become stale over the winter.

Monique had tied her long silken hair with a large handkerchief to keep it out of her face, while she scrubbed the marble foyer. She did not notice him at first, nor did he her. Then, almost at the same moment, one looked up and one looked down. Blinding sun outlined his form and obscured her view of the stranger that walked through the door, uninvited. She stood, squinted, and shielded the light by placing her hands over her eyes. For but an instant could she see his features, but it was moment enough. Color left her cheeks and all strength left her body.

She dropped the sponge and then whispered, "Mon trésor."

Her knees buckled and she fainted, crumpling as a wilted blossom. Timetravellar rushed to her and knelt.

"My love, you have seen me?"

His transformation of the day before, it seemed, stayed with him. How wonderful! Finally, he could hold her, be with her, and love her. An instant before an armed sentry came into view on the second floor walkway, Travellar realized the danger that now existed.

The sentinel's eyes froze upon the intruder, and he rushed to one of the many brass alarm bells strategically located around the estate. "Captain of the guard!" he shouted.

The time knight deliberated. Should he try to gather Monique into his arms and flee, or should he stay and slaughter as many as he could? Circumstances that followed made the decision for him. Two more elite ambled through the front doorway, at the same moment the bell rang. Drawing their weapons, they rushed the kneeling Timetravellar. Cold determination in his eyes, he stood and loosed four feet of wicked steel from its lair. One sweeping swing bit both aggressors, and each fell into a puddle of his own liberated blood.

A horde of summoned attackers poured down the steps, as did a throng from the left palace wing and one from the right. Fifty soldiers in Lazare's service answered the bell call and charged the antechamber.

"Damn you, Emilien Lazare. I *shall* return."

Timetravellar burst through the open doorway into the sunlight and searched for an ally. There was but one. A horse, immaculate white in color, stood tied to a post in the front courtyard. Dashing to untie its bridle, he vaulted onto its bare back. Insistent heels urged the magnificent stallion to full gallop, but before he could pass through the wrought iron barrier, a guard slammed it shut.

Without prodding, the horse abruptly turned and circled in the courtyard. There was no escape and the Scot submitted to the idea that he must dismount and fight. Chronos, as he would later be named, broke so abruptly that he nearly threw Travellar from his back. To the human's surprise, the animal bolted for the seven-foot fence. The rider's eyes bugged, as Chronos accelerated and then lunged almost vertically into the air. Travellar grasped the neck of his mount and closed his eyes, waiting for catastrophe, but catastrophe did not come. For what seemed like minutes, the mount and rider soared up, then over the barricade. When the stallion made its landing, it stopped and reared of its own accord, as if to taunt the palace guards.

"By God!" MacTavish marveled. "You are *quite* special, indeed, my friend."

Chronos turned and galloped for the meadow. Palatial archers took their posts in the fortress turrets, and thirty zinging crossbow arrows whizzed passed the escape artists. Twenty yards from the forest edge, Timetravellar began to laugh at the impossible escape that he and his new friend had managed. But, his celebration was premature, as one of the last arrows fired incredibly found its mark. The wooden shaft penetrated the swordsman's right shoulder blade, its metal broadhead protruding through his muscular chest. The full agony of his wound had not yet taken, when he looked down at the blood-covered arrowhead.

"This is not good, my mount," he said, as Chronos trotted into the woods.

Travellar knew they would follow and led the horse deep into the seclusion of his new home. The waterfall was far from the lavish manor, and he would likely be safe there. Tentative in his gait, Chronos walked gingerly, sensing his rider's peril. Streaming, divergent trails of crimson stained the perfect musculature of the equestrian. While he could not he killed by the arrow, it took him to death's door and there he lingered.

The initial impact of the arrow was sharp, but void of sting. As Chronos delicately chose his steps through the undergrowth, the wound quickly began to throb and escalated to agonizing pain. Wooziness seduced the immortal to unconsciousness, but he fought to keep his senses. Slumped on the steed's bare back, his head bobbed, as though his neck were broken. The extraordinary mount altered the rhythm of his steps to smooth the bumpiness of Travellar's ride. The waterfall was but one hundred yards away. Had it been two hundred, the knight would have surely fallen.

Instinctively, Chronos located nature's picturesque fountain. He found a patch of soft, tender grass at the pool's edge, then stopped, and waited. Moments after coming to a halt, Timetravellar submitted to the forces of pain and fell onto the green berth.

Deep in the refuge of senselessness, he dreamed. Some of the hallucinations were absurd, surreal scenarios that were meaningless. Still, some in the deepest part of his psyche were quite real. Of those, most were dreams of Monique, all sweet and tender. A voice in that inexplicable realm bade him stay there, urging him to never return to consciousness. That messenger was deceitful, a consort of the dark reaper. It was tempting to the spirit warrior, because all was beautiful, there. Monique was there. Subtle suggestions that she would always be in the dark realm drew the immortal's spirit deep into his mind, almost beyond his ability to return.

Sense of purpose and quest remained strong in his great heart, though, and that conviction proved more powerful than the trickery of the reaper and his crones.

Late in the afternoon of the first day, his eyelids slowly, arduously opened, as the setting sun attacked his sensitive pupils. His massive body glistened in the waning light of day while his saturated hair chilled the back of his neck. Chronos waited at the tree line and remained watchful of his master. No harm would come to his rider, as long as he stood guard.

Travellar's weakened state prevented him from even raising his head, but on that first occasion when he opened his eyes, he beheld a beautiful black swan. It was drifting at the pool edge, not ten feet from where he lay. He could not ascertain if it was one of his beautiful dreams, or if it was reality. The immortal Glynn MacTavish looked for signs of Vampyra, but she did not come, so he knew it must be reality.

Pain from his shoulder was intense. His mind traveled back and forth to avoid dealing with that which was unbearable. As he looked upon the swan with half opened eyes, he thought, "I do wish Monique was here to see this. She loves beautiful things."

The swan responded to his unspoken wish, "But, she is not here, nor can she be. You have come here because of your great love for her, but it will seem an eternity before you will again feel the touch of her skin."

Timetravellar's eyebrows knitted, as he listened. "I know you don't I?"

"Indeed you do, Glynn MacTavish. I have spoken to you as wolf, as goat, and now as swan. Let me speak to you by the name you know me as. I am Ian, your mage...and friend...of days long gone by. My son, your journey is a difficult one, one that will try the armor of your spirit. Still, you must prevail."

Smiling the knowing, unsurprised smile of delirium, the immortal said, "Ah, Ian my friend. It has been too long." The cavalier's eyes closed and the conversation ended and he returned to the mystical place where he could be with his passionate love, Monique.

Waking in the deepest part of night, his eyes opened for the second time. The glare of a yellow light masked the stars presence. Dulled from his injury, he was not keen enough to turn his head and see the blazing fire. Instead, he remained motionless and stared straight up.

The melodious hum to his left finally coaxed him to turn and look. In the fire's light, he watched the hypnotic flames, never questioning that a fire raged without his building it. He wondered what the multi-pitched hum was, but did not care much. Nonetheless, he would, in but a passing moment, see the remarkable producer of the sound. Eyes transfixed on the dancing blaze, a minute figure hovered into his field of vision. She was only six inches tall and her wings beat furiously, while she tended the fire.

"Milady...,"

She gasped, squealed, and darted into a clump of lilies. Peering from behind the wildflower's elongate leaves, her expression was one of mistrust and regret. The firelight barely extended to her hiding place, and the warrior strained to see her.

"Please, do not be frightened."

"And what makes you think I am frightened, giant?" she huffed.

A whimsical smile came to her patient, as he postulated, "Perhaps because I *am* a giant?"

"Impudence!" she scolded. "I'll have you know that I am of fae blood, and unafraid of the likes of you. Do not be deceived by my size. I have great magic!"

"Yes, I'm sure that you do. I meant no offense."

"Your very presence is offensive, I am afraid," she scoffed.

Travellar's expression turned serious, almost irritated. "Well...no one is forcing you to stay."

"That is true, but I am here because I was commissioned by a great magician. Keep you in mind that I am not smitten by your pretty face. I come in service to a great sorcerer, that is all!"

"Hmmm," MacTavish growled, remembering that Ian had come some time before. "I am not so sure he is *that* great of a magician. I would certainly question his taste in wee fairies."

"Indeed!" she snorted. "And what about me gives you the right to question his greatness?"

"Because you are a bitch from fairy hell, I would say."

The half-foot nymph angrily stepped out of the foliage and stomped toward Travellar with clenched fists on her tiny hips. Smoldering eyes sent their reply before her small voice could. "Because my femininity does not flood at your presence does not make me a bitch!" she fired. "I do have passion, but I am chosen because the native fairies of this forest are too taken by you. You are *their* responsibility. I am summoned here from my home forest in Britain because of their giddiness. You...," she stopped in mid-sentence and peered at Timetraveler with concern.

The brief conversation had exhausted the wounded swordsman. He missed most of her damnation, mercifully in sleep. Walking more lightly, she approached him. Without indication, her wings raised and beat rapidly for a short burst, until they could levitate her to his chest. Landing softly on the crag that he was, she studied his face.

"He is rather pretty," she thought.

* * * *

The morning sun brought wildlife chattering their "good mornings." MacTavish opened his eyes and, for the first time, sat up. The fire burned brightly; it had been recently stoked. At first, his panning eyes identified nothing, but the second pass detected what he sought. Behind a large cedar, he saw a few strands of wavy blonde hair. Watching curiously, he anticipated movement, but movement never came. This one was stealthy and experienced in the ways of the wood. Still, while he knew it was a woman, he had expected a six-inch woman to be lurking about. Judging from the height of the amber locks above ground, this fawn of the forest was around five feet tall. He would not challenge her seclusion though, and scooted back so that he could sit and lean against a small birch. It felt as though the arrow was still hung in him, but when he looked down, he could see that it had been removed. The entry point on his back and the exit wound on his chest were bandaged and coated with a pungent salve.

Turning his attention to the clear pool, he again observed the dark swan floating toward him.

"Did we speak on last eve, or was it my delirium?" he asked the swan.

"It was indeed I, warrior," Ian replied.

"If you are the wolf, the ram, the swan, and my friend, then tell me mage, what manner of trickery do you cast upon me? If indeed you are my kind mentor from years gone by, then share with me your magic such that I may vanquish Lazare and retrieve my sweet Monique."

Warping and undulating, the swan's shape struggled with a bizarre and violent transformation. A dark image stretched upward above the water and then stopped. Details of the ambiguous form became clearer, while subtle fluctuations rippled from top to bottom. Then, from nondescript mass to identifiable form, the likeness flashed to a dark-robed Ian, the Magician. His navy garment with matching glengarry rendered him a scholarly looking figure. He stepped from the water surface onto the smooth shoreline pebbles, and the clean-shaven white-haired sorcerer proceeded to his disciple.

He held his hand up in the illuminated Scot's face to beg him not to rise. The ancient conjurer bent at the waist and hugged his charge of so many centuries.

"Ah, Glynn. It has been so long, so very long."

He squatted, held his open palms to the fire and then rubbed them together.

"She feels badly you know," Ian continued.

"Who?" Timetravellar asked.

"Why, Sylvie of course. The fairy that tends to you while you are injured."

"Ah, yes the sharp-tongued, winged wench, about so high," MacTavish replied, holding his hands half a foot apart.

Ian chuckled and then said, "Yes, you have met her I see, but do not be too hard on her, Son. She is faithful and obedient. I asked her to be your guardian, when you were felled. Rightfully, the fairies native to this Ténèbres should be your attendants, but it seems they are too impressed by your stature, and the cut of your chin. I wished not to leave anything to chance and I called her from the forest near Camelot."

"Last night I saw her before sleeping and she was so small, but today, I catch a glimpse of her and she is...of normal size."

"Aye, different sizes, different shapes, she is quite skilled in the ways of magic, quite skilled indeed. You will find her a great ally, as you follow your quest," the mage said.

"Well now, at least you strike the mark. My quest is to kill Lazare, before he can curse Monique with the wickedness of undeath," Travellar declared.

"That my son, is not your quest at all. Monique Dubois was cursed with undeath, before you ever laid eyes upon her."

MacTavish interrupted, "Then I shall go back farther in time, before she met me. I am immortal after all. I can traverse the millennia. You have shown me that, I am here, now," he preached.

"Glynn MacTavish, I am old...and tired. My journey

soon comes to an end, so you must listen very carefully."

Like an undisciplined child, the younger, again, interrupted. "An end? But you are a mage, immortal,

"I think we may be here until you are as old as me, if you do not learn to seal thy lips and listen." He smiled. "If I may continue. Yes, immortal by magic, but I have seen all that I have wanted to see and I have done all that I wanted to do. It is by choice that I expire and move on. Existence, on this earth, in this time, is one of many. I do not evaporate into nothingness. Rather, I move to a plane that others do not understand. My journey to that new place begins soon. It is for that reason that I summoned Sylvie to take you the rest of the way, until you are victorious in your crusade."

Timetravellar's head bowed and his eyes watered. So many cruelties it seemed accosted him. To be without form only to find it, only to be driven from his heart's desire once she could see him. Now, his great teacher, his friend heads off on a course of self-expiration. Misery seemed to abound at every turn.

"Wait a damned minute! What do you mean you summoned Sylvie to take me the rest of the way? She is a caustic, bitter little wench. What she needs is a leprechaun with a gigantic penis to bend her over a toadstool and drive her home! I'll go nowhere with her, Ian," Timetravellar declared indignantly.

The petite winged fem fatale stepped out from behind the massive cedar trunk, lightning bolts building in her eyes. She raised her hand to sling a savage retaliatory spell upon MacTavish, but Ian raised his hand in kind, and she submitted.

"Beyond this day, I shall not be here to rescue you from her wrath, Glynn-boy. It would be in your interest to cool thy hot tongue. After all, you will stroll down time's path with her for quite a lengthy journey."

MacTavish's face reddened at the prospect of spending even a moment with her. Ian implied that she possessed power that he should fear, or at least respect. The thought of securing an alliance with one so snotty was preposterous. The immortal glared at the sprite the way an estranged school child might glare at another, after being reprimanded by the teacher.

"I *told* you she felt badly," Ian snapped. "If you will *just* give her and me a chance, perhaps, we can finish this before the sun sets."

MacTavish conceded, sensing the mage's frustration and bid him continue.

"As I was saying before we detoured to the adequacy of your chosen fairy, your quest is not to vanquish Lazare, at least not now. You have been directed here to indeed watch over Monique, to indeed repel the crawlers of night. For five centuries, they hunt her like dogs. Lazare himself is wicked enough, but him you cannot thwart."

Timetravellar could not contain himself and interrupted, "But why, great magician?"

Ian cocked an eyebrow and continued, "All things, at least those things relating to Emilien Lazare, must happen throughout time, just as they did the first time. The cretins that hound her are of no consequence over the course of history except to torment her further. Their relentless pursuit was almost more than she could bear, when compounded with Lazare's cruel punishment. From them, you may give her relief."

"Do not be angry Ian, but I must know why it is that I must allow the dark parasite to deploy his evil upon her."

"As you recall, when you were executed, Monique was with child," the mage noted.

"Yes! I do remember! But, what came of my child?" Timetravellar asked, as if awakening from a dream.

"When Quenton and I visited you in the dungeon,

you asked that we return with a legion and remove Monique and your son to Scotland where they belong.

"Soon after your death, an army of vampire killers from all parts of Europe united and descended upon Emilien's palace. He was the most infamous of all vampires, and to bring him to his end would be a great trophy for any one of them.

Monique had just bore your son..." He paused knowing the Scot would not be able to contain himself.

"A son?" He sighed with all the pride of Scotland.

Smiling and nodding the mage pushed forward. "In the midst of all the confusion associated with the vampire hunters' coming, it was easy for me to come and take your boy. Monique fled, when Emilien abandoned all his possessions here. Her existence became that of a nomad, and though Lazare would find her from time to time, her existence fared better away from this place. Your son was raised by me, while your woman was free to wander, as all vampires must."

"Please forgive me Ian, but...,"

"Did you ever know my last name?" the sorcerer asked slyly. "I gave it to your son, as a matter of safety."

Calvin stroked his chin. He had never considered it, never figured that a magician would have a last name. "No," he admitted.

"My last name is...MacLeish. In later years the 'a' was dropped so that it came to be spelled 'm-c-l-e-i-s-h.'"

Glynn MacTavish's mouth fell open, "Like the man whose mind from which I sprang?"

"Precisely. The man whose soul you were a part of is a direct descendent of your son. It is the vampire blood in Calvin McLeish's veins and his forefathers', that kept you alive in a time-purgatory of sorts."

Timetravellar stood, oblivious to the throbbing in his chest and shoulder. This was too much to comprehend, but still he tried.

"Calvin is a descendent of mine?" he finally asked.

Ian continued, "In a manner of speaking, but since you do not have vampire blood in your veins, the family heritage changed dramatically when little Calvin was born."

"Little Calvin?" MacTavish probed. "You named my son Calvin, like Calvin McLeish in nineteen-hundred and...whatever?"

"Just a coincidence Glynn-boy. Or...perhaps it was providence. No matter."

"Ian, this is all quite interesting, but I have been patient. Tell me now why it is that I may not destroy the dark rapist."

Ian nodded, "I am glad to finally be shedding this burden. You can be quite irritating, you know, not near the discipline of your father, Lachlan. If you recall, the same Calvin that we speak of exists no more. He sacrificed himself so that you could be born...as an immortal."

Timetravellar's face contorted. He recognized the truth in Ian's words. He had not even been thoughtful of Calvin's forfeiture. All that he had done was for himself and Monique. He was ashamed to have been so thankless for Calvin's selfless gift. A moment of reverent silence, and then he continued. "Again, I ask you old man!" MacTavish growled.

"God give me strength!" Ian pleaded. "This is the rest of it. When I finish, I am finished. Ask me no more.

Calvin McLeish does not exist in the future, as we speak. His wife exists, his neighbors exist, and his children exist. Yet, the man that you once knew is vanished from the face of the earth," the mage coached.

"But it was by his choosing, great mage. Calvin was miserable in that existence, just as I was in his mind. In some way, do you not think that he is liberated from the prison of his mind, and the prison that his life had become?"

The shaman rose from his squat, turning his back to the fire for warmth. "Yes, my son. It is true that changing places with you, and now being the resident of your mind is easier, more peaceful for him. However, his destiny and yours are intertwined. When you, Glynn MacTavish, came into being, as the immortal Timetravellar, the balance of things was greatly upset. Your love for Monique Dubois is more powerful than any magic that I have seen in all my millennia. That great passion coupled with the fact that your son passed down blood of the undead allowed you to return from oblivion to be with your heart's desire. Up until this point, superficially, all seems well.

"You must understand, though, that there is a great void in the future. Calvin is *gone*, and Calvin plays a vital role in history. You see, when Calvin entered cyberspace, he was on the cusp of creating something that is vital to Scotland. That creation was a book that he was writing titled *The Legend of Glynn MacTavish.*

His research, combined with the myths of your mortal years, will result in a work that will become magnificently well received, worldwide. Scotland, its history, and even it's culture will be brought to the forefront of the twentieth century population's attention. That scrutiny and recognition will affect our country's politics, its wealth...its future. Calvin's place in the future must be preserved, yet he is not there."

Tension vanished from the magician's face, as he had finally completed a task that began with a promise to his great friend, Lachlan MacTavish, some five hundred years earlier. Timetravellar plucked a weed from where it grew and contemplatively chewed on its sweet stem. Ian watched, anticipating the inquisitiveness of his ward.

"Calvin...had fallen deep into despair when you came as the wolf. The spirits that he drank were taking their charge. He even considered ending his own life with a weapon of the future. How could he have accomplished something so important as you describe?" Timetravellar asked.

"This is the last of it," Ian smiled. "Calvin entered cyberspace and met his maternal ancestor, Monique Dubois, oblivious to the fact that there was any relation. Had things followed their proper course, he would have developed a relationship with her on his own, much different from the one he developed when you were a factor.

Her writing, the great passion and empathy that exist in Monique's words, her pain, all represent her essence. Those powerful emotions and feelings had things gone as they should have, would have inspired Calvin to once again write. In the proper course of events, Calvin would mention his ancestry and she would unwittingly be an invaluable resource for him. The book would have been completed; Calvin would have reunited with his wife, and his life would have taken a marvelous turn for the better. As things stand at this moment however, none of it will be.

Perhaps now you can understand Glynn Timetravellar MacTavish. Your existence, as immortal, serves to resurrect a passion more powerful than any I have seen in two thousand years. Yet, that is all that it serves. You may walk through time with your love, but you must stand at the edge of the shadows," Ian concluded.

Timetravellar's head dropped, as he fully comprehended the implications of Ian's sermon. This seemed a cruel revelation, but now his quest was fully revealed. He spoke not, as his mentor walked away from him far out onto the surface of the lake.

Turning before departing, he offered a final consolation. "Our paths shall not again cross great warrior. Of you I am most proud, and in you I have the most faith. As for the fairy, your squire of centuries to come, be kind to her. She too has great magic...and a great heart."

As the old Scottish wizard stood atop the water in the center of the transparent pond, light sparkled and darted from his garment and it was clear that his time in this world was at its end. Yet, before the colorful light show finale, his last words emanated from the spectacular display.

"When the book is written, five hundred years from now, that will be the time, when you may finally put an end to Monique's suffering. Then, you may destroy the one who so richly deserves it."

Light streamed and streaked in all directions from his ethereal being. The shooting, darting bolts of light imploded into a single, cataclysmic point of illumination, and he was gone. Timetravellar watched in marvel, and in dismay. The sorcerer who had been his teacher, advisor, and pedagogue was gone forever.

Chapter 38

V

Seven mischievous, crooked smiles peered from behind the campsite's surrounding ferns and large Amanita mushroom caps. Hiding at the edge of darkness, just beyond firelight, they watched. Those winged pixies had never seen a human size faerie, and Sylvie was a wonderment to them. One by one they gained enough courage to step out from their hiding places. Snickering with giddiness, they approached the giant that so much resembled them.

Sir Ian had scolded them for being taken with the visitor, Timetravellar. By right, he should be under their guardianship. Ténèbres was, after all, their domain, and Timetravellar was their duty. Still, Ian could leave nothing to chance. This pack of winged imps was a promiscuous lot, moreso than most faeries, and their fixation with his physical grandeur was a threat to the magician's plan.

Whereas the seven wee beauties were distinct in that way from other nymphs, so were they different in the way they that they were not a jealous bunch. To them Sylvie was an enchantment, something marvelous, perhaps, a new playmate.

Sylvie breathed deeply from the wine-induced sleep and occasionally emitted a brusque snore that would cause the welcoming entourage to flinch and break for the cover of foliage. Realizing what happened, they would stop, burst into laughter and then muffle their voices for fear of waking the giant. Noemi, their leader, covered her mouth to mute the escaping belly laughs, but despite her intent, tears of hilarity rolled down her cheeks.

Finally, the mystical troop established a sense of control and warily approached the sleeping Sylvie. Beside the giant was a goatskin flask, and they were betting among themselves, silently, that there might be wine within. Noemi signaled to Babette, Celena, and the rest, and they all took their turn at tugging on the large cork. Babette was the last to pull, and the cork which she could barely get both hands around, sent her sprawling onto the dirt, as it became dislodged. Again, the minute seven squalled in unrepressed laughter, but quickly silenced to inspect the vessel. Celena reached her hand inside the large bladder, licking her fingers to sample its juice.

Smacking her lips, she concentrated for a moment to determine if it was as they hoped. Her eyebrows did a little dance and then that trademark crooked grin creased her lips. Each of the pack ran to the surrounding flora and plucked leaves that would be folded to make drinking cups. Reaching inside the skin neck, they filled their containers and began celebrating their good fortune.

At first, they stood in a circle smiling, drinking and endeavoring not to stir the immense one. Yet after a couple of rounds, their inhibitions and wariness of Sylvie floated away somewhere, perhaps into the forest. It was

Hyacinthe whose hips first started swaying, as the music of wind and waterfall struck her attuned ears. Nadège pulled a wooden flute from the belt of her abbreviated tunic and began playing a mirthful ditty. Zoé grabbed Aurélie and in the absence of a male took the dance-step lead. Noemi leaned against Sylvie's right breast and laughed, as her girls all began dancing around the low light from the fire's glowing coals.

Sylvie sat up unexpectedly and Noemi somersaulted backwards onto the ground. The giant rubbed her eyes, blinked, and gazed at the other six celebrants that were still unaware of her rising. She smiled.

Sylvie watched in quiet respect, as a legendary figure, a myth of gigantic proportions, went to the beyond. He had been her mentor as well, and the skill of her craft was learned almost entirely from him. She stood modestly at the brink of forest shade, her face softer than when she sparred with Timetravellar. The brief, tan, furless skin that comprised her tunic almost perfectly matched the bronze of her skin. Aquamarine eyes welled with sorrow. Just as Ian had been a second father to MacTavish, he had been her only guardian.

A mother of fairy blood and a father of human blood created a tragic union. The mother she had never known died at childbirth because of the mixture of her child. Her father, hated by all for his desecration of a pure fae, was felled by an assassin's arrow. While the Druid priests marginally accepted Sylvie, fairy folk scorned her for being of mixed blood.

Faries were a unique, wonderful lot, but not above extreme jealousy and vindictiveness. Ian had comforted Sylvie as a child, when she would burst into his cave wailing from their abuses.

Smiling compassionately he would say, "Don't cry Sylvie. It is likely your clear green eyes, your honeyed hair, and the shape of your bottom that drives them to such remarks. You could not choose your parents any more than they could. Still, it is a convenient stone to cast at you. In truth, it is your beauty that makes them envious." He would wipe her tears, pat her backside, and send her back out into the world a little stronger and a little more confident. In as much as he had enriched Glynn MacTavish, so too he had endeared himself to the nymph. Now, at the mage's call, she was flung into a confederation with the likes of this Scot. Eyes down, she was unsure of how to approach him. Awkwardly, slowly, she paced toward the sinewy, sitting figure. "Let's have a look at your dressing," she offered.

Timetravellar continued to stare at the center of the lagoon where Ian had been. His grim stare spoke of the barrenness of his heart. Sylvie reached to pull his tattered shirt to the side, but he held his hand up, as if to say, "Leave me." Although she did not leave, she did retreat to the forest edge, twenty yards from where he sulked. She petted Chronos's nose and grappled with a moment absent of gracefulness. Finally, she did speak.

"We have not been properly introduced. I am Sylvie. It seems that our mutual friend has bound us together for sometime to come. Shall we make the best of it?"

Travellar did not reply. His mind boggled with the cruelty of his destiny. He had come back to his home time, yet was not at home. He had returned to liberate his lover, yet he was forbidden to see her, or intervene on her behalf. His great friend had gone to some new dimension where he could not go, and lashed him to the company of a fairy. Bitterness would pass, but for the moment, his outlook was bleak.

After perpetual silence, he stood and walked into the heavy shade of Ténèbres, without saying a word. Hours passed, as he walked and pondered his fate. Perhaps he would disobey the mystical patriarch and rush to the palace and rescue Monique. But what of

Scotland at the turn of the millennia? Why was it incumbent upon him to endure such a harsh sentence, to secure the future of his homeland? Yet, as quickly as the rebellious thoughts came, they also receded. Honor was, after all, the foundation of his character, and perhaps that is why Ian had so challenged him.

A huge rock eight feet tall and eight feet wide sat in a sunny clearing in the center of the woods. He climbed upon it, and there he sat until the sun slid onto the horizon. Deep thought was normal for Glynn MacTavish, and in the coming months, the boulder would become known to he and Sylvie as the Thinking Rock.

She approached without making a sound, or perhaps it was because he was so deep within his own mind that he did not hear her. Flinching quickly, he was startled when the forest beauty placed her arm around his wide shoulders.

"Come back to the camp," she begged. "All is not so terrible as it seems, please."

For the first time in their short relationship, he smiled graciously. Without a word exchanged between them, they walked through the stand of ancient trees back to camp at the edge of the lagoon. Travellar gathered wood, and Sylvie brought forth a prize. It was a large pheasant she had taken with bow and arrow. During that time when he wandered alone, she hunted. The bird was a peace offering.

"You do realize, fairy, that I am not mortal and do not require sustenance," he said politely.

"Nor do I, time voyager, but you do enjoy the taste, do you not?" she asked submissively.

"Yes, of course."

Pulling the strap from her shoulder, she showed him a goatskin bladder filled with dark red wine. "And do you enjoy this, as well?"

"Aye, even more," he laughed.

The two new compatriots roasted the bird, feasted, and drank into the night. Sylvie's delicate giggles and Timetravellar's deep bursts of laughter echoed into the boundless night. It was a respite, a time for joking, and to a degree, an interlude for the fairy and him to bond. For a short time, his heart was light, and the rare twinkling of merriment blessed the lives of one wanderer of time and one woodland pixie.

Sylvie stood, staggered, and then snickered at her own drunkenness. She made her way behind one of the trees near the camp and returned with two large beaver pelts. The first she folded and placed on the ground where she had been sitting. The second, she folded and handed to MacTavish. His eyes opened wide revealing that he did not understand her purpose.

"It's a pillow, silly," she said smiling.

Weary from the day, and sleepy from the wine, she lay down on earth's mattress and quickly fell asleep. Timetravellar's head tilted to the side, as he marveled at her. She was quite beautiful when she was not reprimanding him for his transgressions. Her eyelashes were long with a sweeping curl. Skin dark from living in the outdoors perfectly complemented the dark blonde ripples that were her hair. The wine had stained her lips, and he dwelled on her beauty. As soft as she was on his eyes, her pretty form only served to make him think of Monique in the palace just beyond the forest. Covering the sleeping Sylvie with his cloak, it took but a motion of his head to beckon Chronos. Leading his new steed to the path in the woods, Timetravellar walked gingerly, so as not to wake the fairy. He climbed upon his ride, once out of earshot, and made his way in the waxing moonlight.

He traveled on Chronos' back until he reached the meadow at the far edge of the forest. There, he dismounted and left his pristine white steed. Even at night, the moonlight would have reflected brightly off the horse and alerted the sentries.

Travellar crossed the meadow and hiked to the back courtyard. There, as he had done before, he climbed the trellis to the third floor and made his way along the ledge to Monique's chamber window. Candlelight shone through the panes, and he knew that she was still about. Stealth was essential. He could not give himself away. Looking on Sylvie had made him yearn for the one who was rightfully his, and if he could not hold her in his arms and stroke her soft hair, then at least he could gaze upon her.

The evening was chillier than the past nights, and condensation had formed on her window. Sitting to the side of the sill, he carefully peered around the stone to have a look. Her distorted image appeared at the vanity. She was probably brushing her hair before bed. Tearing a piece of fabric from his sleeve, he dried a small circle of the dew so that he could see into the room. When he looked in, he saw but a glimpse of her before she blew out the candle. He pulled his head back from the window, sat on the ledge, and stared at the moon.

Timetravellar's heart begged him to tap at the window, but the mage's words were more compelling, still. Starlight and moonlight danced off the single tear that carried the pain of his heart. In the future, this time would pass so quickly for Monique, but for him, it was without end. Midnight came and left, as did one o'clock and as did two o'clock. Finally surrendering to his fate, he stood and began to negotiate the ledge back to the trellis. He paused contemplatively and then returned to the window, before his final departure.

The following morning Monique Dubois rose from her straw mattress and yawned. She made her way to the washstand and poured a bowl full of water from a ceramic pitcher. Shuddering from its greeting, she reached for a towel to dry her face. She turned and looked, as offensively bright sunlight forced its way into the room.

Although, the evening dew had evaporated from the pane, the remnants of something wonderful remained.

It was but a smear now, but still quite legible. Her heart and her lips smiled, as she looked upon a smudged heart drawn on her prison window glass. An arrow pierced the symbol of passion, and joined in its center were the initials G.Mac. + M.D.

* * * The Vigil * * *

Towering beyond the hamlet of Lahr in Central Europe, were the foreboding mountains of der Schwarzwald. Shadows cast over the village by the cold, threatening, peaks at sundown symbolized the fear that invaded the villagers' hearts, as night approached. To the east, within a five-mile radius, were seven ominous castles. Townspeople could see any one of them from opposing mountaintops, but not until this night had anyone ever dared approach the stone structures housing the *evil ones*.

    A January blizzard approached, as Hans and Karl hurried down the moonlit path. If they did not succeed in their mission, it would be spring before they could make another attempt. It would be spring before they could again muster their courage. The two, both village merchants, would obtain the entire wealth of Lahr if they could prevail. Even in their minds, the chance of success at all seven castles was infinitesimal. But, it was greed that drove them on, on through the piercing gusts of hellish cold.

    There was but one path that led from the village to the mountains. From the first granite castle, Vampyra's, the others could be accessed. Still, it was Vampyra that Hans and Karl feared most. The other undead would be formidable, perhaps invincible. It was Vampyra, though, who was credited with one hundred nineteen villagers' disappearances over the last eighty years. In truth, the vampiress had only been positively identified twice in the last one hundred years, but myth, folklore, and rabid imaginations, told of her being spotted almost weekly. Insane fear drove Lahrians into contracting Hans and Karl to slay the Vampiress of Schwarzwald, and the purse was made fat.

    Scurrying around a bend in the brilliantly lit path, the two approached a great boulder. Had they looked higher and been less distracted by the numbing cold, they might have noticed the motionless figure at the top of the boulder. The cloaked sentinel was as still, as cold, and as quiet as the rock itself. Walking past the huge stone monument, a shadow flashed before them, as the watchman fell from the dark heavens.

Thundering on the dirt and gravel road, the vigilante landed, appearing from nowhere. The merchants whose courage was already failing, jumped backward in astonished disbelief.

"My God man, you've frightened the wits out of us!" Karl cried out. "Are you lost? Do you know where you are?"

"I am not lost," the cloaked stranger answered calmly.

"You are not from these parts," Hans interjected.

The stranger, wearing a freshly grown beard draped and frosted with his breath's crystallized condensation, did not reply immediately. He was neither from that region, nor was he from that time. Finally, he queried. "Where do you travel on this bitter night?"

"We go to that castle." Karl motioned to the west. "We go to exterminate the vermin of our land."

"And who might that be?" the dark figure asked. "The vampiress...Vampyra," Karl replied. "And what is your name, Sir?"

"My given name was Glynn MacTavish, but now I am simply called Timetravellar. What do your have in that bag?"

"Stakes. We have stakes!" Hans answered.

Timetravellar threw back his head and laughed.

"There must be twenty in there, gentlemen. Are you sure you have enough to kill one woman?"

"Aye, there's enough. And, kill her we shall, after we've had our pleasure with her. She is said to be a fine wench. Seems an awful waste not to have tasted her, before we send her to hell," Karl boasted.

Travellar's eyes narrowed, as a silent fury raged inside him. Had the two merchants looked more closely, they might have seen the inferno that escalated within the stranger.

"How long have you been out here?" Hans asked, realizing that it was a night not fit for any manner of creature.

Grasping the hilt of his broadsword the Timetravellar replied, "A little over two hundred years."

* * * * *

Hans Keppling and Karl Guenther's names were added to the town's registry. The role call of the Schwarzwald dead had now grown to one hundred twenty one. As always, Vampyra was credited with the kills. Although she herself had taken Lahrians as needed, neither she nor the town, would ever know that the vigilant watchman, the Timetravellar, had intervened. It was a task he performed many times over the centuries, but it was a labor of love, and he performed it flawlessly. The vampiress' enemies were many, but during that time, when he was in her time, he protected her.

Author Bio – Steven R. Cowan

Steve Cowan lives in rural South Georgia with his wife Mary and children, Forrest and Hannah. He is forty-five years old, while his writing career is only eleven years old.

His first novel was inspired by a nightmare, but prior to that time, he had no aspirations to write at all.

Since that dream in late 1989, he has written four novels, *Gothica: Romance of the Immortals* being the second. His fifth and current project, tentatively titled, *The Shadow Shifter* is expected to complete in the spring of 2001.